THE EARL OF RAYMORE WANTED NOTHING TO DO WITH LADIES

Once he had adored an angelic creature who had turned out to be a devilish minx in disguise. After that, the only females he cared to know were women who catered to his body without laying claim to his heart.

MISS ROSALIND DACEY WANTED NOTHING TO DO WITH GENTLEMEN

Unlike her best friend, the beauteous and biddable Lady Sylvia Marsh, Rosalind found flirtations a fearful ordeal and the game of love one that she could only lose. Better to be happy with herself than suffer a man who would only use her and mock her dreams.

Clearly Raymore and Rosalind were in perfect harmony in assiduously avoiding each other—until the night the unthinkable happened, and the impossible had to be faced. . . .

Red Rose

SIGNET Regency Romances You'll Enjoy

Red Rose

Mary Balogh

A SIGNET BOOK

NEW AMERICAN LIBRARY

NAL BOOKS ARE AVAILABLE AT QUANTITY DISCOUNTS
WHEN USED TO PROMOTE PRODUCTS OR SERVICES.
FOR INFORMATION PLEASE WRITE TO PREMIUM MARKETING DIVISION,
NEW AMERICAN LIBRARY, 1633 BROADWAY,
NEW YORK, NEW YORK 10019.

SIGNET TRADEMARK REG. U.S. PAT. OFF. AND FOREIGN COUNTRIES
REGISTERED TRADEMARK—MARCA REGISTRADA
HECHO EN CHICAGO, U.S.A.

SIGNET, SIGNET CLASSIC, MENTOR, PLUME, MERIDIAN and NAL BOOKS
are published by New American Library,
1633 Broadway, New York, New York 10019

First Printing, March, 1986

1 2 3 4 5 6 7 8 9

PRINTED IN THE UNITED STATES OF AMERICA

Song

My Luve is like a red, red rose,
    That's newly sprung in June:
My Luve is like the melodie,
    That's sweetly play'd in tune.

As fair art thou, my bonie lass,
    So deep in luve am I;
And I will luve thee still, my Dear,
    Till a' the seas gang dry.

Till a' the seas gang dry, my Dear,
    And the rocks melt wi' the sun;
And I will luve thee still, my Dear,
    While the sands o' life shall run.

And fare-thee-well, my only Luve!
    And fare-thee-well, a while!
And I will come again, my Luve,
    Tho' 'twere ten thousand mile!

ROBERT BURNS

1

The coachman gave his horses the signal to start, and the old traveling carriage, its blue paintwork faded, its coat of arms chipped and shabby, slowly moved past the tollgate and onto open highway again.

"That be the last un," he said with some relief. "We'll be drinkin' our ale in Lunnun tonight, me lad."

"Be it far, then?" asked the lad, a footman of a mere thirty years.

"Keep yer poppers open when we top yonder rise," his companion said, pointing his whip ahead a couple of miles to where the road disappeared over the crest of a hill, "an' yer'll be able to see Lunnun spread afore ye."

The footman leaned forward eagerly, as if he thought the action would bring him sooner to his first view of London.

Inside the carriage, Lady Sylvia Marsh sat forward as soon as it jolted into motion again and scanned the countryside eagerly. "We must be getting close now," she said. "Surely we will be able to see the city soon."

"You have been saying so for the last five hours, Sylvie," her companion pointed out with a sigh. "Do please sit back and sleep or look out the window to enjoy the scenery. You will not bring our destination one inch closer by being such a jack-in-the-box."

Sylvia turned large blue eyes on her cousin. "Oh, Ros," she said pleadingly, "can you not feel any excitement at all? I know you did not wish to come, but since you had no choice in the matter, will you not allow

yourself to feel some eagerness at least? It is April, the
height of the Season, and we are to be part of it all.
This is what I have dreamed of for several years." There
were tears in her eyes.

"Yes, I know you have, Sylvie," Miss Rosalind Dacey
replied, her expression softening somewhat, "and I know
that you have had to wait a whole year longer than you
should because we have been wearing black."

"Do you think nineteen is dreadfully old to be making my come-out?" Sylvia asked anxiously.

Rosalind smiled and shook her head.

"Poor Papa!" her cousin continued. "He was going to
bring me himself more than a year ago, for all that he
hated town life so. Aunt Lavinia would have chaper-
oned me. And I would have been barely eighteen—just
the right age."

"Well, you are looking remarkably well-preserved for
one so advanced in years," Rosalind assured her. "If
you keep your back to the light at all times, no one may
notice your wrinkles."

Sylvia let out a peal of laughter. "What a tease you
are," she said. "You know very well what I meant. And
anyway, I do not begrudge Papa that year of mourning.
I did love him so, Ros. He was the best of fathers."

"Yes, and the best of uncles," her cousin agreed. "*He*
would not have forced me to come to London. He was
quite willing to let me stay at Raymore Manor while he
took you to London. I should have been quite happy
there, even though he had invited Cousin Hetty and
her poodles to come and bear me company. Indeed,
Sylvie, I wish he had not died."

"What do you think Cousin Edward will be like?"
Sylvia asked.

Rosalind raised her eyebrows. "Do you realize how
often you have asked me that in the last year?" she
asked with a sigh. "We both know only what the lawyer
told us when he came to inform us of the contents of
your papa's will. Your father's heir, and our guardian, is
two and thirty, unwed, a fashionable man about town.

He has made no attempt to see us or to visit his new property at Raymore. Until three weeks ago I hoped he had forgotten our existence. But he had not. To satisfy some whim, he has summoned us to town, and insisted that I accompany you, even though I wrote to ask if I might stay at home."

"He probably plans to find husbands for us during the Season," Sylvia said. "Oh, how splendid it will be, Ros. New clothes and balls and such"

Rosalind examined her ungloved hands, which were clasped in her lap. "There can be nothing there for me," she said with quiet resignation. "Do you think he will let me return home when he knows, Sylvie?"

Sylvia gazed with sympathy at her cousin. "It may not be as bad as you think," she said. "You are an heiress in a small way, after all, Ros, and somewhere there must be a man who does not care about the other."

She was still staring at her cousin's downcast face when her eye was caught by something different in the landscape beyond the carriage window.

"Oh, look," she cried, pointing, "London, Ros!"

Rosalind turned and looked, too, at the distant skyline of buildings. She felt none of the excitement that was bubbling from her companion. She felt only a sinking feeling in the pit of her stomach, a threatening sense of panic.

It was all very well for Sylvia to be overjoyed, Rosalind thought, turning her gaze to her cousin, who had now moved to the seat opposite hers and was sitting with her face pressed to the window. Sylvia was beautiful, there could never be any question about that. She was small with a trim figure that looked very feminine even in the unfashionable muslin gown Miss Porter had made for her. Her hair was so blond that it was almost silver. And it was the sort of hair that would adapt itself to any style, it seemed. Her complexion was perfect, her cheeks always flushed with a color more perfect than any that could be created with rouge. Her teeth were white and even and often in evidence. Sylvia smiled and laughed frequently. Her large blue eyes seemed constantly to be dancing. Rosalind might have resented her. But who could resent a girl whose nature was almost constantly sunny, whose heart was always warm? Those who did not know her might have felt that she had recovered all too quickly from the death of her mother from pneumonia four years before, and of her father from a heart seizure fifteen months before, but Rosalind knew that the girl had genuinely loved and grieved. Her happiness now did not exclude the very deep attachment she would always feel for her parents.

Yes, it was all very well for Sylvia to look upon this summons to London as the great opportunity of her life, Rosalind thought. She would enjoy the activities of the *ton* to the full. She would soon have every man below the age of fifty (and some above) dangling after her, as she had at Raymore since she was fifteen years old. She would probably fall in love half a dozen times in as many weeks. At home she had ritually fallen in love with every man who smiled at her, and many had smiled. She would probably end up making a brilliant match.

But how different things were for herself, Rosalind thought. Not by any stretch of the imagination could she be called beautiful. She was tall—she had topped Uncle Lawrence by one inch. She had an embarrassingly and unfashionably full figure. For five years now, ever since she was seventeen, she had persuaded Miss Porter to let out the seams of her dresses so that they would disguise her curves as much as possible. Her hair was almost black, an inheritance from her Italian mother, she assumed, and heavy and straight. It was almost impossible to coax it into any fashionable style. Rosalind usually wore it in a smooth chignon, as she did today. Her eyes were large enough and thickly lashed, her best feature, in fact. But they too were very dark. She wished they were blue, like Sylvia's, or gray at least.

There was nothing remotely delicate or feminine about her appearance, she concluded.

But it was pointless, anyway, to wish for delicate eyes and brows, wavy hair, a shorter stature, and a more svelte figure. What good would beauty do her when there would always be the one great defect? Nothing could ever change that. Uncle Lawrence had understood. He had never forced her to socialize. On the few occasions when she had been forced into company, he must have noticed as well as she the reactions of strangers: distaste, embarrassment, pity. He was quite willing to let her stay at home with her books, her painting, and her music, or to ride freely around the estate on her mare, Flossie.

By what right did this Edward Marsh, the new Earl of Raymore, order her to come to his residence in London? She was two and twenty years old and no direct relation of his. She resented her dependence on him. The only complaint she had ever had against Uncle Lawrence had come after his death. She had never understood why she, as well as Sylvia, had been put under the guardianship of his nephew and heir until her marriage. He had known that she would never marry.

"You are very quiet, Ros, and you are not even looking out the window," Sylvia said in exasperation. "Do look. We are about to enter the outskirts of the city. Oh, it is so easy to imagine why people used to expect the streets to be paved with gold, is it not?"

Rosalind obligingly turned her attention to the window, but both girls were soon exclaiming in dismay over the dirty streets and the ragged, grimy people that crowded them.

"That child is crying," Sylvia said, pointing at an emaciated little ragamuffin who was rubbing both fists against his eyes. "Oh, do you think I should call Ben to stop and give the boy some pennies?"

"I think not," Rosalind decided. "There are so many others, Sylvie." She looked, troubled, into her cousin's

tearstained face and lowered her eyes to the hands in
her lap until Sylvia began exclaiming with more cheerfulness at the buildings and conveyances of a more
fashionable part of London. She gazed with every bit as
much curiosity as the other girl at the imposing man-
sion in Grosvenor Square at which Ben the coachman,
slowed the carriage.

"This be her," Ben was saying to the gawking footman, who had to be prodded in the ribs before he
remembered that it was his duty to jump down from
the box and knock on the large oak front door facing
onto the cobbled courtyard.

Even in the middle of the afternoon there were two
games in progress in the card room at Watier's Club.
Both groups of players were silently intent upon their
hands. The few spectators were hushed too, all of them
standing around the table that was farthest from the
windows. Here young Darnley was in too deep. Everyone knew that the comfortable competence left him by
his father a mere two years ago had been all but dissi-
pated on reckless living. If he did not cut his losses
soon, some of them felt, he would be living in dun
territory before the summer was over.

The young lord sat forward, his manner careless and
relaxed. The only key to his true state of mind was his
flushed cheeks and his eyes, which darted constantly
from his own hand to the cards held by his companions,
as if he could divine what they held if he only looked
often enough.

The object of Darnley's most penetrating glances was
the man opposite. He sat with a look of cool boredom,
one well-manicured hand holding his cards, the other
toying with the crystal glass on the table, which held an
inch of brandy still. His eyes never once strayed from
his cards, not even to glance at the pile of bank notes
and vouchers that lay neatly stacked before him.

Finally he laid down his cards and spread them so
that all could see. Only then did he lift ice-blue eyes to

the young man across the table. But his face was expressionless. All three of his fellow players threw their own cards onto the table, two of them with a resigned shrug, Darnley with an involuntary exclamation of annoyance.

"Luck ith with you today, Raymore," he said casually. "Mutht leave now. Appointment to dwive Lady Awabella Matthewth in the park. Muthn't be late. Will call tomowwow to pay my debt, dear fellow."

The sixth Earl of Raymore looked steadily and cynically at Darnley. "I shall be at home over the luncheon hour," he said, "though, of course, you may always see my secretary if I am not at home. Sheldon's door is always open."

Darnley bowed stiffly and left the room with his head held high. The onlookers drifted away, some of them to the other table, where the play was still in progress, others to another room.

"Not entirely fair, Edward, to rub it in quite like that," the player to Raymore's left said quietly. "You know very well that Darnley will not call on you tomorrow. He don't have the blunt."

"Then he should admit as much, Henry," Raymore said with a careless shrug as he tapped the vouchers and bank notes into a neater pile before him. "He should have asked for more time."

"Come now," Sir Henry Martel replied with an uneasy laugh, "you must allow a man some way to save his dignity. It takes some courage to admit to having played beyond one's means, especially in this club. Have a heart, man."

Raymore regarded his friend coolly. "If he chooses to gamble when he has not the means, he should be man enough to take his losses," he said. "I have no sympathy. Do not try to make a bleeding heart of me, Henry."

His friend laughed outright. "I should know better than to try, should I not," he said, "with you, who have no mercy and compassion on any man, least of all yourself? Why have we been friends these ten years, Edward? I am sure I cannot fathom the reason."

"Originally it was because I never competed with you for all the prettiest girls," Raymore answered dryly, "and later it was habit, I suppose, though perhaps you think that my title has added something to your consequence in the last year? There was a suggestion of a smile about his mouth.

Sir Henry clapped his friend on the back and rose to his feet. "You have penetrated my darkest secret," he said with a hearty laugh. "And, indeed, my friend, I owe you lifelong devotion for having introduced me to Elise when you did not wish to partner her yourself for a dance. Come, let me buy you a drink before I go home. I must not linger long. Elise has only two weeks to go before her time and becomes nervous if I am from home too long. Though what she expects me to do if I am there when the pain begins, I have no idea. Perhaps it will be a comfort to her to know that I will be downstairs in the drawing room wearing a path in the carpet." He laughed again.

The Earl of Raymore rose to his feet and followed his friend across the room. He kept his voice low in deference to the serious game that had now attracted several spectators at the table close to the windows.

"I'm damned if I would ever do so much for any woman," he said. "Why get so excited when they are performing the only function for which they are of any use?"

"I say, Edward," Sir Henry said rather sharply as he seated himself in a deep leather chair in a lounge that adjoined the card room, "coming a trifle offensive, my boy. Anyway, you seem to find at least one other use for the fair sex, or was that your maiden aunt you were driving in the park yesterday afternoon?"

"I was talking about wives," his friend replied. "Mistresses, of course, have a different function. And I admit that it can be quite pleasurable if the female will just keep her infernal mouth shut."

"The delectable one in the park did not?" Sir Henry asked, grinning.

"We discussed bonnets for all of one hour," Raymore said, raising one eyebrow in his friend's direction. "Pardon me, we exchanged views on parasols for perhaps ten minutes of that time. To relieve the monotony, you see. Her elocution lessons slipped once or twice, too. Pure cockney beneath the veneer, Henry."

Sir Henry laughed. "But good in bed, Edward?"

"Mm, quite a shapely armful," the earl agreed. "But one cannot quite wipe out memories of the featherbrain attached to the body, except perhaps at moments of the deepest involvement. There is a delicious little redheaded beauty at Covent Garden. New this week, I believe. Probably not under anyone's protection yet."

"But soon will be, I assume," Sir Henry commented. "When are your wards arriving, Edward?"

His companion took a long drink of his brandy before replying. "Probably today, if they left yesterday as I directed," he said.

"And you are not there to greet them?"

"Good God, no. Inheriting the title and the property hardly makes up for being saddled with two female wards." Raymore shuddered.

"Why bring them to London if their existence is so distasteful to you?" Sir Henry asked.

His friend raised haughty eyebrows. "Is the reason not glaringly obvious?" he asked. "This is the marriage market of the nation, Henry, and this the height of the buying and selling season."

Sir Henry looked at him with interest. "You have no intention of getting to know them, Edward? One of them is your cousin, is she not?"

"Daughter of the fifth earl," Raymore replied. "They are females, Henry, of marriageable age. Doubtless they have their heads full of nothing except finding husbands. I intend to oblige them."

"Do you have anyone in mind?" There was an undertone of sarcasm in Sir Henry's voice.

"I shall have to look them over first," Raymore replied with an arctic smile. "They both have dowries large enough to add to their attractions. But the better-looking they are, the higher we can aim. Either way I shall be done with the obligation before the Season ends."

Sir Henry Martel drained his glass. "Yet if you were selling some of your cattle, my friend," he said, "you would take a year or more if necessary to ensure that you had found a suitable buyer."

The earl shrugged. "But then girls are not horses," he said.

His friend rose to his feet, shaking his head. "I must be going," he said. "Coming my way, Edward?"

"No," Raymore replied. "I shall stay here to dine. Good day to you, Henry."

The Earl of Raymore summoned a waiter and ordered another brandy. He waved carelessly to a group of acquaintances across the room, who were engaged in a lively discussion, but made no move to join them. He allowed his mind to dwell on the topic that had been depressing him for days. For how long would his home and his peace of mind be invaded by a pack of females? Cousin Hetty had arrived two days before, accompanied by three pesky little poodles. Fortunately, she was a reasonably sensible woman, though she did like to talk rather more than was necessary and in a somewhat strident voice. However, her presence was absolutely necessary while his two wards were in residence with him.

He shuddered at the thought of being saddled with two hopeful debutantes for the rest of the Season. His cousin Sylvia had been eighteen at the time of her father's death, the lawyer had told him. He had never met her and, in fact, had met his aunt and uncle only once or twice in his life. His father had never been close to his brother, the Earl of Raymore, and had rarely visited him. Would the child be pretty? Silly? Shy? And what about the other girl? The earl felt particularly annoyed about his position as her guardian. He had really just inherited her from his uncle. She was not even related to him; she was a niece of the dead countess. She was a few years older than Sylvia, the lawyer had told him vaguely. How many years older? Raymore hoped that she would not too certainly have joined the ranks of the old maids. He could find it very tricky to get her married off if she were too old. And then he would be stuck with her for life, forever moving the fading creature around from one home to another, wherever he happened not to be.

Raymore took a snuffbox from his pocket and gazed absently at the ruby-studded lid, his thumbnail against the catch, though he did not immediately open it. How he hated women. He wished to heaven that he never need have anything to do with any of them. He should have entered a monastery, he thought with cold humor. But then, of course, that would not have served his purpose. There was that base bodily craving that had to be satisfied—and satisfy it he did with the type of woman he most despised. He always chose his women with care, assuming almost without conscious thought that physical beauty might compensate for the fact that he despised both the woman who gave her favors for money or expensive baubles and himself who bought.

Raymore flicked open the lid of his snuffbox with a practiced thumb and placed a pinch of his favorite blend on the back of his right hand. He sniffed delicately, first through one nostril and then through the other. He soon felt more himself. But he could not force himself to move. He had told Cousin Hetty that he would return for dinner. They would await his arrival. Yet he had told Henry less than an hour before that he would dine at the club. Confound it, and he would, too. Let the girls wait to make his acquaintance. Perhaps he would have more stomach for the introductions in the light of day.

He placed one booted foot against a stool and gazed gloomily at the high gloss of the black leather. Women had always been the bane of his life. His own mother! He had vague memories of her. He believed that she must have given him much attention. The memories mostly involved her leaning over him with a gentle smile—whether to soothe away a headache, or to admire a daisy chain, or to bid him good night, he could not clearly recall. But he had loved her, trusted the permanence of her love. She had run away with the curate of a neighboring village when he was seven, leaving him behind. He had suffered cruelly from his sense of loss and rejection and from his father's drunken rages.

And then there had been Rachel, his father's second wife. She had been Edward's governess for three years, and all the while had been sweet and attentive. She had seemed to devote herself entirely to the lonely child, and he had gradually allowed himself to love and to depend upon another human being again. He had felt deeply shocked, even betrayed, when he knew that she was to marry his father. How had she been able to get to know him when she spent all her time with the boy? But he had talked himself into accepting the marriage. After all, it would be infinitely better, more permanent, to have her as a mother than merely as a governess.

It was only six months after the wedding when Edward, exploring the upper hallway as he often did when playing imaginative games, opened the door to a room that he knew was not occupied by any of the servants, and found two people threshing around on the bed. They both turned alarmed faces at the sound of the opening door. The woman with her head on the pillow was Rachel. The man on top of her was his father's head groom. There were no covers over them. They were both naked.

Edward had not understood what was happening, but he had rushed outside and hurtled his way into the closest clump of bushes, where he had vomited for several minutes. He knew after that that he had Rachel in his power. He had never used his advantage, though she had pleaded with him later that same day and watched him out of anxious eyes for weeks afterward. After that she had fawned on him, praised him in his father's presence, bought him gifts. And he had gradually withdrawn more and more inside himself, refusing for the rest of his father's life to so much as recognize her existence. She had married the groom one week after his father's death, five days after Edward had dismissed the man from his service. He could still not understand why they had left that door unlocked.

"Your table is ready, my lord," a waiter said with a discreet cough at Raymore's elbow.

The earl indicated by raising his half-empty glass that he would adjourn to the dining room as soon as his drink was finished. He must have been a slow learner, he thought, a sneer marring his face, to have trusted another woman. But during his first full Season in London, fresh down from Oxford, he had fallen in love with Annette Longford—tiny, vivacious, pretty Annette. He had spent hours dreaming of her, and as many hours contriving meetings when they could converse with some privacy and perhaps touch each other. She was the sweetest, truest person he had ever known. When he gazed into her wide hazel eyes, he beheld perfect innocence.

They had been formally betrothed after three months, and Edward had accepted an invitation to spend the summer months on her father's estate. They were to be married at the end of August. The months had been bliss, heaven on earth. As they were betrothed and so soon to be married, they had been allowed more freedom than Edward had ever expected.

In the middle of August he had explained to her a theory of his. The idea was that a betrothed couple could best show their love and their total trust in each other's vows by giving themselves to each other. He realized that for her this would be a greater commitment, but she could show him the way she would totally entrust herself to his keeping by giving him now what most girls withheld until the wedding night. He had been utterly sincere in this suggestion. It had not been an elaborate seduction ploy.

He had expected denial, or reluctance, or at best a sweet and shy surrender. They were on a deserted hill at the time, sitting on the grass before a Greek-style folly. He had not expected her to get to her feet, as she had, and begin to remove her shoes and stockings and turn her back with a smile for him to unfasten her dress. He had been delighted, but puzzled, by her total lack of embarrassment as he uncovered her body in the bright sunlight and then undressed himself. He had been unprepared for the way she lost no time in lying down and positioning herself for him, reaching up with eager arms to pull him onto and into her. She had not been a virgin.

She had told him afterward, as he lay bewildered at her side, one arm beneath her neck, that she would marry him because her papa wished it and because she now discovered that it would be great fun in addition—this with her innocent, wide-eyed smile. But he must not expect her to be faithful. She already had lovers—she named two men, with both of whom Edward was acquainted—and intended to continue the liaisons. She would not, of course, ever make mention of his own lapses. But she would, naturally, always observe the proprieties as she expected him to do.

Edward had dressed and stood looking down to the lake at the bottom of the hill while Annette clothed herself in more leisurely fashion. He had told her, coldly, that she would find some reason to put an end to their betrothal. If she did not, he would disclose the fact of her affairs, including the names of her lovers. He had walked down the hill without looking back.

And he had learned his lesson well that time. In eleven years he had had no relationship with a woman. He bedded one when he felt the need, sometimes the same woman on more than one occasion if she were beautiful enough and if she satisfied his needs well enough. But he had never set up a mistress and had never come closer to a woman of his own class than the occasional conversation at a dinner table or the rare dance at a ball if he felt he could not avoid it.

The Earl of Raymore set down his empty glass on the polished table at his right elbow and moved into the dining room.

2

———————◆◆◆———————

Sylvia and Rosalind were awed when they entered the Earl of Raymore's home. The hall was enormous, the marble floor echoing beneath their footsteps. White marble busts lined the walls, huge paintings hung above them, gleaming chandeliers were suspended from the high ceiling. A broad marble staircase ascended from the center of the hall, two branches leading to an upper gallery and the upstairs apartments.

A wooden-faced butler conducted the two young ladies past impressive liveried footmen and ushered them into a salon. He bowed himself out and closed the double doors behind him.

"Surely Carlton House cannot be grander than this," Sylvia whispered. Somehow it seemed inappropriate to speak aloud in such surroundings. "Our guardian must be enormously wealthy, Ros."

Rosalind was standing with her back to the room, her attention caught by the painting over the mantel. "It is surely a Rembrandt original," she said in awe.

"Oh, do you think so?" Sylvia asked, glancing briefly at the painting. "Ros, I feel decidedly nervous. How long will he keep us waiting here, do you suppose?"

Rosalind too glanced hastily in the direction of the doors and sat down abruptly in a nearby chair.

They were not kept waiting for long. A footman opened the doors only a couple of minutes later and stood aside while a lady rustled into the room. The girls had a swift impression of a large, big-bosomed lady, fashionably dressed in a day dress of silver-gray silk, her face rouged, her gray hair frizzed and piled high on her head beneath a white lace cap, a lace handkerchief waving from one heavily ringed hand.

"My dears," she said, "I knew you would arrive today. Did you have a dreadfully tedious journey? I hate being cooped up in a carriage myself, especially in fine weather like we have been having. But no matter. You are here now and will be rested in no time. Would you like some tea, or would you like to be shown to your rooms immediately? Of course, you must need refreshment. I am sure your coachman did not stop for any, once he knew that he was close to the end of his journey. Come up to the drawing room. Gracious, how I shall enjoy having your company, girls. I have not had the excuse to go into society a great deal since my dear Arnold died twelve years ago. Now I have the come-out of two charming young ladies to arrange, and I shall enjoy every moment of it. I always regretted that I had no daughters of my own. Now, which is which of you two? That is a silly question, of course. You must be Lady Sylvia Marsh, my dear. You have the family coloring. And you, of course," she said, turning to Rosalind, "have inherited your dark hair from your Italian mother. Now, am I right? And how stupid of me. You must both be wondering who I am, since I am very obviously not the earl. I am Sylvia's papa's Cousin Hetty."

She paused for breath and smiled broadly.

Rosalind, still seated, felt overwhelmed. So this was the Cousin Hetty who had been going to stay with her while Uncle Lawrence accompanied Sylvia to London for her come-out.

"I am pleased to meet you, ma'am," Sylvia was saying, extending a hand. "Is his lordship not at home?"

"He is expected for dinner," Cousin Hetty replied. "But there is plenty of time before that for you to drink tea and to retire to your rooms to change and freshen up."

She led the way from the room and up the marble

staircase to the drawing room above. While Sylvia seated
herself and Cousin Hetty rang the bell for tea, Rosalind
forgot herself enough to cross the large room.

"What a beautiful pianoforte," she said, running a
hand reverently over the highly polished wood. "Does
the earl play?"

"No, my dear," Cousin Hetty replied, "but he is a
well-known patron. He holds a concert in his home
each year. But not in this room. If you think this a
beautiful instrument, wait until you see the music room."
She nodded her head.

Rosalind recrossed the room to take a seat beside
Sylvia.

"Did you hurt yourself on the journey, my dear?"
Cousin Hetty asked her with concern.

Rosalind blushed hotly. "No, ma'am," was all she
could say. She knew that for politeness' sake she should
have explained, but she did not, and the moment passed.

The Earl of Raymore did not return for dinner. Rosalind was both disappointed and relieved: disappointed
because she wanted to get the ordeal over with, relieved because she was tired and was glad to postpone
the meeting until another day.

All three ladies retired early to bed at Cousin Hetty's
insistence. And indeed she was tired, Rosalind reflected.
She hoped she would sleep. She had seen the music
room during the evening and had been awed by the
magnificence of the pianoforte there. It was a work of
art just to the sight, but its tone when she ran her
fingers over the keys was exquisite. She was excited,
too, to discover a harpsichord. She had never seen one
before and had thought them to be quite out of fashion.
But she was delighted by the harsh and yet dignified
sounds that it produced when she played a few bars of a
Bach fugue.

Rosalind sat up in the four-poster bed and gazed
around her at the elegant bedchamber that was to be
hers during her stay in Grosvenor Square. She clasped
her raised knees and laid her chin on them. Would he

allow her to return home again? He would know immediately that she was no candidate for a marriage market.
She would not be able to endure much of this. It had
been ordeal enough today just to know that the butler
and those footmen had witnessed her defect, in addition to Cousin Hetty. Surely he would never insist that
she go out in public, though Cousin Hetty had talked
constantly during dinner about all the social events that
they would attend after his lordship's ball the following
week had introduced them properly to the *ton*.

It was not that Rosalind was not interested in marriage. She had all the normal impulses and cravings of
any other girl. She was two and twenty already. The
last four or five years had been long and lonely ones,
especially when Sylvia grew old enough to attract the
admiration and attentions of almost every young man
who set eyes on her. Rosalind was not jealous of Sylvia—
she was too close to her cousin and the girl was too
sweet-natured for that. But her cousin's constant presence in her life did serve to emphasize her own defi-
ciencies as a woman.

Rosalind compensated for what was missing in her
life in several ways. She rode a great deal when she was
at home, using up energy and challenging herself by
galloping Flossie and jumping hedges and fences that
could quite easily have been avoided. Indoors, she
occupied herself with music, both playing and singing,
and with painting and reading.

And Rosalind had a dream companion. He never
could be a real man, she realized that. He was too
perfect. He was tall, with broad shoulders and narrow
hips and long legs. He had thick blond hair and deep-
blue eyes. It was the eyes that she could imagine most
clearly. Their expression could change from humor to
deep concern, but they were always focused full on her,
and there was always a smile lurking in their depths.
He loved her. To him she was perfect. He loved her
black hair and pale skin; he told her that her defect did
not make a mockery of her shapely figure. It was a

lovely woman's body, he said. And he would discuss for
hours with her the books she read, the dreams she had.
It was not a physical relationship. She never imagined
him kissing her. She did sometimes rest her head on
his comfortingly broad shoulder, though, as they talked.
She called him Alistair. He had no last name.

He comforted her now as she slid down on the bed
after blowing out the candle and tried to sleep. She was
beautiful and she was a person who mattered a great
deal to him. She was important. Rosalind almost believed him as she fell asleep.

The Earl of Raymore found out from his valet very
late that night that his wards had indeed arrived. But
he was in no hurry to meet them. It was Hetty's job to
entertain them, take them shopping and sight-seeing.
That was what he had brought her here for. His own
task would not begin until the ball the following week.
At least his wards would be well on display then, he
thought with an unamused smile. His invitations had
been accepted by almost everyone to whom they had
been sent. It was no ordinary event to be invited to a
ball given by the Earl of Raymore. Very few of the *beau
monde* could even remember what the ballroom of his
house looked like. Most of them had seen only the
music room in recent years.

It was quite late the following afternoon when the
earl finally presented himself in the drawing room,
where his cousin and his wards were taking tea. Hetty
dropped a miniature poodle to the carpet and came
hurrying toward him to make the introductions. The
earl largely ignored her. His eyes swept the two girls,
who had risen to their feet and were curtsying to him.

His eyes were drawn first to the little blonde. Pretty.
Quite beautiful, in fact, once she had been got into
more fashionable clothes and had something done to her
hair. Thick clusters of ringlets had never appealed to
his taste. She was blushing a becoming shade of pink
and had large, innocent blue eyes fixed anxiously on his

face. He immediately distrusted the eyes. He bowed coolly and turned to the other girl.

A more tricky proposition, he decided immediately. Her coloring would not please easily. Dark hair was not fashionable, and hers was positively black. She was too tall also, and had nothing for a figure; though it was hard to tell what was beneath that ill-fitting sack of a gown that she wore. Her face was too pale, though the eyes were fine enough. He did not like the expression on her face. Although she watched him as wide-eyed as the other girl, there was a tightness about her jaw that suggested a stubborn will. Well, she had a good-enough dowry, he reflected. There would be some fool who would think her an acceptable-enough bargain. He bowed, his face as expressionless as when he had entered the room.

Rosalind was finding it impossible to relax. If she unclenched her teeth, her whole body would start trembling and she would crumble. Alistair had never looked at her like that: coldly, a sneer on his lips, as if she were a piece of unwanted merchandise. Yet he was Alistair! The same height, tall enough to make her feel petite, the same magnificent build, the same hair and eyes. Strangely, she had never pictured Alistair's mouth, but it must surely be the one feature that was different. She would never have created that sensuous mouth, certainly not with the distortion of a sneer. And the eyes. She could see through Alistair's eyes into his very soul. These were opaque. It would be impossible to know what went on in this man's mind. She shivered involuntarily.

The earl was seated now, making polite but stiff conversation with Sylvia, who was glowing, seemingly undisturbed by the sneer and the empty eyes.

Cousin Hetty was talking. "And Miss Dacey plays quite beautifully," she was saying. "You would be impressed, Cousin Edward."

"Indeed?" he said, not bothering to hide his skepticism. He was accustomed to having his sensibilities

murdered by eager debutantes who thought they could
play the pianoforte divinely. He frequently amused himself by imagining the expression on their faces if he did
what instinct directed him to do and slammed the lid
down onto the dabbling fingers. He had never put his
fantasy to the test. He intended to quell the preten-
sions of his ward without delay. He had no wish to hear
his precious instruments abused by a mediocre talent or
no talent at all.

"Come, ma'am," he said coldly, rising to his feet and
extending a hand in her direction, "I must hear you
perform."

"Oh, no, pray, my lord," she protested. "You are a
connoisseur of the arts, I am told. I play merely for my
own pleasure."

"Let us have no false modesty," he said impatiently,
looking steadily at her. "If you are good, I shall tell you
so. If you are not, I shall also tell you."

Rosalind's heart was beating so erratically that she
was having a difficult time breathing. The moment had
come, then. The pianoforte was at the opposite end of a
very large room. She had prepared herself for this,
dreaded it. But now there was no postponing it. Already the earl's face was showing signs of growing impatience. She stood up and began to cross the room.

"Have you sprained your ankle, Miss Dacey?" he
asked sharply from behind her.

She turned to face his frowning stare. "No, my lord,"
she answered coolly. "My limp is a permanent disability."

His eyes narrowed. "Explain, please," he ordered.

"I fell from a horse when I was five years old and
broke my leg," she explained. "The physician who attended me set it poorly. When I recovered, it was to
find that the injured leg was shorter than the other."

He stared at her blankly. "The doctor must have
been drunk," he said.

"I have been told that he was," she replied calmly.

"Sit down, ma'am," Raymore said, the pianoforte
forgotten. The only thought in his head was that he had

been cheated. No one had ever hinted to him that one of his wards was a cripple. How was he ever to find her a husband? He would be forced to support her for the rest of his life, a permanent millstone around his neck. To say that the girl limped was to put the matter kindly.

The earl did not seat himself again. He made his excuses, bowed with stiff formality, and left the room.

Sylvia followed Rosalind upstairs a short while later. "Is my cousin not quite gorgeous, Ros?" she bubbled as they climbed the staircase together, Rosalind holding on to the rail.

"Quite devastatingly handsome," she agreed dryly.

Sylvia giggled. "Is it permitted to marry one's guardian, I wonder?" she said, opening the door into her cousin's room and following her inside.

"I imagine there is no law against it," Rosalind replied, "but he is your cousin, Sylvie."

Sylvia clasped her hands and smiled broadly. "But he is not yours," she pointed out. "You must set your cap at him, Ros. The Countess of Raymore!"

Rosalind smiled and sat on the bed. "If I had your looks, I might be tempted," she said with a lightness she did not feel, "but I think I shall settle for being an old maid. She held up a hand when her cousin made a face and would have spoken. "Besides," she added, "I don't like him, Sylvie."

"Why ever not?" that young lady replied. "I thought him excessively polite, Ros, and he did not insult you when he saw you limp. I thought him quite kind when he told you to sit down instead of making you walk quite across the room to the pianoforte."

"Did you not notice his eyes, Sylvie?" Rosalind asked. "They are cold and unfeeling. And his mouth sneers. I felt that the man holds us in the utmost contempt. The less we see of him, the happier I shall be."

"Pooh," Sylvia protested, "you are imagining things just because you were embarrassed to have him see you walk."

Rosalind shook her head. "You must go and dress," she said, changing the subject. "I somehow feel sure that his lordship would not take kindly to our being late for dinner—if he deigns to give us his company, of course."

Rosalind did not follow her own advice well. She changed rapidly enough into a blue silk gown that fit as loosely as her day dresses. But her hair gave her trouble. She pinned and unpinned, coaxed and teased, but to no avail. She was not concentrating, she concluded. Finally she threw the brush with a clatter onto the dressing table and stared despairingly at her image in the mirror. She felt terribly betrayed. She had accepted her own ugliness; she had accepted the fact that no man would ever look at her with anything but revulsion. She had not become bitter, had not allowed herself to become jealous of Sylvia or of any of the other young ladies of her acquaintance. All she had was her dream. And she had felt safe with Alistair. Because he was unreal, a creation of her own imagination, he would remain with her through life, soothing her through the lonely years, giving the illusion of love and acceptance.

And now, in one day, just when she needed him the most, he had been destroyed. By what uncanny coincidence of fate had she imagined a man who was physically identical to her guardian? She doubted that she would ever be able to resurrect Alistair with his kind eyes and his platonic love that was completely centered on her. The stiff manner, the sneer, and the disapproving air of the Earl of Raymore would always intrude.

She hated him. Perhaps that was unfair. He had, as Sylvia said, acted with politeness. He had said and done nothing discourteous or unkind. Even when he had noticed and questioned her limp, he had not said anything to disclose disgust. But because he resembled Alistair so closely, she was unusually sensitive to the hard core of dislike that she was quite sure he felt for both of them. And he had no reason to feel that way. He did not know them. They had not imposed their presence on him. He had summoned them. Yes, she hated him.

Tomorrow she would go to him and ask to be sent back home. He surely would not refuse. He was a physically perfect man and he obviously cultivated beauty around him. His house was furnished with tasteful objects and priceless works of art. He was known for the first-class musical talent that he engaged yearly to entertain his friends. He must agree that she could merely be an embarrassment to him. She must convince him that she would never impose upon him in the future. He could forget her very existence.

He had been right about the doctor, though. He had been drunk, just like everyone else who had gathered on her father's estate for the hunt. The hunt was an annual affair, her aunt had told her much later, but was more an excuse for an orgy of drinking and feasting than a sporting event. Rosalind had been at home with her parents. She lived mostly with her uncle and aunt, the Earl and Countess of Raymore, because her parents traveled almost constantly. But their times together were very intense. Her mother had taught her to sing, her father to ride. She remembered them as a vibrant couple, whom she had loved passionately, though she realized now that they had been very selfish people.

On that particular occasion, Rosalind's father had insisted that she ride, although she was far too young to join the hunt. He had urged her, laughing, toward a fence higher than any she had jumped before. She could almost remember the sound of her own laughter as she had spurred her pony toward it. She could not remember anything else except the tedium of days and weeks spent in the house and, later, the garden, while her leg healed beneath the splints.

Everyone had laughed and teased her when the splints were first removed and she had limped and hopped excitedly around the house. But Rosalind could remember her father's towering rage when it became obvious that the limp was involuntary and when someone—her mother?—had measured her legs. She was not now sure if her father really had gone and horsewhipped the doctor, or if she had just made up that detail to satisfy her child's imagination.

But her father had insisted, cruelly almost, that she overcome her terror of climbing back into the saddle again. Only later, after his death, would she thank him for his foresight.

"We will make of you the finest horsewoman in the damned county, my little Rosalinda," he had promised, "and everyone will see you as a creature of grace and beauty." He had fingered a shiny lock of black hair lovingly as his gaze strayed to his wife.

They had both died of the typhoid a year later while visiting her mother's relatives in Italy. Rosalind had not suffered outwardly. She had never seen a great deal of her parents. But inwardly something had been lost. The first of her dreams had died.

And now a second, she thought grimly, picking up her brush again and tackling her mane of black hair once more.

The Earl of Raymore was also not making any great effort to get ready for dinner. He had gone to the library after leaving the drawing room and still sat there.

He had a problem, there was no doubt about it. The cousin was all right, at least. She was lovely and appeared not to be unduly shy. Raymore had not taken too much notice of what she had to say during the few minutes he had sat talking to her, but he was sure that she would take well. She would probably have a large following of eager bucks within a few days of next week's ball. All that would be required of him would be to choose the most eligible without delay.

But the other! What was he to do with her? His first instinct had been to send her back where she had come from. But that would not answer. He was responsible for her until she was married. He would never be able to forget about her, never be free of her, if he admitted defeat at this point. He would have to think of some way of getting her married. Surely there was someone who would be willing to take her off his hands, someone who really needed a wife and did not much care what she looked like or how she walked. Not that the girl was exactly ugly. If she dressed more becomingly and did something with her hair, she would be presentable, at least. He did not like her, though. She had been almost willing to argue with him about playing the pianoforte, and he had not liked the way she had looked directly and defiantly into his eyes when she had told him about her lameness. The girl did not know her place, he guessed. He would have to remind her, if necessary, of who was the guardian and who the ward.

The earl thought with distaste of the ball that was planned for the following week. He frowned. That was too long to wait. He must begin the campaign before then, especially for Miss Dacey. She would certainly not show to advantage at a ball. He made a mental note to speak to Hetty the next morning and instruct her to take the girls to a modiste to have new wardrobes made and to a stylist to have more fashionable hairstyles. They must be ready with at least one outfit apiece by the following day. He would take them to the theater and let them be ogled from the other boxes. A limp was not apparent when one sat at a play.

Raymore rang the bell at his elbow. When the butler appeared, he was informed that his lordship would not dine at home. White's Club was a more congenial setting for this particular evening than his own home.

3

The Earl of Raymore entered his house late the following morning and made his way, as usual, to his secretary's office to examine the morning's post. He was feeling quite pleased with himself. He had had his promised talk with Hetty earlier and she had been most eager to comply with his demands. She had been delighted at the prospect of preparing her charges for a visit to the theater. Henry had just agreed to join the party, provided there had been no further developments in his wife's delicate condition by the following evening. And, best of all, Raymore had just thought of Sir Rowland Axby. A middle-aged man of unprepossessing appearance and totally lacking in personality, he had nevertheless succeeded in finding a bride fifteen years before and fathering a brood of six youngsters before his wife died. His efforts to find himself a new mate were fast becoming a standing joke with the *ton*. Miss Dacey would be perfect for him. Axby would want a wife who would be prepared to rusticate with the children. His ward would doubtless be grateful to have her future settled and to be removed from the embarrassment of a public setting. He instructed Sheldon to send an invitation to Sir Rowland to attend his ball the following week.

"Miss Dacey has asked to· speak with you on your return, my lord," Sheldon said.

"Eh?" said Raymore, looking up from a letter that he held in his hand. "Has she not gone shopping with her cousin and Mrs. Laker?"

"I believe they have postponed the outing until after luncheon, my lord," the secretary replied.

Raymore put the letter down on the desk in irritation and frowned at Sheldon. "What does she want?"

"She did not say, my lord."

"Send word that she may attend me in the library at once," the earl directed and strode from the room. The infernal chit! He had known she would be trouble.

Rosalind assumed a confidence she did not quite feel as she waited for a footman to open the library doors for her. Her guardian was seated behind a heavy mahogany desk at the far side of the room, sunlight streaming in from the window behind him, making a halo of his blond hair. She felt that he had deliberately placed himself there so that she would be forced to undergo the ordeal of limping across the room toward him while he watched her steadily. His elbows were on the desk, his fingers steepled beneath his chin. Alistair with a stony expression!

"Have a seat, Miss Dacey," he said, motioning to a straight chair at the other side of his desk.

Rosalind sat down, her back straight. He did not initiate any conversation. He sat and stared at her.

"My lord, will you please allow me to return home?" she blurted, and watched his eyebrows rise haughtily. She had not intended to broach the subject quite so bluntly.

"Home, Miss Dacey?" he queried, ice dripping from each word. "You are at home, ma'am. This is your home as long as I choose to make it so."

Rosalind blushed and bit her lip. "I mean to Raymore Manor, my lord," she said. "Indeed, I appreciate your kindness in inviting us here. For Sylvia it is a dream come true to be in London during the Season. But you did not know when you invited us here that I am disabled. I cannot mix with society, my lord. My presence would merely be an embarrassment to you and to myself. I am sure you must agree."

"Must I?" he asked quietly.

Rosalind paused, uncertain of his reaction. His eyes gave no clue. "Will you allow me to return?" she asked.

"No, I will not," he replied.

Rosalind swallowed. "Why not?"

His eyebrows rose. "Because I choose not to allow it, Miss Dacey," he said. "This is reason enough."

Her jaw clenched. "You have given no reason at all," she snapped unwisely. "Kindly make yourself clearer, my lord."

His palms lowered to the desk and he rose to his feet without hurry. He did not remove his gaze from Rosalind's face. "I shall make myself clear, ma'am," he said very softly, coming around the desk to stand towering over her, "crystal-clear, I trust. I am your guardian. Until you marry, you are my responsibility. I shall choose what is best for you and you will not question my decisions. Perhaps my uncle allowed you to question him and dictate your own terms. You will not find me so amenable. I tell you now that you will remain in London until the end of the Season or until I have found you a husband. At the end of the Season I shall tell you where you will be going. You do not need to concern yourself with the matter. You will not be consulted. Do I make myself understood, ma'am?"

Rosalind had sat crimson-faced through most of this icily delivered monologue. Now she looked at him with an expression of incredulity. She laughed scornfully. "You speak like a character from a gothic romance," she said. "I am two and twenty, my lord, a grown woman. Do you believe you can browbeat me as if I were a child? You have it within your power, I suppose, to keep me here against my will. I am reminded that the place I call home is in reality your home now. But this idea of totally ruling my life as if I were a mindless imbecile! I would remind you, sir, that we moved out of the Dark Ages a significant time ago."

His jaw clenched. "By God, ma'am, you will learn who is master here," he said. "If you must speak with a shrewish tongue, you may do so, but not with me as an audience. And you will remain in this house at my pleasure and do as I bid you. You have a ball to prepare for next week, and I believe that at the moment you are delaying a shopping expedition."

Rosalind rose to her feet and glared up into his face. "And that is another thing," she said. "I believe you have commanded us to have new clothes. I thank you for Sylvia, my lord. She is most excited at the prospect. I need nothing new. I am quite satisfied with the clothes that I have."

"You do not have to look at yourself wearing them," he sneered. "A sack would become you as well as the gown you are wearing now. Look at you!" He rashly reached out a hand and grasped a handful of fabric at her waist, startling himself when his knuckles came to rest against the shapely curve of a hip.

Rosalind jumped back, slapping at his hand and colliding clumsily with the chair as she landed on her weak leg. "Don't touch me!" she hissed.

He stood staring at her for a moment, his hand still outstretched. Rosalind turned and limped her way to the door, uncaring that her hasty progress merely emphasized her ungainly motion. His voice stopped her as she grasped the door handle.

"You will accompany Mrs. Laker and your cousin this afternoon," he said, "and you will purchase the garments that I have instructed Hetty to help you choose. If you fail to do so, Miss Dacey, I shall take you shopping myself tomorrow."

Rosalind, seething, had no doubt that he meant what he said.

Madame de Valéry, to whom Cousin Hetty conducted her charges as one of the most fashionable modistes on Bond Street, was a busy woman. A demand to have two new evening gowns designed, made, and delivered by the following afternoon was one that she would not normally have complied with. But when Mrs. Laker dropped the name of the Earl of Raymore, she thought that perhaps she might oblige if her seamstresses could be prevailed upon to work through the night. Madame did not personally know the earl. He was unmarried and did not keep mistresses, as far as anyone knew. But he was enormously wealthy. If it suited his fancy to rig out these two young ladies—even the crippled one—in the height of fashion, she would go out of her way to please him.

The younger of the two was every dressmaker's dream. Petite and very pretty, she also had enough interest in the clothes that were to be made to stand through the tedious business of being measured and to point out designs, fabrics, and trimmings that she liked. She was also flatteringly willing to take advice. With her coloring, did she not agree that the spring-green satin would make a more dazzling underdress for the white lace that she had chosen for her come-out ball? Oh, yes, Lady Sylvia Marsh thought that was a splendid idea.

The older one was a different kettle of fish altogether. She had the most unfortunate limp, which would surely ruin her chances of cutting any sort of dash. But she need not be such a dowd. She had fine hair—a trifle dark for fashion, of course, but thick and shiny. She made it quite clear to her long-suffering chaperone, though, that she would *not* have it cut and styled just to please his lordship. It suited *her* very well the way it was. Her figure, too, was good. Madame de Valéry learned this after winning a battle in which she insisted that she could not make miss's clothes by measuring the ones she wore. She must measure miss herself. Miss Dacey stood with set jaw and angry eyes while Madame discovered that beneath the loose, ill-fitting walking dress was a figure that many an actress or opera dancer would have killed for: full breasts, tiny waist, generous hips, and long slim legs—though, of course, there must be something wrong with them to cause her to walk the way she did.

The young lady took almost no interest in the styles that were chosen for her, but she did plead with Madame when her cousin and Mrs. Laker were out of earshot to please make the gown loose-fitting. She did not wish to display herself to the gaping *ton*. The poor dressmaker protested that her professional reputation was at stake. She would lose half her patrons if it were seen that she had outfitted the protégée of the Earl of Raymore in a sack. She did, however, agree to neck-lines that were more modest than she favored, and to high-waisted gowns with skirts a trifle less figure-hugging than most young ladies desired.

Rosalind had to be satisfied with the small victories she had won.

It was only the following afternoon that Sylvia and Rosalind discovered the reason why one gown each had had to be delivered that same day. They were to attend the theater, it seemed, with their guardian and his friend Sir Henry Martel. The great Edmund Kean himself was to play Shylock.

"Oh, I do think it kind of his lordship to arrange entertainment for us so soon," Sylvia said to Cousin Hetty, her eyes shining. "I feared that he did not like us, that we were a nuisance to him, as he paid only that one brief call on us two days ago. But he has arranged this for us, and the ball next week."

"Cousin Edward is not accustomed to having ladies around him," Hetty explained, attempting to tie a bow in the red ribbon that she had placed around the neck of one little poodle. "He does not know quite how to behave in female company, I believe. He is shy."

"Oh, do you believe so?" Sylvia asked, her eyes large with sympathy. "I had not thought of that. We must make an effort tonight to set him at his ease, Ros. Shall we?"

Rosalind smiled fleetingly. "I must disagree with Cousin Hetty," she said. "The man is not shy. He is arrogant and he is a tyrant."

"Oh, I do not feel you should speak that way about his lordship," Cousin Hetty said, flustered. "Hold still,

Pootsie, my love. After all, my dear, he has invited each of us into his home and has seen to it that we have every comfort."

Rosalind did not reply. She had no wish to begin an argument. She was relieved to find during the conversation that ensued, though, that the earl was to dine with his friend and that the two of them would return in time to escort the ladies to the theater. During the play she would be able to direct her attention to the action on the stage. Only during the carriage ride would she be forced to make conversation with that horrid man. She dreaded seeing him again. Her interview with him the previous morning had convinced her that he was the kind of man she most disliked. To him women were not persons at all. They were mere chattels who were made to be seen and not heard, who were to kiss with gratitude the ground before the man who deigned to notice them. Rosalind had never been a rebellious girl. She had been used to living her own very private life while sharing a home with relatives she loved and respected. But she neither liked nor respected the Earl of Raymore, and she had no intention of allowing him to rule her life. She had decided the previous day, after her meeting with him, that there could be nothing but open warfare between the two of them. She would cross him at every opportunity that presented itself.

The earl himself was having similar thoughts. He had avoided meeting his wards after that first formal introduction. He had no wish to exert himself in making the kind of polite and inane conversation that women seemed to enjoy. And he did not wish to give that Italian spitfire a chance to cross swords with him again. He knew now beyond a doubt that she was trouble, but he would handle her. He had been pleased to learn from Hetty that she had attended a modiste along with his young cousin and had been fitted for all the garments that would be necessary during the Season. Perhaps she had learned that it was pointless to argue with him. But Raymore doubted it.

When he entered the drawing room of his own home after dinner with Sir Henry, he was pleasantly impressed. His cousin Sylvia now looked perfect for her part. Her hair had been trimmed so that the blond curls molded her head and trailed down a very delicate neck. She wore a gown of the palest blue that appeared to be a perfect match for her eyes. She would do very well. This evening's appearance would whet the appetites of those men who were on the lookout for a beautiful heiress. And who was not? he thought cynically.

His other ward was looking almost promising, too, if one ignored the look of hostile defiance in her dark eyes. She wore a gown of royal-blue velvet with modest neckline and rather wide folds falling from the high waistline. Madame de Valéry had done a rather clever job of hiding the girl's lack of shape, he decided, ignoring the incongruous memory of the feel of her hip beneath his hand the morning before. Her hair, too, was dressed becomingly in heavy coils high on her head, loose curls trailing her neck and temples. She looked striking, he decided, even if not handsome.

Sir Henry, having been introduced to the ladies, scooped an indignant poodle pup out of the nearest chair and sat down. Sylvia took the little bundle from him and soothed it in her lap as she talked to her new acquaintance as if she had known him all her life.

The Earl of Raymore turned to Rosalind. "I compliment you on your appearance, Miss Dacey," he said unsmilingly, "but I see that you did not have your hair styled."

"You can perhaps force me to buy clothes, my lord," she answered coolly, "but my hair is part of my person. And I will allow no one, not even you, any control over that."

He turned away from her, showing no visible reaction. "Shall we go?" he said to the room at large. "The carriage is waiting."

"A trifle early, are we not, Edward?" asked Sir Henry. But he rose to his feet when his friend did not reply.

Raymore had good reason for leaving early. He wished to have Rosalind seated in her box before a large number of curious eyes could watch her arrival.

His plan succeeded. The boxes were almost empty when he seated his wards. Only a few young men had taken up their positions of vantage in the pit, where they could ogle all the ladies as they arrived.

"Oh, look, Ros," Sylvia exclaimed, grabbing her cousin by the wrist. "That man is entirely pink. Even his hair!"

She stared quite openly at a tall young man who stood languidly in the pit, surveying some new arrivals in the box opposite through a quizzing glass.

"That is one of our most prized exquisites, Lady Marsh," Sir Henry said, smiling and leaning forward. "Lord Fanhope. He turns a different color for each day of the week. He even wears a patch on his cheek. It is somewhat unfortunate that the color is pink tonight. The patch cannot be easily distinguished from this distance."

"If you keep staring at him, cousin," Raymore added, "he will be your friend for life."

"Well, I think he looks remarkably silly," Sylvia decided, and she turned her attention away from its unworthy object.

"Does your wife not enjoy the theater, Sir Henry?" Rosalind asked, having heard him refer earlier to a wife.

He smiled at her. "Elise would love to be here," he said, "but she is not going into company these days. She expects to be confined any day now."

Rosalind gave him her full attention. "Oh, how splendid!" she said, her face glowing. "Is it to be your first, sir?"

Sir Henry was unused to anyone talking about the expected event. Pregnancy was generally considered to be an ungenteel topic of conversation. Most people would politely choose not to notice when a lady was missing from society for a few months.

"I should be so delighted to meet Lady Martel if I may, at a time convenient to her, of course," Rosalind continued. The greatest regret she had about her physical condition had always been that, because she would not marry, she would also not bear children.

The Earl of Raymore, standing at the back of the box, was pleased. His cousin, of course, would take with no trouble at all. But even the other girl was glowing at the moment. She looked almost handsome with her bright dress, and her dark hair and eyes. For once she even had some color in her cheeks. He let his eyes stray casually around the other boxes and the pit, all of which were now full. The attention of several people was directed at his box. His plan was working well, it seemed.

The evening continued well. During the intermission, Sir Henry left to greet some friends in another box. And several of Raymore's acquaintances paid a call in his box with the obvious purpose of being introduced to the two young ladies. The earl, his manner cool and detached, performed the introductions and mentally assessed each visitor. Mr. Victor Parkins, balding, paunchy, was obviously taken with his cousin. Rich enough, well-enough connected, but not a dazzling-enough catch. She could aim higher. Charles Hammond, charming, handsome, also set out to dazzle Sylvia. Not a bad connection, but something of a rake. The chit looked interested, too. He must be careful that Hammond did not get too close to her at next week's ball. Sir Bernard Crawleigh was eminently suitable. He had the connections, the presence, and the wealth to win Raymore's approval. The earl watched in some fascination, though, as the young man directed his interest, not at Sylvia, but at Rosalind. He had no chance to observe her reactions as his attention was claimed by the arrival of Sidney Darnley, come to view the newly arrived heiresses.

By the end of the evening, Raymore was still feeling satisfied with himself and his wards. He should be able to get them off his hands by the end of the Season. Even Miss Dacey need not be a hopeless case if she could find a way of hiding her deformity and if she would keep her caustic tongue still.

He lingered with his party until most of the audience had left the theater. He let Sir Henry lead Sylvia out and then offered his arm to Rosalind. He drew her arm through his and held it firmly against his side as he led her down the stairs and out to the pavement, where his carriage had now found an empty spot in which to wait.

Rosalind fumed and shrank away from the hard masculine body against which she was being pulled. "My walk may not be elegant, my lord," she said quietly, for his ears only, "but I am capable of moving unassisted from place to place."

He looked sidelong at her, his eyes glacial as usual. "I hoped to save you from embarrassment," he said.

"You could do that very effectively," she retorted, "by allowing me to return home."

"*Touché*," he answered. "You do enjoy having the last word, Miss Dacey, do you not?"

He handed her into the carriage and jumped in after her. Sir Henry excused himself as soon as they arrived back in Grosvenor Square. He did assure Rosalind, though, that his wife would invite her to visit whenever she felt well enough. The earl, too, left the house again to visit one of his clubs, having seen his wards safely into the care of Cousin Hetty and the dogs.

Rosalind and Sylvia spent a fairly quiet time for the five days that remained before the ball. They went shopping with Cousin Hetty a few times and helped her walk the dogs in the park during the mornings. But they could neither receive nor accept any invitations until they had made their official come-out.

Sylvia was impatient, but happy. The shopping expeditions and the arrival of the bulk of their new wardrobes filled her with excited anticipation. And the visit to the theater had whetted her appetite for more meetings with society.

"Did you not think Mr. Hammond exceedingly charming, Ros?" she asked one afternoon when Rosalind sat on her bed while Sylvia held her new clothes against herself one at a time and surveyed the effect in a long mirror.

"I certainly noticed that he was handsome," Rosalind replied with a smile. "Do you like him?"

"Do you suppose he has been invited to Cousin Edward's ball?" Sylvia wondered, answering the question indirectly.

"He must be acquainted with our guardian or he would not have come to his box at the theater," Rosalind said. "It is likely that he will have received an invitation."

"Oh, I do hope so," Sylvia said.

Rosalind tried as far as possible to forget about the coming ball. She was pleased two days after the theater visit to receive a note from Lady Elise Martel, inviting both Sylvia and herself to call on her during the afternoon. Sylvia declined, as she had already agreed to go with Cousin Hetty to a milliner's for the purchase of several new bonnets. Rosalind was glad of the excuse to avoid having to go with her, and she genuinely looked forward to meeting Lady Elise. She had liked her husband very much.

The Earl of Raymore's carriage delivered her to Sir Henry's home. A butler took her bonnet and gloves and showed her into a light and airy sitting room. Lady Elise rose to greet her. She was a smiling, auburn-haired lady, very pretty, Rosalind decided, despite her large bulk.

"Miss Dacey?" she said, coming forward, right hand extended. "This is a most unorthodox way to meet, but I am so obliged to you for coming. Henry was very taken with you the other evening and mentioned that you hoped to meet me. I hope you have not come merely out of the kindness to a poor pregnant lady who is confined to the house."

"Indeed I have not, ma'am," Rosalind assured her. "I do not like to be seen in public, either. I would rather be here with you than on Bond Street with my cousin Sylvia and Mrs. Laker."

Lady Elise smiled and motioned Rosalind to a chair. "Is it because of your limp?" she asked candidly.

Rosalind was surprised at her own lack of embarrassment. "Yes," she admitted. "I hate to be noticed by everyone, especially for such an ugly defect."

"I can see that it would limit your activities," Lady Elise agreed. "You would not want to walk too much in the park, I imagine, and I suppose you cannot dance. But I would advise you not to be overly conscious of the fact that you limp. When people have once noticed, they will disregard it, you may be sure. And you have other assets."

Rosalind shrugged in a resigned manner. "I know that I am ugly," she said, "but I have learned to accept the fact. All I ask is to be allowed to live my own sort of life."

Lady Elise chuckled. "And Edward will not allow you to do so. Henry said that he thought you and your guardian do not see eye to eye. I can imagine how trying it must be for you. He hates women, you know. But, my dear Miss Dacey—may I call you Rosalind? —why do you call yourself ugly? You are no such thing. It is true that you do not have the peaches-and-cream look of the typical English debutante. You must have foreign blood, do you? French?"

"Italian."

Lady Elise nodded. "You are not pretty," she said frankly. "Your hair is too dark and your features too strong. But you could be quite extraordinarily handsome if you chose. You should wear your hair high on your head and hold your shoulders back more and your chin high. And your clothes should be more carefully made to your figure." She frowned and unexpectedly wagged a finger at her guest. "I would wager that you are deliberately hiding a good figure. Am I right?"

Rosalind did not know how to reply. She was saved from her embarrassment when Lady Elise laughed suddenly. "My manners have certainly gone begging," she said. "Goodness, we have just met. It is most impertinent of me to pick you apart the way I just did. Please forgive me. Put it down to my condition. I am living in a rather unreal world at the moment, where the usual rules do not apply."

Rosalind immediately relaxed. The conversation switched to a discussion of the coming event and Elise's fervent hope that she would bear a boy. She assured Rosalind, though, that Henry would not be at all disappointed with a girl. The visit lasted for more than an hour. Rosalind felt as if she had known her new friend for years. She promised to return the following week, after the ball, if the new arrival had still not put in an appearance.

The visit to Lady Martel occupied only a single afternoon. Rosalind helped keep her mind off the ball for much of the rest of the time by busying herself with music and reading. She paid a few visits to the library at times when she knew that the earl was not at home. She discovered a volume of Mr. Pope's poems and carried it off to her room, where she spent many hours reading his poems carefully. She thoroughly enjoyed "The Rape of the Lock" and read it many times. But on the whole she found his tone unnecessarily caustic. Much of what he wrote was the product of a bitter mind. And he had had some deformity, she had read somewhere. She shuddered. She hoped she would never allow her physical condition to warp her mind or her attitude to life.

And she spent many hours in the music room. She was fascinated by the harpsichord and played it often. It was especially suited to the music of Bach, she found. But it was the pianoforte that became her particular love. She played Haydn, Mozart, all the music she had ever learned, in fact. And she sang to her own accompaniment. She sang old ballads and newer love songs.

In the music room she could completely forget herself. It was a large room at the far end of a wing of the house that contained none of the apartments that were in daily use. The instruments stood in the middle of the room, far from windows and doors. Here she could play and sing undisturbed and undetected. Here she could be happy and forget such things as balls and society and stubborn, arrogant guardians.

She would not have felt so contented had she known that on an afternoon three days before the ball the Earl of Raymore, on his way to his room to change from his riding clothes into an outfit more suited for dining out, heard the distant sound of music. He stopped in his tracks and listened. His jaw set in annoyance when he realized that the sounds were coming from the music room. Only carefully selected guests, including the professional performers that he invited to play at his annual concerts, were allowed to touch the instruments there. One of his wards must be tinkling away in her best schoolroom manner. What sacrilege!

He changed direction grimly and strode toward the door of the music room. It was probably Rosalind Dacey. She was the one who fancied herself as an accomplished musician, he seemed to remember. He would make it perfectly clear to her that she was welcome to practise in the drawing room when he was not there, but that the music room was very definitely out of bounds.

He stopped just outside the door, his hand stretched toward the handle but not quite touching it. She was singing. He did not recognize either the words or the melody, but the song was so simple and so haunting that it halted his progress completely:

> My Luve is like a red, red rose
> That's newly sprung in June

Raymore felt a momentary sharp pang whose source

and meaning he could not identify. She should always sing. She had a contralto voice that was soft and throbbing with feeling. It was sheer beauty.

> And I will come again, my Luve,
> Tho' 'twere ten thousand mile!

The song was finished. The earl's hand had fallen to his side, but he still stood and listened as she continued to play the melody. After a while she began to hum again.

When she started to play Beethoven, the Earl of Raymore moved away from the room without opening the door. She was good, he was forced to admit. He would leave her alone with her music. She could probably do no harm to his prize possessions, after all.

He did not intend to, he did not particularly want to, but he found his feet taking him toward the door of the music room for the following two afternoons. The first time she was playing the harpischord. He did not hear it very often. Most of his guests avoided it as an outdated instrument inferior in versatility to the pianoforte. But she made Bach sound brilliant, as if the harpsichord were the only instrument that would bring his music to full life. The second time she was singing again, an old ballad of valor and love and death. She made him feel all the grandeur and all the pathos of the old story. That must be how the ballads had been sung all those years ago, when song had been the chief method of communicating news as well of entertaining.

Raymore retreated abruptly when the music stopped and did not immediately resume. He had no wish to be caught spying or, indeed, to come face to face with his ward. Rosalind Dacey, musician, he had been forced to recognize and respect in the last few days. Rosalind Dacey, the woman, was a different matter altogether. He could live quite happily if he never encountered her again.

Rosalind had much the same thoughts in reverse during those few days. She saw very little of the earl.

But she still seethed with resentment over his refusal to allow her to return home and over his insistence that she attend the ball. She did not intend to submit meekly to her fate, though. She smiled several times to herself, thinking of the plan she had made to make the Earl of Raymore see things her way.

4

---·••·---

The servants and extra hired workmen bustled around all the day of the ball, preparing for the three hundred guests who were expected in the evening. The hallways and grand staircase were scrubbed and polished and decorated with lavish floral displays. The ballroom underwent similar treatment. By late afternoon the whole house smelled of roses and carnations.

Sylvia and Rosalind had been sent to bed by a firm Cousin Hetty after lunch. They were to rest, she insisted, even if they were too excited to sleep. A hair stylist was to come later to dress their hair and then it would be time for an early dinner and all the bustle of getting ready before joining the earl at the receiving line.

Surprisingly, Sylvia was ready first. Flushed and excited, she tapped on Rosalind's door and let herself into the room without waiting for an answer. Rosalind swiveled around on her stool, disregarding the dresser whom Cousin Hetty had insisted she allow to help her to dress. The woman was attempting to fasten a string of pearls around her neck.

"Oh, you do look lovely, Sylvie," Rosalind exclaimed. "Just as a young girl should look at her come-out, I believe."

"Starry-eyed and heart aflutter?" her cousin asked, laughing. "It is absurd to be in such high spriits, is it not, Ros, but I cannot help myself. Will I do?" She held the sides of her lace overdress and twirled for Rosalind's inspection.

The green underdress had been an inspired choice, Rosalind thought. Sylvia looked as fresh and innocent as spring. The lace was delicate and made the girl look ethereal. Her silver-blond hair, combed into soft, shining waves, was threaded with a green ribbon. Her cheeks glowed with natural color. There was just enough bosom displayed above the scalloped neckline of her dress to indicate that she was a woman and no longer a schoolgirl, yet not enough to draw undue comment.

"Indeed you will outshine everyone, Sylvie," she said with sincerity.

"Oh, but I shall not outdo you," her cousin answered loyally. "There will probably be a score of girls to resemble me, Ros, but no one could compare with you."

Rosalind grimaced, unable to see that comment as a compliment. She turned back to face the mirror and allowed the dresser to attach her pearl earrings to her ears. She was not displeased with her appearance, but she would need all the confidence she could muster to see her through the ordeal of the hours ahead.

Conceding the fact that she could not change the color of her hair, she had to admit that the style was good. Lady Elise had been right. It did suit her to have it piled into complicated swirls and twists on the crown and back of her head. But the hairdresser had allowed enough loose ends to curl around her face and along her neck to give her a softly feminine look. The dresser had insisted on a little rouge to relieve the paleness of her skin. And it was so artfully applied, blended so carefully along the line of her cheekbone, that it looked natural.

Rosalind stood and examined her gown in a long mirror. One thing she had insisted upon during her reluctant fittings at Madame de Valéry's. She was two and twenty. Although this was officially her come-out Season, she refused to behave like a debutante and wear pastel shades. They would serve only to accentuate her age and to emphasize the darkness of her coloring. She wore a deep rose-red gown of unadorned satin. The neckline was modest. Madame had cunningly fashioned the bodice so that it flared loosely from just beneath the breasts. The skirt was full but not illfitting. It swirled around her as she moved. Rosalind was not given to pointless longings, but she did catch herself thinking wistfully of being able to dance as she gazed at the rose-pink slippers that peeked beneath the wide hem of her dress. She gave herself a mental shake, drew on the elbow-length white gloves that the dresser was holding out to her, and turned to Sylvia with a smile. "Shall we go down," she suggested, "before his lordship comes looking for us, breathing fire and brimstone?"

He was waiting for them in the drawing room, looking magnificent, Rosalind conceded reluctantly. Her eyes took in the dull-gold knee breeches and coat, the brown waistcoat and snowy white linen and lace at neck and cuffs. He was truly handsome from the neck down, but his face looked more like that of a man contemplating his own execution than of one about to host a ball for the *ton*.

He bowed unsmilingly and placed his empty glass on the mantel. "You are both to be complimented on your appearance," he said. "Shall we join Hetty in the ballroom? Our first guests should be arriving soon."

He offered Rosalind his arm, but she pretended not to notice and turned and limped out of the room ahead of both him and Sylvia. She would not allow him to treat her like an invalid.

In one of his few meetings with his wards in the previous few days, Raymore had instructed Rosalind on how she was to conduct herself at the ball. She had felt like an enlisted soldier taking orders from a general. He had not asked or discussed or coaxed; he had told. She was to stand next to him in the receiving line, with Sylvia on her other side. If she became tired of standing, she must take his arm and lean on him. When the dancing was to begin, he would lead her as unobtrusively as possible to a sofa close to the door, after which he would begin the dancing by leading out Sylvia.

He and Cousin Hetty would introduce her to various guests; she assumed he meant various young men. Her inability to dance would be attributed to the fact that she was somewhat lame. He had considered telling everyone that she had twisted her ankle, he told her frankly, but had decided that that would not serve, as she could expect to be in London for at least two months and she could not convince everyone for the whole of that time with the twisted-ankle story.

On no account was she to move from the sofa. If no one else offered to bring her a plate of food at supper-time, he would do so himself. All she had to do was smile and be charming to all who came to converse with her.

It was while he talked that Rosalind devised her plan to get even with this man whom she had come to detest. Only this enabled her to sit outwardly serene as he talked about her quite candidly as if she were a piece of spoiled merchandise that a buyer would have to be tricked into purchasing. She would show him!

The first part of the evening went as planned. The Earl of Raymore was satisfied with the appearance of his wards. His cousin, of course, looked inviting, as he had expected. But he had been half-prepared for some resistance from Rosalind. He had thought that she might try to appear in an old gown or with a plain hairdo. He had been quite prepared to march her back to her room and threaten to take her inside and dress her himself if she did not immediately cooperate and dress herself becomingly. But he was impressed. In her own way she looked almost magnificent. Not in his style, of course, or quite in the style that was likely to take well with the *ton*, but certainly she was quite acceptable. If only she did not have that ugly limp!

She did not take his arm at all during the hour in which they stood greeting guests, even though he offered it several times when there was a lull in the lineup. But he could not complain about her attitude. She was not sullen. She smiled and shook hands with each person who passed. Raymore was pleased that he had taken such a firm stand with her from the beginning. She had obviously learned to accept his way as best for her.

When even the last trickle of guests appeared to have passed into the ballroom, Raymore sent Hetty and Sylvia in to draw the eyes of his guests, while he ushered Rosalind to the sofa that had been reserved for her.

She watched with something between amusement and wistfulness as the earl led Sylvia into the first set of country dances. She had never been to a ball, but had watched her cousin have dancing lessons at home. It was a silly pastime, she had decided in self-defense. But she did feel a momentary pang on this occasion as she watched so many elegantly dressed men and ladies move gracefully through the intricacies of the dance. It must be wonderful to be able to move with such grace.

She was not left long to brood alone. After the first set, her guardian approached with a young man who was trying to look at ease in a coat that must have taken three grown men to squeeze him into and collar points that held his head almost completely immobile. Although she conversed with him for almost half an hour, Rosalind could never remember afterward so much as his name. She was watching Sylvia dancing with a string of dazzling partners, including Mr. Charles Hammond, who looked even more dashing tonight than he had at the theater.

Rosalind remembered Sir Rowland Axby afterward, mainly because he sat with her during the supper dance and insisted on bringing her a plate of food and sitting beside her while she ate, though she urged him not to miss the gathering in the supper room on her account.

She felt a little sorry for the man. Nothing in either his looks or manner was particularly attractive, and such must have been the case all his life, she judged, because he talked very fast, holding her eyes with his

anxiously, as if he were accustomed to being interrupted. Rosalind had been bored even before his arrival. She might as well listen to him and give him a
little happiness, she thought resignedly. He talked about
his home, his possessions, his friends (she suspected
there was some fabrication there), and his children,
who ranged in age from twelve down.

The Earl of Raymore was definitely gratified. He had
already assessed the ball to be a resounding success
before supper was over. He had never enjoyed a ball,
of course, and could not be said to be enjoying this one.
But both his wards appeared to be well-launched. Sylvia had had a dizzying array of partners, many of them
eminently eligible and many of them appearing smitten
by her beauty and her sunny manner. He had noted
with particular interest that Lord Standen had danced
with her twice and had escorted her to supper. That
would indeed be a dazzling match. The man had rank,
looks, wealth, everything that could commend him to a
prospective bride.

And Rosalind was not to be the utter disaster that he
had feared. He had seen to it that she was partnered
during each dance but the first, and was pleased to see
that she was making an effort to be agreeable. As he
had hoped, she and Axby seemed to be dealing well
together. The girl apparently had sense. She must realize that she could not aim much higher and was prepared to consider his suit. And Axby looked very
interested. He had certainly seemed undeterred when
Raymore had explained to him that the girl could not
dance because she was lame.

And indeed, Raymore thought, for someone like Axby
she was a prize. She looked quite handsome tonight in
the richly colored gown and her hair dressed that way.
"A red, red rose" flashed through his mind, and he
looked at her curiously as the orchestra tuned up again
and Axby bent over her hand, saying his farewells. Tonight it was not so impossible to imagine that rich contralto voice as belonging to her.

Before Raymore had a chance to select another partner who might not object too strongly to sitting out a dance and talking to his ward, he noticed that Sir Bernard Crawleigh was standing before her. Raymore turned his attention to Sylvia, checking her partner for this dance. Standen's younger brother was leading her out for a quadrille. Raymore almost smiled. Was Standen trying to protect his interests by cutting out as many rivals as possible? He must have instructed his brother to dance with Sylvia. The two brothers were as different as day and night. Nigel Broome had none of the advantages of his brother, neither height, nor looks, nor confidence.

Rosalind was explaining to Sir Bernard why she could not dance. "To put it bluntly, sir," she said, looking frankly into his eyes, "I am crippled and have been ever since I had a riding accident at the age of five. Oh, I can walk," she assured him as his eyes strayed to her feet, "but only with a rather bad limp."

He smiled. "I wondered why you have been sitting here all evening, ma'am," he said. "May I join you?"

"If you really want to," she replied, "though I would not have you feel obliged to do so. I see several young ladies who look very eager to dance."

He grinned and sat down beside her. "This evening cannot be much fun for you," he said. "Are you here by choice or do I detect the heavy hand of Raymore in this? I can well imagine him playing the tyrant."

Rosalind smiled conspiratorially and found herself conversing quite easily with him for the next half-hour. She surprised herself. She was usually markedly self-conscious in the company of young men, especially ones as handsome as Sir Bernard, with his dark wavy hair, dancing brown eyes, and very charming smile. As she talked, she began to see how she might best put into effect her plan to teach her guardian a lesson. She certainly could not put it off much longer and was becoming quite agitated at the thought.

When the music stopped she smiled at her compan-

ion. "It is excessively hot in here, sir. Would you escort
me to the balcony for a breath of air?"

Sir Bernard did not immediately reply. "The balcony
is across the room from us, ma'am," he said, "across an
empty dance floor. Would you be embarrassed to have
all eyes upon you as you walked?"

Rosalind flushed. She would be extremely embarrassed but had decided that this plan was one sure way
of convincing Raymore to send her back home. At least
she would never again have to face any of these people.
"I perceive that *you* would be embarrassed to be seen
with me," she said.

He smiled slowly. "On the contrary," he said. "Do
you know, Miss Dacey, I have a sister who is constantly
into mischief. You remind me of her at the moment.
You are up to something, are you not? Now, what is
it?"

Her eyes twinkled back at him for a moment, but her
heart was also beating uncomfortably fast. "Shall we
go?" she asked, rising to her feet and extending an arm
to take his.

The guests, congregated around the edge of the dance
floor in small groups, gradually found their attention
caught by the slow progress right across the center of
the room of Sir Bernard Crawleigh and Miss Rosalind
Dacey, the ward of Raymore who had been seated all
evening and who was rumored to be lame. They all
become shockingly aware that the rumor was quite
true. Although the girl was rather splendidly dressed
and bore herself like a queen, she moved in a rather
ungainly manner. Why she chose thus to disclose her
deformity no one could imagine, but she appeared quite
unperturbed. In fact, both she and her companion
seemed engrossed in conversation, apparently unaware
that almost three hundred pairs of eyes were on them.
Having crossed the room, they disappeared through the
open French doors leading onto the stone balcony
outside.

The Earl of Raymore, conversing with a group of

acquaintances, had frozen at first. When he realized that his senses were not deceiving him, he ruthlessly suppressed his first instinct, which was to rush across to his ward and drag her out through the closest doorway. He smiled lazily and resumed his conversation. He waited until the music began again, made his excuses, and circled the room in leisurely manner until he too could leave through the French doors.

He could not remember ever being so angry in his life. The girl had done that quite deliberately. It was a well-calculated move to show her contempt for her guardian. And how well she had succeeded. Little fool! Did she think that any man would willingly be seen with her after this? Even Axby must have taken her in everlasting disgust. His one aim now was to find her so that he might have the satisfaction of placing his hands around her throat.

He did not have far to look. She and Sir Bernard were sitting on the bottom step leading onto the lawn that circled the house, laughing softly.

Rosalind looked over her shoulder when Raymore stood three steps above them. She had expected this encounter, was prepared for it. She looked up at him with a mixture of defiance and triumph in her eyes. He held her eyes with his, his expression impassive.

"Crawleigh, I wish to speak to my ward, please," he said softly and pleasantly.

"Miss Dacey was about to faint with the heat," Sir Bernard explained gallantly. "I suggested that I escort her outside for some fresh air."

"I thank you for your concern," Raymore said, his eyes still on his ward. "Would you leave us now, please?"

Sir Bernard glanced uneasily at Rosalind, but he really had no alternative but to turn and climb the steps again and disappear into the ballroom.

"Stand up," Raymore instructed, still very quietly and pleasantly. He descended the remaining steps until he was standing in front of her.

Rosalind knew without a doubt that if she did not

comply immediately, she would be yanked quite unceremoniously to her feet. She stood.

"Take my arm," he said, extending it with the utmost courtesy.

"Where are we going?" Rosalind asked suspiciously.

"Would you prefer to walk there with me and find out, or to be carried over my shoulder like a sack and find out that way?" he asked, his words quite at variance with the air of courtesy that he still assumed.

Rosalind took his arm. They walked in silence along the lawn close to the house until they came to a servants' entrance. Raymore opened the door and ushered her inside. He grasped her elbow and led her along dark passageways until they arrived unexpectedly in the main hall. He guided her across to the library, opened the door, and ushered her inside.

Rosalind drew a deep breath, walked across to the desk, and turned to face her guardian, her chin held high. He busied himself for a while lighting candles that stood on the mantel and then turned to her, his eyes for once alive—with blazing anger, she realized.

"You will explain that exhibition you just put on for the benefit of my guests," he said.

"I needed air, my lord," she replied defiantly.

"Don't lie to me, ma'am," he snapped. "It was for my benefit, was it not? Your revenge for what you consider to be tyrannical treatment?"

"Yes," she said, a light of triumph in her eyes. "You insisted, my lord, against my wishes, that I meet the *ton*. Well, tonight the *ton* met me. Me!" She pointed to herself emphatically. "If people are to meet me, they must know that there is more to me than black hair and dark eyes and clothes that Madame de Valéry has made as flattering as she can. They must know that there is more to me than a name and a comfortable dowry. They must know that I have two legs, just like them, but that one is shorter than the other. I showed them what you had so carefully tried to conceal."

"Fool!" he said through his teeth. "Do you expect that any man will wish to ally himself with you now that you have shown such shocking lack of taste? I have been working for your own interests, trying to find you a husband. You seem bent on alienating everyone who is anyone."

"Do you think I would care for any husband who was tricked into offering for me?" she cried. "Do you think the only purpose of a woman's life is to find herself a husband? If I ever marry, my lord, it will be to a man who loves me just as I am, limp and all, to a man who will not care that much"—she snapped her fingers above her head—"for the fact that I cannot walk elegantly or dance."

"Love!" he said, throwing a world of scorn into the word. "Have you been living with your head in the clouds all those years in the country? Here you will learn that marriages are alliances, carefully made for the advantage of both parties. And who would wish to ally himself to a woman who can so brazenly make herself the laughingstock in public?"

"Then let me go home," she said, "where I may dream of love if I wish and you can forget about alliances."

"Home!" he mocked. "Is that what this is all about? Have you been hoping that I will pack you off back to the country? You can forget that, my dear. Raymore Manor is my home. Do you think I wish to encounter you there every time I decide to visit?" The words were meant to be brutal and had their effect.

"Then I shall stay," she spat out at him, "and you may find me a husband if you can. But from now on, my lord, your prospective buyers must see *me*. Bring them here to the house and I shall strut up and down the drawing room for them. If any man can tolerate what he sees, he may make you his offer."

Her voice had risen to near-hysterical pitch. She held

her arms out to the sides and demonstrated the strut she had described. She greatly exaggerated her limp as she walked the length of the library and turned to walk back again.

"Stop it!" he hissed.

She looked across at him haughtily and continued to move. "Can you not see me walking down the aisle of St. George's, Hanover Square, toward my bridegroom, my lord?" she goaded. "On your arm?"

"Stop it!" he repeated. When she continued to prance past him, he strode across to her and grabbed her by the shoulders. "Stop it, do you hear me?"

"Perhaps you would like to offer for me yourself, Edward," she said, her voice becoming even more shrill. "You spend little enough time at home and would not have to look at me often. I might be prevailed upon to accept, you know. You are handsome enough." She smiled dazzlingly and tried to whisk herself away.

"Stop this, Rosalind," he ordered again, pulling her against his chest. "Enough!"

And because indeed she had no more to say, Rosalind did stop. They glared at each other for a few seconds, both breathing hard, and then inexplicably his mouth was on hers, pressing her lips against her teeth quite mercilessly.

They both jerked away almost immediately and gazed with something like horror into each other's eyes. There seemed no sensible reason why a moment later they were kissing again. This time his mouth came down across hers open, and it seemed the most natural thing in the world, when his tongue pressed insistently against her lips, to open her mouth to receive it. Heat flared between them as his arms drew her closer and as she molded her body to his, thighs, hips, breasts straining for closer contact.

His hands moved around to explore her breasts as his tongue stroked the warm recesses of her mouth. Her hands twined into his thick hair as she moved against his hands. They were both in the grip of raw desire.

It was Raymore who finally succeeded in pulling his mind free of his physical passion. He grasped her arms and put her from him as if she were a deadly snake. He watched her heavy-lidded eyes resume normal consciousness.

"So!" he said, imposing iron control on his voice. "It is now crystal-clear how you have occupied your time in the country, ma'am, and why you wish to return there. How many lovers have you had to roll you in the hay?" The usual ice had returned to his eyes and his voice. "It was nicely done. Did you think to bend me to your will by offering me your body when your defiance had failed? You forget, Rosalind, that your body disgusts me."

Rosalind felt unexpectedly calm. "I hate you," she said quite dispassionately. "I did not expect ever to dislike anyone as much as I do you. No one else matters in your life except the Earl of Raymore, am I not right? You were born with a heart of stone, my lord, and are totally incapable of feeling the finer emotions. Love, kindness, compassion: they must be just words to you. You think you can hurt me by making cruel references to my physical appearance? You are far more crippled than I will ever be, Edward. You do not have the power to wound me."

She turned and walked from the room with as much dignity as her limp would allow. She went immediately to her room, undressed without the aid of her dresser, and climbed into the big four-poster bed.

5

Most of the flowers and decorations that had adorned the hallways, staircase, and ballroom of the Earl of Raymore's home had been removed by midmorning of the following day. But they were soon replaced by the countless bouquets that began arriving before luncheon. Most of them were from gentlemen who had danced with Sylvia. Two were for Rosalind: one bouquet of pink and white carnations from Sir Rowland Axby and one of red roses from Sir Bernard Crawleigh.

Sylvia danced into her cousin's room at noon and pulled back the heavy curtains from the windows to let in the sunlight. "Oh, do wake up, sleepyhead," she begged. "I am simply longing to talk to you about last night, Ros."

Rosalind groaned. She had not fallen asleep until long after daylight came, and even before conscious memory returned, she knew that she did not want to wake up.

"Was it not a perfectly splendid evening?" Sylvia gushed. "All the ladies so friendly, Ros, and the gentlemen!"

Rosalind knew from experience that there was no fighting such high spirits. She pushed herself up to a sitting position on the bed. "And with which of them have you fallen in love?" she asked.

"Oh, I really do not know," Sylvia replied seriously. "Mr. Hammond is very handsome and charming, but do you think he smiles too much, Ros? Lord Standen is very grand. I believe Cousin Edward favors him. He is quite distinguished-looking, too, and very elegant. Perhaps if I met him a few more times, I should be as comfortable with him as I was with his brother, Mr. Broome. Of course, I had not met him before, either, but perhaps he is more easy in his manners because he is not a lord and does not have an air of such consequence."

"Ah," said Rosalind, "I did not notice that young man. Is he also handsome?"

"Oh no," Sylvia said candidly, "not at all. Pleasant-looking, perhaps. Ros, you should see all the flower decorations downstairs. Some from gentlemen I cannot even remember! You must come and see. There are some for you, too."

"Indeed!" her cousin replied dryly. "I cannot imagine who would want to remember me after last night."

"That perfectly gorgeous man we met at the theater is one of them," Sylvia said.

"Sir Bernard Crawleigh?"

"Yes, him. Oh, Ros, he is the one you walked across the ballroom with, is he not? How could you do such a thing? I thought it excessively brave of you."

Rosalind rested her forehead on her raised knees. "I really do not wish to discuss that," she said. "Give me five minutes, Sylvie, and I shall come and inspect this flower garden with you."

A feeling of oppression stayed with her for the rest of the day, but she had no chance to give in to her mood. After she had dutifully inspected all the flowers with Sylvia and read all the cards, it was time for luncheon and a long conversation about the previous evening's successes between Sylvia and Cousin Hetty. Visitors began to arrive in the afternoon, almost all of them male.

It was during these visits, when the drawing room was crowded, that the Earl of Raymore put in his only appearance of the day. Rosalind, talking at the time with Nigel Broome, stiffened. She was afraid to look directly at him, but was constantly aware of his moving about the room, greeting the various visitors. She could breathe freely again only when she became aware, after twenty minutes, that he had left.

Later in the afternoon both cousins were taken driving in Hyde Park, Sylvia by Lord Standen, Rosalind by Sir Rowland Axby. The latter made no reference to the embarrassing spectacle Rosalind had made of herself the evening before. In fact, no one had done so except Sylvia. Rosalind was content during the drive to listen to Sir Rowland talk on about his family and about his house and to try not to imagine what half the people riding and walking in the park must be thinking of her.

The Earl of Raymore had a great deal more time than his ward during the day to brood on what had happened the evening before. After very few hours of fitful sleep he rose early and saddled his fastest horse. Hyde Park was not the ideal place for an uninhibited gallop, but it was the best he could do under the circumstances. At least he did not have to worry about endangering any other riders or pedestrians. The mists of early morning had still not lifted as he drove his spurs into the horse and galloped quite recklessly across the green lawns.

How could he have so forgotten himself and propriety as to have kissed his own ward? He disliked the girl intensely. She was everything he most detested in a woman—proud and independent of spirit, making no secret of her scorn for men. She was bold and had no sense of modesty. What other girl would have walked across an empty dance floor during her come-out ball even if she had the prettiest of walks? She had quite openly shown her contempt for the whole *ton* by making such a public demonstration of her deformity. Physically, she was not attractive at all to him. He had never admired tall women or dark coloring. Only fragile, fair beauty had ever tempted his appetites. Yet, despite all these things, he had given in to some madness the night before. For the span of a few minutes, he could not deny it, he had wanted her more than he had ever wanted any woman. It was only by some miracle that he had come to his senses when he had. A few minutes more, seconds even, and he would have passed the point of no return. The thought did not bear contemplation. Raymore turned his horse and urged it back in the direction from which he had just come. He tried desperately to keep his mind blank.

Uncharacteristically, the earl stayed at home after breakfast, first consulting with his secretary and checking his morning mail and then retreating to the library, where he sat at his desk and stared ahead of him. Why had she allowed such an unchaste embrace as they had shared last evening? God, in this very room! He would never have guessed that she was a practiced flirt. He would have expected that someone with her obvious lack of beauty and with her deformity would have been completely untouched. But apparently not. She had shown no signs of shock at finding that a kiss was not always just a meeting of the lips. She had shown no shame or embarrassment about fitting her body against his. She had invited his hands on her breasts. He had no doubt at all that she would have allowed him to undress her and lay her down on the library carpet. The slut! He drove one fist into the other palm and swore out loud. Why was he still capable of feeling surprise at anything that women could do? He had considered Annette to be just an innocent little doll too, had he not?

He had made another discovery the night before. Those loose clothes that Rosalind Dacey chose to wear hid the most curvaceous feminine body that he had ever touched. Perhaps it was that discovery that had made him come so close to losing his head entirely. But why would she hide the one asset that might make some man ignore the unfashionable dark foreign looks and even, possibly, that quite ugly limp? He guessed that he would never understand women.

The belief that he had been taken as a dupe upset the Earl of Raymore a great deal. He had thought himself immune to women. For the past eleven years he had taken women at his own pleasure, always to satisfy a purely physical need, never out of passion or any finer feeling. It was terrible to him to admit that he had lost control, even if only for a few minutes. What made matters infinitely worse was the knowledge that he had erred with his ward. However reluctantly he had accepted his guardianship, nevertheless he had a responsibility, a duty to protect her and care for her needs, a duty to see her suitably married. However willing a partner she had been, and however much she had instigated the whole episode, still he had wronged her by assaulting her as he had in his own home.

Raymore sat a long time silently considering what he must do. The most obvious solution seemed to be to give in to her demands and send her back to the country. Yet he could not display weakness by giving in to her so. He had very little hope left of finding her a husband in the near future. She had effectively prevented that by her behavior in the ballroom.

He had still not found a solution when the butler knocked on the door to ask if his lordship intended to eat luncheon at home. Raymore ordered a tray brought into the library. It cannot be said that he enjoyed his meal. He hardly tasted it, in fact. His mind was dealing with a thorny problem. Did he owe Miss Dacey an apology? The idea was quite unpalatable. She had clearly provoked him into anger. He was very ready to believe that she had lured him into that embrace. Even so, he admitted, he should not have touched her.

Raymore decided that he would join the ladies later in the drawing room. There would probably be visitors. His cousin Sylvia had appeared to take very well the evening before. He would draw Miss Dacey to one side, apologize briefly, and be done with the matter. It was far more desirable to do the job that way than to speak to her in private. She would be sure to make a major quarrel out of it if he did it that way.

In the event, though, Raymore found himself unaccountably uneasy when he entered the drawing room. As he accepted a cup of tea from Hetty and entered into a conversation with Standen and his sister, Mrs. Letitia Morrison, he was uncomfortably aware of Rosalind sitting across the room talking to Standen's younger brother. He talked to each of the visitors in turn, but failed to take the opportunity of moving to his ward's side when Broome moved away to talk to Sylvia. Soon he lost the chance, when Axby took the empty seat that young Nigel had vacated.

Raymore left the room soon afterward without having spoken to his ward. In fact, he had not even looked directly at her the whole time he had been in the room. The earl frowned. What was the matter with him? Was he afraid of the chit? He hurried up to his room and rang impatiently for his valet. An hour later he left the house and remained away until the early hours of the following morning.

The ladies did not have any engagement for that evening, but they spent a productive evening going through the pile of invitations that had arrived with the day's post. Now that they were officially out, Sylvia and Rosalind were entitled to attend as many routs, balls, Venetian breakfasts, soirees, and other events as could be reasonably fitted into each day. Sylvia and Cousin Hetty were trying to decide which of the invitations should be accepted.

"Lady Sefton promised me last evening that she would send vouchers for Almack's," Cousin Hetty said, scratching the ears of a sleeping poodle as she passed an invitation card across to Sylvia.

"Almack's!" that young lady squealed. "How heavenly! Did you hear that, Ros?"

Fortunately for Rosalind, the question appeared rhetorical. Her cousin was already exclaiming over the card

she held in her hand, which promised further delights
at yet another party.

Rosalind did, in fact, escape early to bed, claiming
that she was tired after the ball of the evening before.
She was not exactly lying, she mused as she closed the
door of her bedroom behind her and set down the
candle on the table beside the bed. She was extremely
weary and mortally depressed. Until the night before,
she had buoyed up her spirits with the conviction that
the Earl of Raymore would send her back home without
delay once she had publicly embarrassed him.

But her scheme had failed. Not only was she being
forced to remain in London, but she had succeeded in
embarrassing herself quite dreadfully. The only factor
that had given her the courage to walk across that
ballroom the evening before was her conviction that
she need never face any of those people again. Now it
seemed that she was doomed to face them all many
times.

How she hated her guardian. Even that afternoon he
had appeared in the drawing room, probably to check
on her, like a jailer, to make sure that she was not
hiding in her room. She shuddered at the memory of
what had happened between them the night before.
That he was physically very attractive she could not
deny. She had loved Alistair, his dream counterpart, for
several years. But how had she allowed herself to ignore the very contemptible character that was housed
in the very godlike body? She never would have done
so had she not been furiously angry, she persuaded
herself.

But her own abandonment to the embrace quite disturbed her. Rosalind had never been kissed before.
Indeed, she had rarely had any contact at all with men,
having always avoided the few social events that she
and Sylvia had been invited to in previous years. She
should, then, have been shocked even by the mere
touch of a man's lips. And she had been shocked at
first. She had pulled away from him with the same

instinct as she would have withdrawn her hand from a hot surface. But when she had looked at him, his face had for once been unguarded, the coldness absent. His eyes had had depth, and she had fallen into those depths as he drew her to him again. And she would never be able to explain why she had reacted as she had that second time. Her behavior was frightening to look back upon. Rosalind could explain it to herself only by admitting that she had wanted him. She had wanted to be close to him, closer than she could be even by pressing her body against his. She had opened her mouth when his tongue had asked entrance, though she had not known there could be such a kiss. She had moved against his hands, wanting them to know her. She had always been embarrassed by her full figure, but she had welcomed his hands on her breasts, had ached to have them beneath the fabric of her gown. She had wanted him.

Rosalind was clinging to one of the posts of her bed. She hung her head and closed her eyes. How could she have behaved so, had those feelings with *him*? With him of all people! Had she no shame? Could she be attracted so powerfully to beauty when there was no substance behind it? He was a cold, unfeeling man who just happened to be extraordinarily handsome. Was she to be seduced by external appearances alone?

And why had he participated in that embrace? Rosalind knew that her deformity repelled him. She knew that he disliked her. She knew that she was ugly. Why, then? He could not have been led astray by appearances. She turned her face to the bedpost as she faced the truth as it must be. He had deliberately set out to humiliate her. She had bested him in the ballroom, and being the sort of man who could never allow another to outmaneuver him, he had coldly and calculatedly taken his revenge almost immediately. With practiced powers of seduction, he had drawn her into making a complete cake of herself. Forever afterward now, when he looked at her, he would be able to sneer at the poor, ugly girl who had responded eagerly to an embrace in the library, believing it to be a sign of real attraction.

Rosalind's knuckles were white as she clung to the post. She would get even with him. She did not have the faintest notion of how she would do it, but she would.

The Earl of Raymore rose the next morning with the determination to see Miss Rosalind Dacey as soon as possible, make his apologies, and forget the whole matter. He was heartily sick of the whole situation with his wards. Having them in his house and setting about getting them married was proving a deucedly troublesome business, and that one girl was occupying his mind far more than he could wish.

When he finally sent for Rosalind to attend him in the library just before luncheon, however, something had happened to completely reverse his mood. For the first time in days he was feeling positively cheerful.

"Good morning, Rosalind," he said when she came through the door. He had decided to drop the "Miss Dacey." She was, after all, his ward. He stood with his back to the windows, his hands clasped behind him.

"My lord," she said, nodding coolly in his direction. She stopped inside the door and stood facing him.

"Will you not have a seat?" he asked. "I have good news for you."

She did not move, but her face lit up as she looked fully at him for the first time. "You are sending me home?" she asked.

He clucked his tongue impatiently. "Far better than that," he said, and paused to let his words take effect.

Rosalind's face became shuttered again. She stared at him.

"I have an offer for you," the Earl of Raymore said.

Rosalind still said nothing.

"Come," he said, leaving his place by the window and crossing the room to her. "Are you not eager to know the identity of your suitor?" He had intended to take her by the hand and lead her to a chair. But he stopped ten feet away from her, halted by her utter stillness.

She did not answer him.

"Sir Rowland Axby has visited me this morning and asked if he may pay his addresses to you," Raymore said, frowning briefly. The girl should be ecstatic. What was the matter with her?

"I see," she said finally, her face devoid of all expression. "And did you sell me, my lord?"

"Sell?"

"That is what I said," she agreed. "Sir Rowland has come buying and you have sold, I gather. Me and my modest dowry in exchange for what? Freedom from my troublesome presence? I daresay for you it is a thoroughly satisfactory bargain."

"Why do you persist in seeing yourself as merchandise?" he said irritably. "It is perfectly normal for girls of your class to make marriage alliances. It is normal for fathers and guardians to help make those alliances. It is the way our society works. I fail to see why you apparently object."

"Why has Sir Rowland chosen me?" she asked quietly.

"Why? Because he is pleased with you, I suppose. Because he needs a wife and because you are single girl belonging to his own class."

"You are a liar," she said dispassionately.

Raymore's eyes narrowed. "And you are deliberately trying to provoke me, ma'am," he replied testily.

"You know as well as I do why I am to receive this most flattering offer," Rosalind said. "Sir Rowland is an aging widower who has nothing to recommend him to a prospective bride. He has neither looks, nor intelligence, nor charm. But he does have a large family. He has looked around him for the girl who is least likely to refuse his offer and he has settled on me. Quite admirable, of course. The man has sense, if not intelligence. What does he see?" She held out her arms and looked down at herself. "He sees a girl who is too tall and too dark for fashion, one who does not have a pretty face. And best of all he sees a cripple. Such a girl, of course, is bound to be so beholden to him for the kindness of his offer that she will devote the rest of her life to being a slave to him and his six children and to any other children that he may condescend to give her."

"Are you finished?" Raymore asked, still ten feet away.

Rosalind let her arms fall to her sides again and stared silently back at him.

"The truth of the matter is," he said coldly, his eyes opaque again, "that this *is* a flattering offer. You are *not* ugly, Rosalind. In fact . . ." He hesitated and did not complete the thought. "But you cannot expect to be numbered among the beauties of the Season. Coming, as you do, from a life in the country, I can see that you have not been taught to face reality. The life of an old maid is a frightful one. Such a woman is passed on from one relation to another, always at everyone's beck and call, not wanted by anyone. I do not wish that life for you. Sir Rowland Axby may not be the man of your choice, but believe me, Rosalind, marriage to him will be better than no marriage at all. At least you will hold a respectacle position in society."

"I would rather die," she said.

He gestured impatiently. "Pure melodrama," he said. "I took you for a woman of some sense."

"I, on the other hand, have understood you from the beginning," Rosalind said. "You are a cold, hard man who has so little regard for the feelings of others that you do not even know that those feelings exist."

"Always we come back to your hatred of me, do we not?" he said, moving away from her and walking to the fireplace, where he stood staring down at the unlit logs. "If you hate me so much, Rosalind, I would think you would be delighted to have an opportunity to be independent of me."

"I will not marry Sir Rowland," she said.

He looked up sharply at her. "You will listen to his

proposal this afternoon," he said, "and you will accept, my girl."

"Oh, no, Edward," she said quietly. "Pray do not work yourself into a lather over this. You have no way of winning. You cannot force me to marry anyone and it is pointless to engage in a battle of wills with me. I would guess that most people crumble before your will, but you will find that I shall not."

The Earl of Raymore had gone very still as he watched her. "We shall see, ma'am," he said calmly. "We shall see. You may leave me now."

He stood staring at the door for several minutes after she had taken a quiet departure.

6

Sylvia fell in love twice during the following few weeks. At first it was with Charles Hammond, who pressed his suite quite ardently. He made a point of discovering which events Sylvia was to attend and was always at the same places himself. He was at Almack's to claim her hand the first time she attended that hallowed establishment; he was at a musicale she attended and seated himself next to her to listen to an Italian soprano; he was at a regatta and was in the right place to hand her into a boat. And he was a constant visitor at Grosvenor Square, staying in the drawing room as long as any visitor and being sure to be the first to ask Lady Sylvia Marsh to drive with him in the park afterward.

Perhaps it was his very persistence that caused Sylvia's affection to cool. "He *does* smile too much, Ros, does he not?" she asked seriously one day when the two girls were together in the breakfast room.

"Would you have the poor man frown all day long?" Rosalind asked, laughing.

"No, but no one can be cheerful and lighthearted all the time, can they?" the girl replied. "Anyone who is, is either playing a part, not acting naturally, or is rather empty-headed."

"And which unfortunate description do you think fits Mr. Hammond?" Rosalind asked.

"I do not know," Sylvia replied seriously. "I think perhaps a little of both, Ros."

"Do I understand that you are out of love with him?" her cousin asked, hiding her smile.

"Oh, I do not believe I was ever in *love* with him," Sylvia protested. "But you must admit that he is very handsome, Ros."

The following day Sylvia was in love with Lord Standen, who also made a point of singling her out at most of the social functions they attended, but who did not persist in quite so vulgar a manner as Charles Hammond. He was a good-looking, dignified man.

"And much more serious-minded than Mr. Hammond," Sylvia confided to Rosalind. "I am quite in love with him, Ros."

"Yet you told me when you first met him, Sylvie, that you did not feel quite comfortable with him," Rosalind pointed out.

"Yes, but I feel he is *worth* getting to know," Sylvia replied. "Nigel says that his brother is always a little stiff in manner with people he does not know very well."

"I see," her cousin said. "And after one gets to know him, Sylvie?"

"Nigel says he is a very affectionate brother and kind and generous to his tenants."

"He sounds very admirable," Rosalind said. "So you are quite resolved to have him, Sylvie?"

"Oh, I would not say that," Sylvia replied hastily. "I am in no hurry. But Nigel says that his lordship has rarely shown such interest in any lady before."

Rosalind herself was resigned to spending the remainder of the Season in London. It was obviously pointless to hope that Raymore would consent to her returning to the country. She would wait out the months, she decided. When midsummer came and it became obvious to him that she would never marry, he would have to let her go home. She would just have to be patient.

She had, of course, refused Sir Rowland Axby's offer. He had come a few hours after her interview with

Raymore and she had been summoned to the library.
She had again felt sorry for the poor man, who had
spruced himself up for the occasion and was obviously
very nervous. Rosalind had let him down as gently as
she could. Too gently, perhaps. He had insisted on
believing that her only reason for refusing was that he
had rushed her.

"You are new to the pleasures of town, dear Miss
Dacey," he had said in his slightly nasal voice. "It is
understandable that you do not wish to rush into a betrothal so soon. I shall be patient and trust that after a
few months you will welcome the prospect of becoming
my wife and living in domestic bliss with my family in
Leicestershire."

"I would not wish to mislead you into thinking my
answer may be different then, sir," Rosalind said gently.

He held up a hand. "Say no more, my dear Miss
Dacey," he said. "I perfectly understand. I shall return
at a later date to repeat my offer. I trust that by then
you will have satisfied your quite natural desire for
amusement."

And Rosalind had to be content with that. To give
the man his due, she had to admit that he gave her
room to enjoy herself, had that been her intention.
Although he frequently hovered in the background at
functions she attended, he did not pester her with his
presence. To her surprise, she found that Sir Bernard
Crawleigh was frequently attentive. He treated her with
an amused courtesy. She always felt when with him
that they were partners in some sort of conspiracy. He
understood perfectly her feelings about being thrown
reluctantly into the activities of the *ton* and her resentment against her guardian. She found it very easy to
talk to and confide in him. It was he who found her in a
small anteroom adjoining the ballroom at one ball they
attended.

"Hiding or sulking, Miss Dacey?" he asked amiably,
closing the door quickly behind him as he came in.

"Neither," she said. "I was just thinking. I do not like to watch dancing."

"You are envious?" he asked quietly.

"Well, yes," she admitted, her chin lifting defiantly. "It is not a good feeling to see everyone move so gracefully and know that I can never do so."

"Stand up," he said, "and waltz with me here."

"Don't be absurd," she replied crossly. "You know that I cannot dance."

"Not in public, maybe, but here with me, Rosalind? There is no one to see. Come."

And for the first time in her life she danced, clumsily, it is true, and clinging to her partner's shoulder as to a lifeline, but she was flushed with pleasure by the time the music finished.

"You realize that you will be in trouble now, I trust," he said with a straight face. "I will wager that the patronesses have not yet granted you permission to waltz."

"I shall also be in trouble if Cousin Hetty finds me alone in here with you," Rosalind said, and smiled.

"Since our meeting will be judged quite improper anyway," he said, smiling roguishly, "I might as well do what I wish to do." He held her lightly by the waist and kissed her on the lips. "Delicious!" he said afterward, smiling. "Now I must try to slink out of here without creating a grand scandal."

Rosalind stayed in the anteroom, the door ajar, for a while afterward, smiling to herself and tapping her foot to the music. What a pleasant evening this was turning out to be! It had been a delightful experience to dance. Sir Bernard had held her very firmly so that she had not felt unduly clumsy. And the kiss she had thoroughly approved of. That was what a kiss should be like, something shared, something enjoyed. Not like that horrid experience with Raymore, when she had completely lost control. That had not been at all a comfortable experience. She believed that she was falling a little in love with Sir Bernard Crawleigh.

In those few weeks following her come-out, Rosalind also furthered her acquaintance with Lady Elise Martel. She visited one afternoon soon after the ball, when the baby still had not been born. It was a warm day for early May and Lady Elise was feeling rather uncomfortable.

"How thankful I am to see you," she told Rosalind. "Henry is feeling guilty about seeing me in this condition and wishes to stay with me to share my misery. But I sent him out today. The heat has made me cross as a bear and I was afraid that I would start snapping at him, poor man."

"Oh, dear," Rosalind said, "and are you planning to snap at me instead?"

"Gracious, no!" her hostess protested, laughing. "You are a visitor, you see, and it is easy to be polite to visitors. It is only those nearest and dearest to us who bear the brunt of our ill humor. Have you not noticed that?"

Rosalind enjoyed the visit. She could relax, as with a friend, and talk on topics other than parties and invitations and fashion. She left at the end of an hour, promising to visit again when Lady Elise's health permitted.

The Earl of Raymore stayed away from his wards as much as he possibly could. In the daytime it was very easy. He had never been a conscientious member of the House of Lords, but he found himself attending more often than usual during that spring. His clubs saw a great deal more of him than they ever had. He spent time riding and practicing his fencing and boxing skills. He began a liaison with the Covent Garden dancer that he had mentioned to Sir Henry Martel at Watier's, and convinced himself that she was a very satisfactory bedfellow. He seriously considered setting her up under his permanent protection, but did not do so immediately. He was restless with a nameless dissatisfaction, though he did not know why. She was the sort of woman most likely to please him: red-haired, petite, fragile, and beautiful. Although she was new to London, she had been well taught in the arts of her chief trade. He would wait awhile before doing anything so permanent and so uncharacteristic of himself as to establish her in a residence that he supported.

During the evenings Raymore occasionally sacrificed his own pleasures for the sake of accompanying his wards to some social function. He wished to lend them all the support of his own consequence. And he wished to watch the progress of his plans for them. He was well-satisfied that there would be no problem with Sylvia. His uneasiness over the attentions of Charles Hammond was soon over. After a couple of weeks the girl began to discourage him. Obviously she had some sense as well as a great deal of beauty. It seemed to him very likely that Standen would offer for her before the Season was over. A summer or an autumn wedding seemed a reasonable expectation.

He did not like to think about Rosalind. She had, of course, refused Axby, more to spite him than to serve her own interests, he believed. He had expected that her chances of attaching to herself any other man were remarkably slim. Yet it was not so. Her disability had been displayed very publicly on her first appearance, had shocked those who had witnessed her display, and had been accepted. She had no great following, but she was not ostracized, either. Axby still seemed to retain some hope; a few older men who were not obviously hanging out for wives seemed to enjoy sitting beside her and conversing, and Henry seemed quite fond of her. He gathered that she had visited Elise on more than one occasion. Strangest of all, Raymore noticed that Crawleigh was on easy terms with her and apparently enjoyed her company. If he could be brought to the point, it would be a great coup. Many hopeful mamas had had an eye on him for several Seasons.

Raymore could not understand why Crawleigh was interested, if indeed he was. He watched them together at one drawing-room gathering following a dinner party. Rosalind was dressed vividly, as she usually was these days, in emerald-green satin. Her hair, dressed high in intricate coils, shone and made her neck appear long and slender. She was laughing. Her dark eyes sparkled, her teeth showed very white in contrast to the darkness of her hair. Had her face been so animated when she had first arrived in his house? He seemed to remember gaining an impression of a stubborn will and perhaps a sullen nature.

His eyes slid down her body. The gown became her well. Its bright color and high sheen gave the impression of elegance, although its style was not calculated to reveal her figure. Raymore remembered those full breasts beneath his hands, the tiny waist, the flaring hips. She laughed again as he watched, a pealing, girlish laugh, and laid a hand lightly on Crawleigh's sleeve for a moment. The earl felt anger flaring. She need not set her cap so blatantly at the man. It might be a brilliant match for her if she could accomplish her goal, but he could not like the connection. He did not have a chance to analyze his feeling; his hostess claimed his attention at that point.

Rosalind's sessions in the music room had not discontinued after her come-out ball. In fact, it became almost a necessity to her to spend at least an hour a day playing and singing. Music soothed her and provided some kind of anchor to an existence that she found a great strain. Rarely was she at ease when she was in society. With Sir Bernard and Sir Henry Martel she found she could relax, but she was always aware of other people in the room and she always wondered what they thought of her, especially when she found it impossible to stay seated. But in the music room she could be herself, forget that she was not as other women. Cousin Hetty had warned her that Raymore had one of his concerts planned for later in the spring and that the artists he chose would probably use the music room for a few weeks prior to the performance. But for the time the room was hers. No one else ever used it and no one ever came there to interrupt her. She believed that no one else except Cousin Hetty and Sylvia even knew that she practiced there regularly.

Rosalind began to challenge herself. She had always played to entertain herself. But in the country she had had other activities, notably painting and riding. And riding had always been the big challenge. Because she was disabled, she had prided herself on being an accomplished and daring horsewoman. But here she had nothing but her music. She had never asked if she could ride here. She supposed that her guardian might consent; riding was an acceptable pastime for ladies. But riding in London meant walking, or at best trotting, a horse in Hyde Park. It was yet another social activity. It would offer her no freedom. She forced herself, then, to aim for greater musical achievement. She practiced for hours on the harpsichord, almost exclusively Bach music, trying to achieve the crisp brilliance that she was now convinced his music was meant to sound like.

But Beethoven had always been her greatest love. There was a passion underlying the surface intricacy of his music, she had always believed. And she had been contented to play those pieces that came easily to her. She had often played the first movement of his Piano Sonata Number 14 because it was relatively easy to play and the melody was so breathtakingly beautiful. Some poet had called it the Moonlight Sonata because the music reminded him of moonlight on Lake Lucerne. Rosalind had always tried to picture such a scene as she played, sparkling cold water, snow-capped Alpine mountains all around. But now she tackled the second and third movements too, forcing her fingers through the tricky runs, trying to achieve power and precision and passion in the chords. But for days she despaired of ever mastering the technicalities.

There was a Sevres vase in the music room, a priceless work of art, Rosalind judged, as well as a beautiful one. She frequently spent time just gazing at it and running her fingers lightly over its texture. When her frustration with Beethoven became so powerful that she felt a strong urge to stalk over and smash the vase, she would turn to song and restore her tranquillity with love songs and ballads. She chose songs for their simplicity and emotion. She was never tempted to try opera or vocal music that required more power or expertise.

Part of the charm of her times in the music room was the fact that there she was completely alone, quite free of the necessity to smile, to make polite conversation, to pretend to be enjoying herself. She would have been horrified indeed had she known that the music room exerted just as strong a pull on someone else. The Earl of Raymore despised himself for his weakness. She was, after all, only a girl dabbling in an art that was beyond her talents. But though he was from home far more than had ever been his practice in the daytime, he was drawn back there, against his every instinct, almost each afternoon when he knew that in all probability Rosalind would be singing and playing.

At first he stood outside the door listening, but his constant unease lest someone should come along and find him spying outside a room in his own house or— worse—that she would unexpectedly emerge and find him there, drove him into an adjoining salon. It was a good choice. Part of the wall between the two rooms was merely a thin paneling that could be folded back and always was during his concerts so that a supper could be laid for his guests to feast upon during the interval. He could listen in the salon almost as well as if he were right in the room with her. And it suited him very well not to see her. He tried to ignore the fact that the music that had become almost a drug to him was produced by Rosalind Dacey.

And so the Earl of Raymore discovered with Rosalind the wonder of Bach on the harpsichord, and he suffered with her through her mastery of the Moonlight Sonata. He would find himself sitting forward in the only chair that had been stripped of its holland covers, clutching his head in frustration, sometimes anger, as she repeatedly played over the same bars and repeatedly made the same mistakes. He would grip the arms of the chair, his eyes tightly closed, willing her through a passage that she had finally grasped. And he listened in a kind of agonized wonder when the melody came flowing in all its glory through the intricate runs and crashing chords.

Raymore had to admit to himself finally that Rosalind Dacey was no dabbler. She was an artist. And he always waited for her to sing. There was nothing brilliant about her vocal performances; the music was too simple to demand brilliance. But she brought a clarity of style and depth of feeling to the old songs that gave them power and dignity. He always waited in hope for the song she had sung that first time he had listened, the one about the rose. He had spent more than an hour in his library one morning trying to find the words of the song. But he had had no success. It must be something recently composed, though surely something that would last. It must be by one of the new poets. He had even gone to a bookshop and bought a copy of Mr. Wordsworth and Mr. Coleridge's *Lyrical Ballads*. But if one of them had written the poem, it was not in that particular volume. The song haunted him. He found himself thinking of the singer as a red rose. He could even picture her dressed in the rose-red gown that she had worn on the night of her come-out. But he steadfastly resisted putting Rosalind's face and character into the hazy mental image that he carried with him almost against his will. His rose was becoming a fantasy creature, different from women as he knew them in reality.

Even Raymore, who had judged the progress of Sylvia's connection with Lord Standen quite satisfactory, was somewhat surprised at the speed with which he came to the point. Less than a month after Sir Rowland Axby had paid his morning call to ask for the one ward's hand, Standen was repeating the performance for the other ward.

Raymore had no misgivings. The connection was quite unexceptionable. Standen had rank, wealth, looks, and sense to recommend him. His serious nature would complement Sylvia's exuberance. The two men quickly came to an amicable agreement.

As he had done on the previous occasion, with Rosalind, Raymore summoned Sylvia to the library before luncheon. He awaited her arrival with a feeling of relief. She at least could be counted upon to behave predictably. He was very thankful that it was not Rosalind again. He could not be sure that she would accept any suitor, even if Crawleigh were to offer for her.

Half an hour later Sylvia rushed with undignified haste into Cousin Hetty's sitting room, where that lady and Rosalind were examining purchases made during a morning shopping expedition. "Ros, Cousin Hetty," she began, breathless from her run up the stairs, "Lord Standen has called on Edward and has offered for me."

Rosalind looked up sharply and searched her cousin's face.

"Well, how splendid, my dear," Hetty said, moving across the room to hug the girl and startling a poodle that had been stretched beneath the hem of her dress. "I knew when I saw you that you would make a brilliant match. And Lord Standen is very grand. I do believe you will be most happy. I wonder when the wedding is like to be. Oh, how exciting. We must get to work immediately on your trousseau." She clasped her hands and gazed in rapture at the prospective bride.

"Are you planning to accept his lordship's proposal, Sylvie?" Rosalind asked more soberly.

Her cousin looked at her incredulously. "But of course," she said. "You know that I love him, Ros."

"Are you sure?" Rosalind asked dampeningly. "You have not known him long, Sylvie, and you know that you fall in and out of love very frequently. Would it not be better to wait longer and be quite sure?"

"Ros," Sylvia pleaded, "I thought you would be happy for me. Lord Standen is far different from all the others, you know. They were mere boys. He is a man. Nigel says that he spends much of his time in the country and insists on running his estate himself. He is very kind to his tenants. I think he is worthy of my love."

"I am sure you are right," Rosalind said, "but we do not always love people just because they are worthy. There has to be a real friendship and attraction too, Sylvie."

"He is always very kind to me," Sylvia replied, "and I know that he thinks me quite the most attractive girl he has ever met. Nigel told me so."

"Well," Rosalind said, smiling cheerfully and rising to her feet, "I am sure the man has a great deal of sense. And for your sake, Sylvie, I hope that this time you do remain in love. I am sure he will make a quite admirable husband."

But she could not help wishing that Nigel Broome would let her cousin do her own thinking. Rosalind was not at all convinced that this attachment would prove any more lasting than any of the others.

7

Lord Standen had decided to celebrate his betrothal to Lady Sylvia Marsh with a week-long house party on his estate in Sussex. Even so, his sister, Mrs. Letitia Morrison, felt that such an event called for a larger gathering in London. One week after the announcement appeared in the *Gazette*, she held a dazzling ball in honor of her brother and his fiancée.

Rosalind was becoming almost resigned to such occasions. She had learned to live her own life as far as was possible during the daytime and to accept the boredom of the evenings when she must sit and look cheerful and converse with whoever chose to sit with her. The event at hand gave her some interest in this particular ball. She watched her cousin and Lord Standen with interest when they were together. They danced twice before supper and stood together between dances speaking to their guests and receiving their congratulations. It was very hard to judge if there was a real attachment between them. They did not appear to talk much to each other, but then the occasion did not give them a great deal of opportunity to do so. They looked happy enough. Sylvia's eyes sparkled and her cheeks glowed; she smiled constantly. Standen was gracious and had a word for each of his well-wishers. Rosalind liked him. He seemed to be a man of good sense and stability of character. She hoped that Sylvia had made the right choice.

The Earl of Raymore was also present at the ball. He looked with satisfaction on the newly betrothed pair.

Half of his responsibility at least seemed to have been safely disposed of. Unfortunately, it was the easier half. He frowned in the direction of Rosalind, who was seated at one side of the ballroom talking to Nigel Broome. Axby had not pressed his suit since her rejection of him and it was unlikely that she would look more kindly on him a second time even if he did. He had been neglecting his responsibilities, Raymore decided. The Season was half over already. If he wished to be rid of her before the summer set in, he would have to work very hard. She looked different from her usual self tonight, he concluded, his eyes assessing her from head to toe. The sky-blue lace gown made her look younger, but also made her appear more foreign. He had never been an admirer of Italian women, but to those who were, she was not unhandsome.

Broome might not be an impossible match for her. He was a younger son, but had a comfortable fortune of his own, inherited from his grandmother. He was an unassuming, rather dull young man, bookish, it was rumored. But they might suit. He might see if he could throw them together a bit during Standen's house party, to which both he and Rosalind had been invited. In the meantime, he strolled around the dance floor, talking to acquaintances, considering the possibility of introducing some of his friends to his ward.

Soon after the supper break Rosalind could stand the boredom no longer. She was fortunate enough to be seated close to a doorway that led onto the terrace. She slipped through into the relative darkness of the lantern-lit outdoors while a set was forming for a country dance and no one's attention was on her. There was only one couple on the terrace and they were quite a distance from her, deep in conversation. The air was too chilly to entice many guests out of doors. Rosalind limped in the opposite direction, one hand on the stone balustrade, until she could descend the few stone steps down onto the lawn. She walked on the grass, taking deep breaths of fresh air, glad to be free of prying eyes for just a few minutes. She shivered.

"It is a full-time task keeping trace of your where-abouts," a cheerful voice said from the bottom of the steps. "One blinks and you are gone, escaped into darkness."

Rosalind smiled. "If I had known you cared, Bernard," she said, "I should have had the orchestra play a fanfare to announce my departure."

"Ah, but then I could not have sneaked out here after you for a clandestine meeting," he said, coming across the lawn toward her, his grin noticeable in the moonlight.

"Mm, foolish of me," she replied, and shivered again.

"You are cold," he said. "I had better escort you back inside."

"No," she protested more seriously, "I plan to walk awhile. You cannot imagine how tedious it is to sit all evening and not be free to move."

He smiled with quiet sympathy, took her hand, and tucked it through his arm, They strolled in silence for a while, watching broken clouds scudding in the moonlight above treetops that waved in a strong breeze.

"You are cold, Rosalind," he said after a few minutes. "Come back now."

She shook her head.

"Look," he said, "Letty's summerhouse is quite close by. Let us see if it is unlocked. If it is not, I shall have to come the bully and carry you back to the house or drag you by the hair."

"You would ruin my coiffure," she said. "I shall come quietly, sir, if the summerhouse is locked."

It was not. They moved gratefully inside the glass structure, which was still warm from the sunlight trapped inside during the day. They sat on a brocade-covered bench that circled the outer wall of the structure. They talked amiably for many minutes, until Rosalind realized uneasily that she had lost track of time.

"Cousin Hetty will be worried," she said, standing up. "I had not meant to be gone so long."

He too got to his feet. "I might be persuaded to escort you back if you will kiss me first," he said.

"Gracious!" Rosalind said, eyebrows raised, eyes twinkling. "I have to pay for your escort, sir?"

"Certainly!" he agreed. He winked at her and grinned. "And payment in advance, too, ma'am. I never trust a pretty face."

She laughed outright and put her hands on his shoulders, her face turned up to invite his kiss. He explored her lips warmly with his, holding her loosely in his arms.

"Mmm," he said with a mock growl into her ear.

She drew back her head, grinning merrily, about to remind him that he must now keep his part of their bargain. But his eyes had moved beyond her and his face had sobered.

"I am sure you will both hate me for interrupting this scene before it has reached a more interesting stage," the icy voice of the Earl of Raymore said from behind her, "but I will have to insist that you unhand my ward, Crawleigh."

Rosalind whirled around to face him. "My lord, what are you doing here?" she cried, and cursed her own reactions even as they were happening.

His eyes raked her body so that she felt quite naked before him. "Rescuing you from a fate worse than death, by the look of it," he said with cold sarcasm.

"Look here, Raymore," Sir Bernard said from behind her, his voice sounding testy, "this is not quite the way it seems, you know."

Raymore raised one eloquent eyebrow. "Forgive my foolishly suspicious mind," he said. "How could I possibly have believed that there might be anything improper in your being alone with Miss Dacey in a secluded summerhouse in the middle of the night? And how could I possibly have been alarmed to find you mauling her like a milkmaid? After all, she is still standing and still fully clothed."

Rosalind was so furious that she was momentarily

deprived of speech. She glared into his mocking face, lit dimly by the moonlight.

"You misunderstand the situation, Raymore," Sir Bernard said quietly. "You interrupted a proposal of marriage. I was about to ask Miss Dacey if she would do me the honor of becoming my wife."

His two listeners became absolutely motionless, their eyes locked, strangely enough, on each other. Rosalind watched Raymore's face slowly lose its sneer and become taut with . . . what? Fury? She was surprised to find that when he spoke, his voice was quiet and almost pleasant.

"I see," he said. "And was I to be consulted in the matter, Crawleigh?"

"Of course," Sir Bernard replied. "But Rosalind is a grown woman, Raymore. I wished to consult her wishes before discussing terms with you."

Rosalind turned and looked up into his face, troubled. "Bernard," she began.

He took her hand and squeezed it hard. "Not now, love," he said, smiling fleetingly down at her before returning his attention to her guardian. "We must see about returning Rosalind to her chaperone," he suggested. "I shall call on you tomorrow morning, Raymore?"

The earl bowed stiffly, his face still tight with that expression that Rosalind could not read. He stood aside from the doorway and the other two occupants of the room passed out before him. Rosalind had never felt so uncomfortable in her life. Sir Bernard held her hand firmly on his arm and reduced his stride to match her halting progress, while Raymore walked at her other side. None of them said a word all the way back to the house. It was a relief to be led back to the sofa that she had occupied for several hours before this escapade. The earl had stopped in the doorway to the terrace. Sir Bernard left her almost immediately after smiling down at her and promising to speak with her the following day. She was joined soon afterward by Cousin Hetty, who scolded her in a cheerful manner about disappear-

ing for such a long time and throwing her into such a
flutter.

Rosalind was happy at least that the ball was almost
at an end. She had to sit looking cheerful for only half
an hour longer. Even the journey home was not quite
the ordeal she had expected. She was very much aware
of Raymore seated opposite her in the carriage, their
knees almost touching, but any tension there might
have been between them was eased by the cheerful
prattle of Sylvia and the lengthy comments of Cousin
Hetty.

The matter was not to be dropped for the night,
though. Sylvia was already halfway up the stairs and
Rosalind had her foot on the bottom stair, Cousin Hetty
close behind her, when Raymore entered the house.

"Rosalind, I wish to have a word with you in the
library," he said quietly.

"Goodness," Cousin Hetty said, "these girls must be
sleeping on their feet, Edward dear. Can it not wait
until morning?"

"I am afraid not," he replied.

Rosalind turned without a word and preceded him to
the library door.

"I shall have warm milk brought to your room, dear,"
Cousin Hetty said. "Be sure to come up in time to
drink it before it grows cold."

Raymore reached around Rosalind and opened the
doors to the library. He closed them again when they
were both inside. He did not waste any time. "Are you
quite bent on ruining a good man's life?" he asked.

Rosalind turned toward him incredulously. "What?"
she asked.

He was looking at her with those ice-blue eyes that
always infuriated her. "You enticed Crawleigh into the
garden tonight," he said, "and into the summerhouse,
so that you might satisfy your lust with him, and now
you have forced him into playing the gentleman and
offering for you."

"Entice? Lust?" Rosalind repeated. She was so furious that her breath was coming in uneven gasps. "How do you dare speak of me so?"

"I have eyes," he said icily, "and I saw how you were kissing him, Rosalind, your hands pulling him down to you. Your upbringing must have taught you how improper your behavior tonight was even without that embrace. And I believe that a few minutes longer would have seen you past the point of a simple kiss."

"Are you mad?" she cried, her voice rising. "You paint me as some sort of seductress. The notion is absurd. Look at me, Edward. Do I look like the sort of woman who would know how to tempt a man even if she wished to do so? I am ugly and deformed."

"You are not ugly!" he snapped, taking a step toward her, his ice turned to fire. "And you forget that I, too, was fool enough on one occasion to taste your charms. I know what you hide under those cleverly designed garments, Rosalind." His eyes raked her again as they had done earlier in the summerhouse, and she felt that she was being stripped of all her clothing. "I shall not be well-pleased if it should become general knowledge that one of my wards is a woman of loose morals."

Rosalind could feel the blood drumming through her head. She fought to keep some control. "If I were a man, my lord," she said, "I should make you take back those words at the point of a sword. You have insulted me beyond bearing tonight. If you have nothing else to say, I shall go to my room."

"Do you intend accepting Crawleigh's offer?" he asked, turning away from her and crossing to a sideboard, where he poured himself a drink.

"He has not yet asked me," she replied curtly. "I will have to discuss the matter with him before I make a decision."

"I would advise you to refuse him," he said, "if you do not wish to have him grow to hate you."

"You would not be able to conceive of the idea that perhaps he loves me and wishes to marry me, would you?" she asked.

"No, I would not."

"Good night, my lord," she said, turning to the door.

"Rosalind!" he said sharply, and when she half-turned toward him she saw that he had crossed the room to her. "You do not have to marry Crawleigh, you know."

She raised her eyebrows and looked at him.

"I believe you were not missed tonight by anyone except me and perhaps Hetty," he said. "Your honor is not seriously at stake."

His face was quite serious, Rosalind observed, not icy, not sneering.

"I never for a moment thought it was," she replied before turning back to the door and leaving the room.

Raymore sat in the library for several hours, one forgotten drink in his hand, his eyes staring unseeing into the empty fireplace. He should be feeling elated. By tomorrow afternoon he should have both wards safely betrothed and there was still a month of the Season left. With continued good fortune, both men would press for an early wedding. He could be free of his obligations by autumn, free to return to his bachelor existence and forget about women as much as he wanted to.

Why, then, did he feel so dissatisfied? He had to analyze the cause. Both men were entirely good matches. Standen had long been an acquaintance of his and was a man of sense and good principles. He would make a good husband. And so would Crawleigh. Raymore could remember a time when the latter had been a wild young man, associated with a dandy set, given to any number of excesses: gaming, women, accepting senseless dares. But he appeared to have outgrown such wildness and had never, in fact, been vicious. He was reputed to keep a mistress in somewhat extravagant luxury, but since he conducted the affair discreetly, there could be no serious objection.

He should certainly be thankful that such an eligible suitor had shown interest in Rosalind. After her refusal of Axby, he had seen little hope of bringing anyone else to the point, certainly not someone of Crawleigh's stand-

ing. He could have just about any lady of quality he
desired for a bride. Why had he felt such opposition to
the match, then, when Crawleigh had first mentioned it
in the summerhouse and when Rosalind was in the
room here with him earlier?

He had felt unease as soon as he had missed her from
the ballroom. He had looked across many times to see
her sitting on the sofa, usually with someone seated
next to her. But he had not seen her go. He did see
Crawleigh leave through the terrace door close to the
empty sofa, though. And he had given them ten minutes before giving in to his impatience and following
them outside. It had taken him another fifteen minutes
to find them. He remembered now his own fury when
he had quietly opened the door of the summerhouse
and found them together, Rosalind's hands at Crawleigh's
neck, his splayed across her back, his mouth at her ear.
For a moment he had wanted to kill, though he was not
quite sure now which of them he had wished to make
his victim.

She had come to epitomize for him all women. She
appeared to be innocent and modest. When he had first
met her, he would have been ready to swear that she
had never been near any high society or any men. Her
handicap and her looks should have ensured that. But
he had been forced to revise that early impression. Like
all women, she had learned to be alluring. She was not,
in fact, ugly. The plain hairstyle and gowns had quickly
been thrown aside once she had had a chance to make
an impression on the *ton*, and he had to admit now that
she could look quite remarkably stunning in the richly
colored gowns she favored and with those thick, shiny
locks dressed fashionably. She was out of the ordinary way.
He found increasingly that she drew his eyes like a
magnet when they were in the same room.

And the demure innocence was just a deceptive fa-
cade, too. He could see now why she had been so
contemptuous of Axby's offer. She was quite capable of
luring a more attractive husband on her own. Had she

been trying to trap him into marriage on the night of her come-out ball? He remembered with some anger the way he had reacted to her. He had been so startled by her almost instant abandonment to his kiss, the passion with which she had offered herself to him, and the glorious shapeliness of her body, that he had almost succumbed to his own desire. By God, she had almost succeeded. If he had taken her on that occasion, he would have been honor-bound to marry her, not only as a gentleman, but especially as her guardian. His jaw clenched. He had not fully realized until this moment just what a fortunate escape he had had. Perhaps she did not realize her own good fortune. He would have seen to it that her life was hell if he had been forced to make her his wife.

And now she had succeeded with poor Crawleigh. Raymore doubted very much if the man had really been about to offer for her. She had obviously been intent on seducing him there in the summerhouse. She doubtless would have succeeded had he not interrupted them. But the end result was the same. Crawleigh had been forced into a situation in which he had no choice. And why should pity be wasted on him? the earl thought bitterly. He had been willing to enjoy her there in the garden. Let him have joy of her for the rest of his life. Raymore thought again of Crawleigh's hands on her back and gritted his teeth.

His rose! In the past weeks he had been lulled again into thinking that the girl who could produce such glorious music must be pure. The truth was that only a person of experience and knowledge would be capable of reproducing the passion of Beethoven and that of her unknown poet.

Raymore pulled himself to his feet. He would be glad to see the last of her. It could not be soon enough for him.

Rosalind, in her room, sitting up in bed, was having similar thoughts. She had to get away from the Earl of

Raymore. The man was pure tyrant, treating her earlier tonight like a child who has no ability to look after herself instead of like the adult she was. And his behavior in the library had been the outside of enough. He had actually accused her of being a seductress, of deliberately setting out to trap Bernard into marriage. If he had called her a whore she could not feel more insulted.

The trouble was that she had a sinking feeling that he was right on at least one detail. Bernard had been forced into that ridiculous declaration. Of course he had not been about to ask her to marry him any more than she had been expecting such a proposal. She liked Bernard excessively and had grown to depend greatly on his friendship. She felt a pleasant attraction to him and had enjoyed both kisses shared with him. She thought she might be falling in love with him. But if they were ever to love deeply enough for marriage, it was likely to be at some future date. Theirs was not a passionate relationship that would develop quickly, but rather an affectionate friendship that might or might not grow into love. At least, that was how she viewed the matter.

And now because of a ridiculous sense of honor, Bernard's hand had been forced. He would call on Raymore tomorrow and then she would be summoned to hear his formal proposal. The whole situation was farcical. She would be downright embarrassed. How could she take Bernard seriously as an ardent suitor? She would tell him, of course, that she could not consider marrying him at present, and that would be the end of the matter. But it was most provoking. Their pleasant friendship would be strained, perhaps ruined, and certainly any chance of love developing would be permanently quenched.

Damn him! Damn Edward Marsh! Why had he had to appear just when he had? That kiss had been so harmless, a joke really. A few seconds later and they would have both been laughing and turning to walk back to the house. And he had been so furious. Rosalind had thought at first that he was about to attack one or other of them. His fists had been clenched at his sides. And she remembered that, inexplicably, she had wanted to go to him, touch him, assure him that what he had seen was really quite deceptive. She had had a vivid memory, looking at him, of what it had felt like to have *his* arms around her, *his* mouth on hers. How thankful she was that she had not given in to the impulse. He had been so insulting immediately afterward, putting the worst possible interpretation on what he had seen.

He was quite insufferable. How could she possibly go on living in his home after the things he had said to her? She was almost tempted to accept Bernard's offer. If she did not, it was likely that she would become an old maid and she would always be bound to this man, would always be at his beck and call. She did not think she could bear it.

Both the Earl of Raymore and Rosalind were still awake when dawn broke.

8

Rosalind was every bit as embarrassed the next day as she had expected to be when a poker-faced butler summoned her to the library. Although she had not fallen asleep until after dawn, she had not slept late but had breakfasted before either of the other ladies was up. She had seen through the morning-room window the arrival of Sir Bernard Crawleigh. He had been closeted with Raymore for upward of half an hour before she was called.

Crawleigh was in the room alone when a footman opened the library doors for her. That at least was a relief. She had been very much afraid that she would have to face both men. But she still found it difficult to look him in the face.

She smiled vaguely in the direction of his neckcloth. "Good morning, Bernard," she said.

"You look as if you are going to your own funeral," he said with a chuckle. "Come, Rosalind, I am not about to eat you."

"Well," she said, relaxing visibly and smiling at him, "I hardly knew how I was to face you this morning. I am dreadfully sorry about last night. I realize that the whole situation was my fault." She limped across the room and sat down beside the fireplace.

"Fault?" he queried. "You talk as if some disaster had occurred. I have come to ask for the honor of your hand, Rosalind."

"Oh, nonsense," she said, giving him a quelling glance.

"That game was perhaps necessary with his lordship, Bernard, but you do not need to pretend with me. Of course you do not wish to marry me."

"Do I not?" he asked, amusement in his voice. He came and sat in a chair opposite hers. "And why not, pray?"

"We are merely friends," she said. "If you were considering marriage, it would be with someone far more beautiful than I and someone who would not be an embarrassment to you in public. Come now, admit that you had not had the fleetingest thought of marriage before my guardian found us together last evening."

"There you are wrong, Rosalind," he said quietly. "I have for some time been thinking of you in terms of marriage."

"Why?" she asked, staring across at him incredulously.

"What a disconcerting female you are," he commented, smiling back at her. "You are supposed to be in transports of delight at the moment, or possibly in a swoon at my feet."

"Fiddle!" she said.

He laughed. "You are one of a kind, Rosalind," he said, "an original. I like your company and I am attracted to your person. Have I answered your question?"

She stared at him silently, trying to understand his enigmatic smile. She had never found Sir Bernard to be a mystery before, but now she did not know what to believe. How much was truth and how much was gallant lying?

"Will you marry me?" he asked. "I would be truly honored, I assure you, and I shall do my best to be a good husband."

Rosalind got abruptly to her feet and crossed the room to the desk. She stood with her hands flat on its surface, her back to the room. "Bernard," she said, "please speak the truth to me. I value your friendship and would far prefer that you speak what you feel rather than what you think you should say. You did not compromise me last night and are not honor-bound to offer for me. Even his lordship admitted that to me when we arrived home from the ball. Please let us be friends again. I do not wish you to come to hate me for forcing you into a course of action that you did not freely choose."

She turned to look at him and found that he had come up behind her while she talked. He was standing now just a foot away. He took her chin in his hand and raised her face to his. "Tears, Rosalind?" he chided gently. "Indeed there is no need to cry. I have spoken the truth to you. I wish above all things to make you my wife. And I ask you again if you will consent to be betrothed to me. The choice is entirely yours, dear. If you wish it, we shall announce our engagement immediately. If you have doubts, you must tell me so and I shall wait." He smiled again into her eyes and lowered his head in order to touch his lips very gently to hers.

Rosalind turned her head away from his hand and fingered a quill pen that lay on top of the desk. "Will you mind very much if I say yes?" she asked apologetically. "I think that I should like to be married to you, Bernard."

He chuckled. "I should mind very much if you said no," he replied. "Now, if we are truly betrothed, may I have a proper kiss, please?"

Rosalind allowed him to hold her and kiss her with more ardor than he had shown on any previous occasion. She even put her arms up around his neck and let her body lean against his. Her mind, in a whirl, was trying to assimilate what she had just done, trying to believe that she had made the right decision.

Cousin Hetty was in an ecstasy of delight. Two announcements had appeared in the *Gazette* within just a few weeks of each other. Both her charges were betrothed and both to extremely eligible young men. She congratulated herself on her accomplishment. She spent many cheerful hours with the latest edition of the *Belle Assemblée*, planning a trousseau for each girl. Sylvia joined in with enthusiasm, Rosalind only halfheartedly. But it was far too soon to make any definite plans. Lord Standen's house party had to be given first consideration.

Lord Standen had decided to celebrate his betrothal in the country with a more intimate group of friends than had gathered for his sister's ball. The visit was to last only a week, as most of his guests would want to return to London for the final events of the Season. But he wished to introduce his intended bride to his widowed mother, who rarely ventured away from his country estate. The party was to consist of his brother, Nigel; his sister, Letitia; her husband, Mr. Thomas Morrison; Sylvia; and her cousin Rosalind. Sir Bernard Crawleigh had been added to the guest list after his unexpected betrothal to Rosalind was announced. Sir Rowland Axby had already been invited when it had been thought that he was the girl's suitor. Two of Sylvia's newly formed friends, Miss Susan Heron and Lady Theresa Parsons, were also to be of the party. The Earl of Raymore, of course, had been invited and was to come for the last few days. He excused himself from spending the whole week in the country on the grounds that he was busy organizing his musical concert, which was to take place soon after the end of the house party.

Sylvia bubbled with enthusiasm. Nigel had told her that his brother's estate was a particularly beautiful place, especially in summer. It was known for miles around for its masses of rhododendrons that lined the mile-long driveway and surrounded the house. Nigel had also told her of the stables and the horses that were the pride and joy of his brother.

"You will enjoy yourself, at least, Ros," she said, hugging her cousin happily on one occasion. "You will be able to ride to your heart's content again. I know you have been missing Flossie, although you have not complained at all."

"Yes, it will be splendid," Rosalind agreed with a rare burst of enthusiasm. "But tell me, Sylvie, do you never talk to his lordship? Everything you know of him and his house you seem to have learned from his brother."

"Oh, Lord Standen is a very reticent man," Sylvia explained airly. "Nigel says that he has always been quiet. I was rather awed by his silences at first, for I wondered if he was disapproving of me. But Nigel says no, it is just his way."

"Oh," was all Rosalind could think of to say. She did not know whether to be amused or uneasy by the constant references to "Nigel says."

On the whole Rosalind was happy about the approaching holiday in the country. It would be delightful to be away from the glare of the public eye. Even though there were to be several house guests at Broome Hall, she felt that there she would have greater freedom to do as she wished. She could avoid the more public entertainments and spend more time alone or—blissfully—out riding. It would be heavenly to be away from the Earl of Raymore for a few days. Her hatred of him had become almost an obsession. She had only to anticipate his arrival in a room, had only to hear his voice, to feel her whole body tense and to lose her ability to concentrate on whatever activity she was involved in. When he was in a room with her, she felt every muscle tighten. She found it difficult to behave or talk naturally to anyone else. It was almost impossible to look at him and almost impossible not to look at him. She would find that in the end she could not resist darting a glance at him with an almost jerky movement of her head, and almost invariably she would choose a moment when he too was looking at her, often with the ice-blue eyes she was accustomed to, sometimes with a still, brooding look that made her breathless and uncomfortable for minutes afterward. It would be good to be free of him for at least a few days. Rosalind hoped that perhaps he would not join the party, after all.

Most of all she welcomed the prospect of a week in the country with Sir Bernard Crawleigh. She felt uneasy about their betrothal. She was not quite certain of her own feelings. She knew that she liked him. She found his kisses pleasant. Certainly marriage to Bernard was like a fulfillment of her wildest dreams. No, not her wildest. Her greatest dream had been to marry Alistair, and no living man could take his place. But had she known a few months before that she would be betrothed to a handsome, charming man of rank and wealth, she would have been ecstatic. For so many years Rosalind had convinced herself that no man would ever want to make her his wife. But now that the impossible had happened, her spirits were curiously flat. Something was not quite right.

She persuaded herself that her unease was due to the fact that she could not be sure of Bernard's feelings. During that morning visit in the library, he had convinced her that he really did wish for the match, that he had intended to offer for her even before Raymore had caught them together. And since then he had been flatteringly attentive, sending her flowers each day, taking her driving in the park, organizing a small party to attend the opera, pressing for an early wedding in the autumn. But she could not help but wonder. Apart from the fact that he had kissed her twice, he had never given a hint of any special attachment before the night of Letitia's ball. His manner had been easy and friendly, frequently teasing, as it still was.

Although Cousin Hetty and Sylvia frequently complimented Rosalind on her appearance, and although Bernard had several times assured her that she was lovely, Rosalind could not free her mind of the habit of thinking herself ugly. It was hard for her to believe that Bernard was not repelled by her appearance, particularly by her limp. How could he love her? And, in fact, she realized, he had never claimed to do so.

These days his friendly, teasing manner was like the surface of a shield. She was not sure if Bernard really meant all that he said, or if his sense of honor was forcing him into an elaborate charade. She looked forward, then, to the stay in the country. Surely if they were together for a week in a more tranquil setting, she would be able to understand her own feelings and she would learn where his wishes really lay.

Only five days were to elapse between the day of her betrothal and the day of the departure for Broome Hall. Rosalind used one of those afternoons to pay a call on Lady Elise Martel, who had finally delivered a son one week before. She was reclining in her private sitting room when Rosalind was announced.

"Do come and sit down, Rosalind," she said eagerly. "How very kind of you to come and visit me when you must have so many more exciting things to do. Henry has told me of your engagement to Sir Bernard Crawleigh. I am so happy for you. I can remember the time when I wished he would pay attention to me."

"Then I must be very thankful to Sir Henry that he put a stop to the possibility," Rosalind said with a smile.

The conversation switched immediately and inevitably to the new baby, who had to be brought from his crib by a nurse to be held and admired by the guest. Holding the sleeping child and examining the perfection of his tiny, curled fingers, Rosalind felt a surge of fierce gladness that she was to be married soon. For the first time in her life she was able to hope and dream of a child of her own.

"Henry wants Edward to be godfather," Lady Elise was saying, "though I could wish that he had a wife so that little Andrew could have a pair of godparents."

"The Earl of Raymore!" Rosalind snorted inelegantly. "I very much doubt that he would come within a mile of the baby. How could he be godfather? By proxy?"

Elise chuckled. "He is a rather formidable man, is he not? I can remember being terrified of him at one time when my mama was trying desperately to match us up. Those piercing blue eyes! But I forgave him all when he introduced me to Henry, though I believe he did so only so that he would not have to partner me himself in that particular quadrille."

"I would not doubt it," Rosalind said dryly.

"But you are quite wrong about the baby," Elise continued. "He came here yesterday with Henry and brought a most extravagant gift. I did not offer to show him Andrew, because I felt as you do. But Henry brought him to the drawing room—he is bursting with the most absurd paternal pride, you know. And Edward actually took the child in his own hands. I just about died of horror. But he put his hand beneath the baby's head and bounced him gently just as if he had a whole nurseryful of his own to practice on, and Andrew did not even cry."

"Amazing!" Rosalind commented.

"Yes, is it not? I told Henry afterward that there is quite a domestic man hidden beneath the rather cold exterior. Poor Edward! If he could just get over his hatred of women."

"Does he hate all women?" Rosalind asked. "Not just me?"

"Indeed he does," Lady Elise replied. "Henry says that he once had a rather unfortunate experience with a broken engagement."

"But it is rather absurd to hate the whole sex because one of us proved to be a jilt," Rosalind said.

Lady Elise smiled and handed the baby back to the waiting nurse. "I quite agree," she said. "But perhaps we do not know the whole story. I would hate to judge Edward too harshly. I must confess to a soft spot for the man."

"Hm," said Rosalind.

"But tell me about your betrothal," her hostess said. "I was never more pleased in my life."

Rosalind found herself confiding the whole to this woman whom she considered a friend, though they had known each other for such a short time.

"Oh, dear," Lady Elise said when Rosalind had finished. "You see? I was quite right earlier when I said that you cannot judge another. I have been feeling very happy for you, assuming that you must be deeply in love. However, you must not despair, Rosalind. I think I can assure you that Bernard would not do anything just for the sake of gallantry. He is close on thirty, you know, and has successfully avoided all the matchmaking females of the last several years. I do not believe that he would have offered for you if he did not really wish to marry you. As you have explained to me, he did not seriously compromise you and could easily have refused to offer had he wanted to."

"Do you really believe so?" Rosalind asked hopefully.

"And you must not give in to overmodesty," Lady Elise said severely. "Because your disability precluded you from many activities as you grew up, you have convinced yourself that you are worthless and ugly. I told you when I first met you that in fact you are not so. And indeed your new clothes and your changed hairstyle make you look quite striking. I might almost say beautiful. I find it not at all difficult to believe that Sir Bernard Crawleigh has developed a *tendre* for you."

Rosalind smiled.

"And do not be afraid of your own feelings," her companion said. "If you love him, Rosalind, admit it to yourself and to him. You must not feel that you are unworthy of his love. "There," she said, laughing suddenly, "Henry always says that sometimes I talk so much that I forget the necessities of life. I have not even rung for tea yet. How rag-mannered you must think me."

Whenever she could, Rosalind spent time in the music room. She felt she would have gone insane without her music. Her uncertainty over her own feelings and those of Bernard, her unhappiness in her guardian's house were all accentuated by the steady stream of visitors who came to congratulate both her and Sylvia on their good fortune. Rosalind, who had been so accustomed to privacy and even loneliness for many years, found the tension almost unbearable. In the music room she could forget. Her singing helped her to escape into an imaginary world of love and dreams. Her pianoforte playing made such demands on her skill and concentration that the real world receded for hours at a time. She had almost mastered the Moonlight Sonata. She wished to eliminate the few remaining flaws and hesitancies in the few days before she left for the country. But it was not easy. She found herself becoming more and more emotionally involved in the music. A few times she found herself actually sobbing as the third movement built in tempo and volume. And she could not understand why. She knew only that her technique was faltering, that she increasingly stumbled over passages that she thought she had mastered.

Raymore, frequently listening in the anteroom, found that sometimes he could not remain seated but paced in frustration, wanting to rush into the music room and shake her, rant and rave at her to concentrate. He sensed her pain but felt powerless either to explain it or to alleviate it. On one occasion, when she had played the same passage through half a dozen times and finally crashed her fingers down on the keys, he felt her despair. He stood with his forehead against the screen, eyes closed, one fist clenched against the lintel above his head. She was his red rose and he fought the impulse to go to her, to hold her to him and soothe away the darkness.

On a seventh attempt, she finally played the passage without a flaw. He opened his eyes, and with sight came the realization that it was Rosalind in the next room. His lip curled in a sneer that was directed entirely against himself and he left the room and the house immediately. He did not go near the music room the next day.

The day for the journey to Broome Hall turned out to be chilly, a brisk wind sending clouds scudding across the sky. But it was a pleasant enough day for a journey. Rosalind and Sylvia traveled together in the Earl of Raymore's new and quite luxurious traveling carriage while their baggage loaded down a second coach. Sir Bernard Crawleigh rode alongside them, occasionally galloping ahead, sometimes riding beside the window, which Rosalind lowered so that they could speak with him.

"I am most honored to be your only outrider, ladies," he said once, tipping his hat further back on his head, "but, alas, there is not one highwayman in sight. How am I ever to convince you of my courage and gallantry if we do not encounter at least one gentleman of the road?"

"Oh, dear," said Sylvia, "do not joke about such things, Sir Bernard. I shall be quite contented if I never see a highwayman."

Rosalind grinned. "Perhaps another time, Bernard, when Sylvia is not with us," she said. "I should be more than delighted to have some excitement to liven up a very dull journey. But Sylvia is so chicken-hearted, you see."

"Ah," he said, and tipping his hat forward again with the end of his whip handle, he spurred his horse forward out of their sight.

Lord Standen and his brother had made the journey a day earlier so that they would be present to greet the arrival of their guests. Sylvia was quite subdued during most of the journey, occasionally giving in to bursts of nervous excitement. The prospect of spending a week in the home of her intended husband frightened her more than she cared to admit. She was not sure that she would be able to spend a great deal of time in his presence with ease. And she was terrified about meeting his mother.

"Poor Lady Standen," she said. "Nigel says that she is frequently in poor health and rarely leaves the house. I do hope she likes me."

"How could she not!" exclaimed Rosalind. "Now, do not go getting yourself into the fidgets, Sylvie. You are the sweetest person I know. If she fails to love you instantly, I shall refuse to be civil to her at all."

"Well, I shall try to please her," Sylvia said anxiously, and lapsed into silence again.

They were the last of the house guests to arrive. Lord Standen greeted his bride-to-be with flattering deference, not waiting for the ladies to enter the house, but coming down the marble steps outside the imposing front doors to help them alight. He did look rather splendid, Rosalind thought, in dark-blue coat and cream-colored buckskins, the white tassels of his gleaming Hessians swaying as he walked. He was a tall man, dark and good-looking. They made a very handsome couple, in fact, Rosalind decided, as he bowed over Sylvia's hand and raised it to his lips. She smiled shyly up at him and then beamed beyond him in a much more relaxed manner at Nigel, who had also come out of the house to greet the new arrivals.

It was hard for Rosalind to see the two men as brothers. Nigel Broome had none of the advantages of his brother. He was half a head shorter and rather too slim to be imposing. His dark hair stood out from his head in unruly curls, and his thin face usually looked earnest. He certainly seemed to have taken upon himself the task of caring for the welfare of his future sister-in-law. He shook hands with her warmly and led her indoors, while his lordship was busy welcoming Rosalind and ushering her into his home.

9

Lord Standen had obviously put a great deal of effort into planning his house party. During the first few days his guests discovered that there were a great many activities in which they could participate, each according to his interests. Yet no one felt as if his life had been organized for him. Each was free to be alone or do nothing if he so chose.

Sylvia had been introduced to Lady Standen in the dining room before dinner on the first evening. The meeting was not such a terrible ordeal, after all. Lady Standen was easily pleased with anyone who would lend a sympathetic ear to her complaints about her health, and Sylvia listened most patiently both before dinner was announced and during the meal itself, when she was seated to the right of her future mother-in-law. Sylvia was a kindhearted girl at all times, but on this occasion her sympathetic manner was largely aroused by awe. The older woman was a wilting creature who nevertheless commanded attention.

Lady Standen appeared to approve of her son's choice, remarking loudly to Sir Rowland Axby in the drawing room afterward that she was a "pretty-behaved gel." Sylvia had escaped to the pianoforte, which she played only indifferently. Nigel followed her there and stood behind her stool, turning the pages of the music. After a while, she stopped playing and turned on her stool to talk to him. Poor Sylvia, Rosalind thought. She had been observing her cousin all evening and guessed that she did not feel entirely comfortable. Standen might have stayed with her and helped her feel at home. But his impeccable good manners had led him to mix with all his guests in order to ensure their comfort.

For the next few days, in fact, Sylvia found that she spent more time with her friends, Susan and Lady Theresa, and with Nigel than she did with her betrothed. He had some estate business to attend to; he had to take his male guests and the more energetic ladies on long rides; he had to spend some time with his mother, whom he rarely saw. Always she seemed to be excluded, whether by her own choice or by his, or even by mere chance, she could not be sure.

With her friends she walked the grounds or sat on the terrace exchanging *on dits* from town or discussing fashions. With them, she discussed her trousseau. With Nigel she played cards and talked about her future husband and home. One afternoon he took her in the gig to visit some of the tenants, with whom she discovered he was on excellent terms. He showed her the schoolhouse, which had been built only three years before at his suggestion. He, in fact, had been the first instructor when he finished at university, but his brother had replaced him with a hired teacher, feeling that it was beneath the dignity of a Broome to teach the children of tenants.

But Nigel still took a lively interest in the school, which now boasted almost all the boys of the estate as pupils. "I dream of extending the building," he told Sylvia, "here on the east, with a schoolroom for girls. Most people think I am absurd. George is quite unconvinced. But I believe that girls can be taught to read and write just like boys, and perhaps they could have some instruction in sewing and drawing and such. What do you think?"

Sylvia's eyes shone. "What a splendid idea, Nigel," she said, gazing at him in admiration. "But could their mothers spare them from home?"

"That is the main problem," he admitted. "But I had

much the same objection to taking the boys into the school at first. Somehow their fathers managed to do without them. I believe that the mothers would too. And think of the advantages, Sylvia. When they are at home, the girls will be able to read to their mothers, to mention just one thing."

"You will do it too. I know you will," Sylvia said fervently. "And will you teach them yourself, Nigel?"

"I think not," he said. "There are any number of ladies who would be thankful for the employment. No, what I really want to do, Sylvia, is to start a school in London for destitute boys. Educate them and train them enough that they can gain employment as clerks or grooms or footmen, perhaps."

He helped Sylvia back into her seat in the gig and drove slowly back to the house, expounding to her the dreams and theories that were dearest to his heart.

Rosalind meanwhile was enjoying herself vastly. The excellence of Lord Standen's stables had not been exaggerated. For the first time since she had left Raymore Manor, she could ride again. On the morning of the first day she went with Lord Standen himself, his sister and brother-in-law, Sir Rowland and Sir Bernard on a partial tour of the estate. She was mounted on a quiet mare that was not quite up to her skills, but she would not complain. Just the feeling of being high in the saddle again, fresh air and countryside all around her, the distinctive smell of horse teasing her nostrils, exhilarated her. She felt comfortable in a new riding habit of wine-red velvet, its wide skirt and fitted jacket neatly fashioned yet not too revealing of her full figure, the jaunty little hat with its curled feather perched precariously on her dark hair. Nothing could quite dampen her joy, even the fact that her mount could not keep up with the others or the fact that she had to converse most of the way with Sir Rowland, who gallantly matched his horse's pace to hers and kept her company.

During the afternoon, when most of the guests were relaxing quietly about the house and gardens, Rosalind again rode out, this time with only Sir Bernard for company. She persuaded the groom to saddle a glossy black stallion for her.

"Are you sure you can handle him?" Sir Bernard asked doubtfully. "Highwaymen I may be able to take in my stride, but I am not quite sure that I relish the prospect of having to rescue a damsel from a runaway horse."

"Me neither," Rosalind replied with an arch glance as she put her foot in the groom's locked hands and mounted lightly to the sidesaddle. "Are you sure you can handle *your* mount, Bernard?" She laughed gaily, turned the horse's head for the exit from the cobbled stable yard, and trotted him down the worn pathway that led to the open fields beyond the house.

For the next half-hour she was completely happy, completely in tune with the animal beneath her. It was perhaps only on horseback that Rosalind ever felt complete. There she could be the equal of anyone in grace and skill. Her deformity mattered not at all. She trotted and galloped the stallion and finally could no longer resist the temptation to ride straight for a hedge. Bernard rode at her side the whole time, not speaking, seeming to recognize her need for silent enjoyment. When he had followed her over the hedge, though, he did catch up to her and pulled his horse close alongside.

"By Jove, Rosalind, you are a neck-or-nothing person," he commented amiably. "Is a poor fearful mortal allowed a rest without losing you entirely?"

She flashed him a smile and skillfully slowed her horse to a walk. "I think the horses probably need a rest," she agreed. "Let us lead them to the water over there." She pointed with her whip to a stream on their left.

They led the horses to a clump of trees close to the banks of the stream. Sir Bernard dismounted and turned to lift down Rosalind.

"You look remarkably fetching today," he said, easing

her down so that her body slid the length of his. "Very Italian."

"Hm," she said, turning away to tether her horse to a tree.

He grinned. "Come and sit over here," he said, moving across to a patch of grass that faced the stream and was shaded from the rays of the sun. Rosalind, having been complimented herself, noticed how handsome he looked, his tall, athletic figure accentuated by the black coat, cream breeches, and black top boots that he wore. He tossed his top hat onto the ground and stretched out a hand to help Rosalind to a seating position. He sat down beside her.

"You may not be able to dance in public," he said, "but you are one of the best riders I have ever seen, Rosalind, and that includes both sexes."

"Thank you," she said. "My father forced me to ride again after my accident, although I can remember being terrified. I believe he realized that I would need at least one method of moving around in which I might be uninhibited."

"Then he was a wise man," he said, circling her wrist with two fingers and then clasping her hand in his.

"This is a lovely estate, is it not?" she said lamely, feeling suddenly uneasy in his presence.

"Yes," he said, laughing, "and so are you. You do not realize that you are beautiful, do you, Rosalind?"

She blushed and laughed in embarrassment. "You do not need to say that, Bernard," she said. "I should prefer that you did not flatter me."

He reached across and took her chin in his hand. "I shall convince you in time," he said softly, and brought his lips down to hers.

Rosalind continued to sit clasping her knees. It was pleasant. She was determined to believe that he really did wish to marry her. She was going to enjoy his company this week and allow herself to fall all the way in love with him.

"Mmm," he said, his mouth moving to her ear, "perhaps this time we will not be interrupted by his damned lordship." He put one arm around her shoulders and drew her against him. The other hand began to undo the buttons of her velvet jacket to reveal the pink silk blouse beneath. Rosalind was so surprised that she did nothing. She continued to clasp her knees with her arms.

"Rosalind," he said, "are you untouched?"

"Untouched?" she asked, the blood beginning to throb at her temples.

"Are you a virgin?" he asked.

Her eyes widened and she could feel her cheeks flush uncomfortably. "Of course," she whispered.

He laughed in amusement. "There is no 'of course' about it. Do you realize how many of the sweet young things who grace the ballrooms with their maidenly pastel shades have lovers, and how many of the very proper matrons at the sidelines also deceive their husbands?"

Rosalind hugged her knees closer. "I think we should be starting back, Bernard," she said. "This is a highly improper conversation."

He chuckled and brought his free hand up under her chin again. "I am sorry, dear," he said. "I merely wished to know how free I could be with you in the coming days. When we return to London, of course, your freedom will be curtailed again, and when I take you to visit my family during the summer, the proprieties must be observed. But here we can begin to get to know each other better."

Rosalind swallowed painfully against his hand. "We should not be alone, Bernard," she said.

For answer he smiled and lowered his head to hers again. Rosalind was forced to put an arm around his neck when she felt herself losing balance. A moment later she felt the grass against her back and head and Bernard's mouth was more urgent on hers, his tongue trying to force her teeth apart. She gasped and squirmed when she felt his hands slide across the silk covering her breasts.

"You are lovely," he murmured, lifting his head and gazing down into her face. He regarded her for a moment and a smile crinkled his eyes. "You are also very frightened, are you not?"

She tried to smile and did not quite succeed. "I just do not think that we should be doing this," she said.

"There is no need to feel guilty," he assured her. "You are going to be my wife very soon."

She smiled with more success this time. It was true, she did feel guilty, though she did not know why. They were betrothed, after all. "Maybe so," she said, "but I am not your wife yet, Bernard, and I should feel a great deal safer right now on the back of that horse over there."

He grinned. "You may be an innocent, love," he said, getting nimbly to his feet and brushing the grass off the sleeves of his coat, "but you have certainly perfected the art of the tease. Just wait until our wedding night, my girl. I shall have my revenge." He reached down to pull her to her feet and kissed her lightly on the lips.

Rosalind limped without further delay to her horse and mounted into the saddle before Sir Bernard could come to offer his assistance.

It was on the night of the same day that Sylvia went to bed in tears. She had entered the dining room that evening on the arm of Lord Standen in a much more cheerful frame of mind than on the previous day. She had enjoyed her outing with Nigel, had spent a comfortable hour with her betrothed in the afternoon inspecting the orchards and flower gardens, and had taken tea with his mother in the latter's private apartments. Her future mother-in-law had treated her with flatteringly kind condescension. Sylvia was prepared to enjoy dinner and the company of her friends. She looked dazzlingly lovely in a primrose-yellow satin gown, gold embroidery sparkling at its neckline and hem. A golden ribbon was threaded through her silver-blond hair.

During the first two courses Sylvia chatted easily and unselfconsciously with Lady Standen on her left and Sir Rowland Axby opposite. Only gradually did she become aware that conversation at the table was becoming more general. Nigel was telling a group of people around him about his dream of setting up a school in London.

"There is certainly a need," he was saying. "You have all seen how the streets of London are crowded with beggars, many of them young children. They have nothing to do except beg and steal, and if they are allowed to go uneducated, they will grow up to produce more children in the same plight. And so the problem will perpetuate itself."

"Papa says that no one need remain idle if he wishes to work," Lady Theresa Parsons commented. "Idleness results from laziness, he says. And if these people are too lazy to work, Mr. Broome, I fail to see that they will take kindly to learning lessons."

"With all due respect to your father," Nigel replied, "I cannot agree. These people need help, and who better to offer assistance than those of us who are privileged?"

The conversation, which was becoming rather loud and forceful, had attracted Lord Standen's attention. "You would go about solving the problem in quite the wrong way, Nigel," he said. "Your plan would help so few children that it would be worthless. The whole social order needs changing. Only then can the plight of the poor be changed."

"I agree with you," his brother said heatedly, "and that should be your contribution, George. You are a member of the House of Lords and can speak out on social issues. I cannot. And while I wait for the whole system to change, a whole generation of boys is growing up ignorant and possibly vicious."

"You must admit that your brother is right, though, Nigel," his mother added from her end of the table.

"The good you could do would be the merest drop in the ocean."

"But—" he began.

"The ocean is made up of little drops, though, is it not?" Sylvia said, and seeing all eyes turn her way in surprise, she was startled to find that the words had come from her mouth. "I mean," she stammered, "without all the little drops there would be no ocean. In the same way, every little child is part of the whole problem. If Nigel can help only a few, he has somehow helped tackle the whole problem." She was flushed and breathless by the time she had reached the end of this long speech.

"I say," Nigel said, his attention full on her, "what a splendid metaphor. I must remember it."

"I think, my dear," Standen said kindly, "that you would be better not worrying yourself over matters that do not concern you."

"But they do concern me," Sylvia cried. She could feel the color high in her cheeks, but seemed powerless to stop herself. "When we are married, my lord, I shall have to be aware of the poor on this estate, and whenever I travel to town, I shall have to pass through those dreadful streets with their wretched crowds. How can I not applaud someone who is prepared to devote his time and his fortune to doing something about the situation?"

"You show yourself to be a lady of great sensibility," her fiancé said, but there was a note of finality in his voice. "I believe we bore our company with such serious conversation." He smiled and turned with practiced grace to Miss Heron, whom he engaged in conversation.

Everyone else appeared to relax and forget the incident. But Sylvia suffered an agony of mortification. The rest of her food tasted like straw. She could never remember being so forward. To have spoken to a whole tableful of people was brazen enough. To have spoken on a topic that was so clearly a male preserve was unforgivable. She had felt Standen's displeasure and believed that it was justified. She could not, though, for dear life see how anyone would not think Nigel's scheme quite irreproachable.

Unfortunately for Sylvia, when the ladies retired to the drawing room. Rosalind, Susan, and Lady Theresa crossed immediately to the pianoforte in search of the music for a song that they had been talking about during dinner. Letitia had gone to her room to fetch her work basket. Sylvia had no choice but to join Lady Standen by the fire. She was scolded, very gently, both for her forwardness and for her opinion.

"Nigel is a dear boy," his mother said, "but he has always been wayward. My elder son has educated him for the Church and has offered him more than one living. Nigel has refused. You see, my dear, if he wishes to serve humanity, as he claims to do, he has ample opportunity to do so in the best possible way. George is a sensible man, you may depend upon it. You must let yourself be guided by him, my dear. He will shape your mind well."

Sylvia had lost the courage that had borne her up for a few minutes in the dining room. She examined her fingernails as her hands were spread across her lap. "Yes, ma'am, I shall try. I am indeed sorry if I caused you embarrassment earlier."

"There," Lady Standen said soothingly, leaning forward and patting Sylvia's hands, "you are a good girl. Just a little impulsive."

Much later, when tea was being served after a noisy game of charades, Lord Standen himself took Sylvia aside. "I was not best pleased with your behavior at dinner," he told her. "I appreciate your loyalty to Nigel, who is to be your brother-in-law, but do you not think, my dear, that your first loyalty should be to me?" He smiled charmingly to soften the harshness of his words. His tone was very gentle.

"I was not intending to disagree with you, my lord," she replied timidly. "I was merely offering an opinion."

He smiled again. "And a very humane opinion, too,"

he said. "It does you credit. But your ideas are unformed, my dear. You are very young, but recently out
of the schoolroom. And you have been without your
father for upward of a year. You must allow yourself to
be guided by me. I shall take the greatest delight in
forming the mind that lies within that pretty little head."
He lifted her hand and touched it lightly to his lips.

A short while later Sylvia sat on Rosalind's bed, still
dressed, watching her cousin take the pins from her
hair and brush out the shining coils of almost black hair.
"*Was* I so very bad?" she asked. "Oh, Ros, I do not
know how I shall face everyone tomorrow."

"Sylvie, you are making a great to-do about nothing,"
Rosalind said. "The discussion was a general one and
you had every right to contribute your ideas. Your
opinion had great validity. I am sure that several people
at the table agreed with you. Mr. Broome certainly did
and I did."

"But, Ros, I spoke against his lordship," Sylvia wailed.

"So what?" her cousin replied. "Must you always
agree with him, Sylvie? You were not rude to him, after
all."

"But I am ignorant and I do have an unformed mind,"
Sylvia said. "I should not set my opinion against his."

"Who has told you that?" Rosalind asked suspiciously.

"Her ladyship was upset with me and his lordship
was displeased."

"Sylvie," Rosalind said, putting down her brush and
giving her cousin her full attention, "you must not allow
anyone to convince you that you are such a foolish
female that you cannot even think for yourself. Please
promise me you will not."

"But he is to be my husband, Ros," Sylvia said
hesitantly.

"Are you quite, quite sure that you wish him to be?"
Rosalind asked impulsively. She was immediately sorry
that she had asked the question. Tears welled up in
Sylvia's eyes. Her cousin was almost overwrought, Ros-

alind realized, and did not need this particular line of questioning.

"He is a very magnificent man," Sylvia said haltingly. "I must consider myself greatly honored to be chosen by him."

"I am sorry," Rosalind said. "I should not have asked that. You are tired, Sylvie. Go to bed now. We have that shopping excursion tomorrow and must be wide awake." She kissed her cousin on the cheek and watched her leave the room.

Sylvia held back her tears until the dresser had left the room, leaving a candle burning on a side table. But then she gave in to her confusion and misery. She had been so sure that she was in love with Lord Standen. It was far too late now to discover that she was not. And she dared not confide in anyone, even Rosalind.

"I am certainly glad that I did not take a hand against you today," Sir Henry Martel said to the Earl of Raymore on the same afternoon as Rosalind took her ride with Sir Bernard Crawleigh. "If I did not know you better, Edward, I would almost think you must have had the cards marked."

"I did do rather well," Raymore agreed, stacking money and vouchers into a neat pile before him. "The opposition was not of your caliber, though, Henry."

The two men moved into the lounge at Watier's, where they sat down to a drink.

"You are very quiet, my friend," Sir Henry said after a few minutes of silence. "I thought you would be elated to have your bachelor freedom for a few days again."

"Oh, yes, quite," his friend replied absently, flicking open his snuffbox and placing a pinch of snuff on the back of his hand. "I have been devilish busy, though, yesterday and today, trying to persuade Hans Dehnert to play at my concert."

"The Austrian pianist, Edward? Is he in England?"

"Yes, indeed," the earl replied. "As a visitor only. He

has refused quite adamantly several people who have tried to persuade him to give a recital."

"I have the feeling you would not tell me this," Sir Henry said, "if you had not somehow succeeded."

The Earl of Raymore allowed himself to smile as he inclined his head. "All is settled," he said. "I can leave for Standen's house party in the morning with a clear mind."

"Tomorrow?" his friend asked with raised eyebrows. "I understood that you meant to put in a token appearance only at the end of the week, Edward."

"I find that I must carry through my responsibility to the end," Raymore replied. "By the end of the summer I should be free of both my wards, Henry. In the meantime, I should supervise their activities through the rest of the Season."

Sir Henry chuckled as he downed the rest of his drink. "Edward," he said, "I do believe that you are becoming a member of the human race. Elise said it was bound to happen sooner or later. I will wager that you are becoming attached to those females and will miss them sorely when they do get married."

Raymore shuddered. "Heaven forbid!" he said fervently.

"Come and dine with us tonight," Sir Henry said, rising to his feet. "Elise has still not been into company since her confinement. She would be delighted to have you as a guest."

The earl declined, pleading a previous engagement. Then he proceeded to sit on in his place, undecided about how to spend his evening. He did not wish to dine at home. He had done that the evening before, believing that it would be bliss to have his home to himself again. Even Hetty had gone away for a few days, to stay with friends until her charges returned from the country. He had found himself unaccountably restless. He had wandered from the dining room to the music room and had stood before the pianoforte pressing down the keys almost at random. Although he was a connoisseur of music, he was not himself a performer. With one finger he tried to pick out the tune of that song she frequently sang, "My Luve is like a red, red rose." He could almost hear it in his mind, but somehow the tune would not reproduce itself on the pianoforte.

He had finally gone, late, to the opera. For once, he had not enjoyed the music. He scarcely heard it, in fact. His sole object had been to watch the little redhead dancer and to meet her backstage afterward. Perhaps she had attached herself to someone else by now. He had certainly neglected her of late. But it was worth a try.

Raymore had spent a most satisfactory night with the creature, who was everything a woman should be. She kept her mouth shut, gave him exactly what he wanted and more, and made no demands afterward for further meetings or for a more permanent arrangement. She had no cause to complain, of course. He had paid her well enough.

He should be satisfied. He had quickly regained his former manner of living. He was free of his wards for a few days and soon would be free of them altogether. He concluded that his restlessness was due to the fact that he knew this breathing space was only temporary. At the end of the week they would be back again and his home would not be his own.

He had decided earlier in the day, as soon as final arrangements had been made with Hans Dehnert, that he would journey into Sussex the following morning, three days before he had originally planned to do so. It might appear ill-mannered if he arrived for only two days when he had been invited for the whole week. And he had to make sure that the engagement was really satisfactory. Rosalind was a schemer, a woman of somewhat loose morals, he suspected, but she was a lady and his ward. If Crawleigh did not truly want her, or if he saw her merely as a plaything, then the betrothal must be ended without further ado. He would send her to live at Raymore Manor when the Season was ended if that was what she really wished. He had other homes in which to stay himself when he tired of town. He need not be troubled by her presence.

Raymore finally left Watier's, taking his hat and cane from the porter. He moved on to White's Club, where he joined a circle of acquaintances for dinner. He spent most of the night playing cards, unable to stomach the thought of searching out the little dancer again. He arrived home with the dawn, somewhat the worse for drink.

10

Rosalind woke up the following morning feeling more cheerful and more energetic than she had done for a long time. She had lain awake for a while the night before, hands clasped behind her head, thinking through the events of the last weeks, assessing what had happened, sorting out her feelings, trying to understand why she had felt guilty with Bernard that afternoon.

It seemed that events had just happened to her, almost without her will, since the summons came from her guardian for her and Sylvia to travel to London. She had been so used to ordering her own life. Suddenly to be catapulted into society had been a shock. She had been sure that after that first appearance no one would want to know her and she would be allowed to return to the way of life she knew. She had been somewhat upset by Sir Rowland Axby's attentions and by her guardian's insistence that she listen to his addresses. And she had been relieved to discover Sir Bernard Crawleigh, who had been friendly and relaxed from the start. Her engagement had been embarrassing because she could never be sure if Bernard had been precipitated into it before he was ready or whether, in fact, he would ever have been ready.

These were the facts she set out before herself to consider. No, there was one more. There was the Earl of Raymore himself. Rosalind frowned and gazed up at the darkened hangings above her bed. What was it about him that always hovered in the back of her mind?

He was an unpleasant man, cold and domineering. It seemed that she could never be near him without all her nerves bristling. Was it hatred that kept him always there on the fringes of her consciousness?

She found him attractive. Now that she was away from him, out of his house, she had to admit that fact. He was gorgeously handsome with that thick blond hair, aquiline features, and perfectly proportioned body. That she could never deny. Her dream man, Alistair, had looked almost identical. Poor Alistair! She had almost forgotten him. But it was not just Raymore's looks that attracted. He had an almost irresistible magnetism for her. She thought of that kiss again and compared it, point by point, with Bernard's caresses. He had taken every one of the liberties with her that her betrothed had taken, and more, and she had not resisted as she had that afternoon. She grew hot at the memory of how it had felt to be in Edward's arms for those brief moments, the very sexual kiss, his hands moving forward possessively from her back.

Yes, she must admit it. It was the only way she might be able to solve the problem. She found the Earl of Raymore a very attractive man. She felt uncomfortable in his presence, partly because she wanted him. She felt infinitely better just admitting the truth to herself.

Having admitted it, she could look at the situation rationally. It was not love that she felt. She disliked Raymore, even despised him. She could not imagine that they would ever find a topic on which they might agree. The attraction was entirely physical. There could never be a relationship between them, even if he felt the same way. And he had made it quite clear from the start that he returned all her feelings, but that he also found her physically repulsive.

Well, then, Rosalind thought with great good sense, she must totally ignore the attraction. It was not worthy of her attention. And having decided as much, she turned her attention to Bernard. Should she continue to feel guilty about having unwittingly trapped him into a betrothal? Today he had not behaved like a man who had been unhappily caught by his own sense of honor. He had quite deliberately invited their tête-à-tête by the stream and he had shown every sign of finding her attractive. His lovemaking had not been merely a dutiful embrace. In addition, he was still friendly and teasing.

The fact was that he *had* proposed, even when she had told him that he need not. She did not have to feel responsible. The only question still to be considered, then, was whether she could be happy with the match. Bernard was a man she could like and respect. And he was an attractive man. She enjoyed his caresses, though she had been somewhat uncomfortable with their ardor that afternoon.

Rosalind fell asleep after determining that, from that moment on, she would accept her betrothal wholeheartedly. She would be confident that she was the woman he wanted to marry and she would allow him to set the pace of the courtship. The Earl of Raymore would exist for the future only as her guardian, and even that position would be his for only a couple of months longer.

All the ladies went shopping the following morning. The village three miles away boasted only a few shops, but the haberdasher's was pronounced to be a very tolerable establishment and Lady Theresa and Sylvia each found straw bonnets at the milliner's that were most becoming.

The gentlemen had had a morning of riding. Both groups were in high spirits at luncheon and greeted with enthusiasm Lord Standen's suggestion that during the afternoon they all walk to the lake that was a mile away through the trees. A picnic tea would be sent by wagon later.

Lord Standen took Sylvia on his arm and led the way through the shady woods to the east of the house. "You will like the lake, my dear," he told her as they walked.

"It is most picturesque. You will be able to sketch here for hours after we are married."

"I never did learn to sketch or paint in watercolors with any great success," she replied apologetically. "Ros was always the artistic one."

"Yet drawing is such an important accomplishment for a lady," he chided gently. "I shall hire you a drawing master and you will soon learn."

Sylvia murmured her thanks. She was soon exclaiming in delight at the beauty of the lake, which was larger than she had expected. "And there are the boats," she said excitedly. "Oh, may we take them out this afternoon, my lord?"

"Of course you may," he said indulgently, "provided one of the gentlemen accompanies you. You will find, my dear, that after we are married, I shall be very insistent that you never take out a boat alone. I should not wish my pretty little wife to endanger herself in any way."

Sylvia looked up shyly into his face to find that he was smiling kindly down at her.

Rosalind was walking with Sir Rowland Axby. He was telling her how his children would enjoy Broome Hall and its spacious grounds. The lake too would delight them and the boats, and an island in the middle of the lake for them to explore. Rosalind began to wonder why he spent so much time away from his children if he loved them so much. But perhaps his need to find them a new mother kept him out in society. Rumor had it that he had offered for two other girls, both new debutantes, since his proposal to her. And he had been particularly attentive to Susan Heron in the last two days, though she had made a determined effort to avoid him this afternoon by grabbing Sir Bernard's arm as if it were a lifeline.

Some of the party sat on the grass by the lake, shaded by the branches of a large oak tree, though Lady Theresa still found it necessary to use a parasol that matched so perfectly the light-blue muslin of her dress that Sir Rowland was moved to tell her that she looked as pretty as a picture. Lord Standen, his sister, and Susan Heron decided to stroll around the lake as far as they could before swampland made further walking impossible. Sir Bernard Crawleigh, Nigel Broome, Sylvia, and Rosalind took to the boats.

Nigel pulled hard at the oars of his boat. He deliberately took a different direction from that taken by Crawleigh, who was rowing at a far more leisurely pace directly toward the island. Nigel said nothing until he and Sylvia were a considerable distance away from anyone else in their party.

"I say," he said at last, shipping the oars and allowing the boat to rock gently on the water, "did I get you into trouble last night, Sylvia?"

"No, really," she denied, "you did not force me to speak."

"I'll wager Mama and George did not like it, though," he said. "They consider me the black sheep, you know. I can stand their disapproval because my conscience tells me that I am right. But I would not for the world have you take my part and incur their displeasure too. Did you get a thundering scold?"

"Well, not exactly a scold," she said unhappily.

"You need say no more," he said a trifle grimly. "I know how both George and Mama can sound so kind and so sincere. They can have one feeling quilty even when one knows that one had done no wrong."

"Nigel," Sylvia said, color rising in her cheeks, "*is* it so dreadful to disagree with one's husband? I would never openly criticize his lordship, you know, and I will try never to fight with him. I am sure he is right when he says that he knows so much more than I and I should allow myself to be guided by him. But surely it is not wrong sometimes to disagree with him and at least discuss a topic. Is it?"

"Of course it is not!" he agreed vehemently. "Don't let George make a little human doll out of you, Sylvie.

You are very sweet and very young, but I have noticed that you feel strongly about some things."

"Yes," she agreed eagerly. "I was very upset when I came to London for the first time and saw the poverty and the dirt. I wanted to stop the carriage and give all my money away. But you have an idea that will really help some people, Nigel, and I do think it so noble of you to want to try."

He leaned forward and touched her hand. "You have a very gentle heart, Sylvia," he said, gazing earnestly into her face, "but you are certainly not a weak person."

She turned her hand so that their fingers clasped. "You give me courage, Nigel," she said. "When I am with you, I feel as if I could stand up against the world."

She tried to smile, but suddenly they were looking intently into each other's eyes. Their hands involuntarily clasped more tightly.

"Oh, God!" he whispered.

"Nigel?" she said, her voice thin and wavering.

At the same moment they snatched their hands away and broke eye contact. Sylvia smoothed her dress over her knees with jerky movements. Nigel snatched up the oars and began to row. They did not look at each other or speak for a while.

"I shall have to go away, you know," he blurted at last. "Tonight."

"Please don't," Sylvia pleaded, her eyes coming back to his face. "Oh, please don't leave me here alone, Nigel."

"Alone?" he said. "You have your cousin here and your friends. You can enjoy what is left of the week."

"No, I cannot," she said, her voice shaking. "Please, Nigel, do not leave. I am mortally afraid of him."

"Of George?" he asked, incredulous. "He won't harm you, Sylvia. He may be somewhat starchy and he may scold a little, but he would never hurt you or be really cruel."

"Oh, I know," Sylvia wailed. "But I cannot be alone with him, Nigel. I do not love him. I have made a terrible mistake."

They stared at each other, Sylvia's eyes wide and frightened.

Nigel finally stopped rowing and shipped the oars again. "I believe it is quite common," he said carefully, staring down at his boots, "for people to panic before their wedding. It is such a final step, you see. But their fear may not reflect their true feelings."

"Nigel," Sylvia said, "I never did love your brother. I thought I did because he is handsome and has such presence. And it felt so wonderful to attract such a great lord during my first Season. Cousin Edward was so pleased and thought it such an eligible match for me. Even so, I believe I would not have become betrothed so soon if he had not been *your* brother, Nigel."

"Did I persuade you to?" he asked aghast.

"No," she replied, "but I liked you so much and I must have felt that I liked him too just because he is your brother."

Nigel ran his fingers through his hair. "It is too late now, Sylvia," he said. "I should be shot. I was so busy courting you for George that I did not fully realize that I wished to court you for myself."

"Oh, did you really, Nigel?" she asked.

Nigel picked up the oars and once more began to row, this time in the direction of the bank. He did not speak until they were close to the small group who had stayed on the grass. "It is no good," he said finally. "I can see no way out."

Sir Bernard Crawleigh, meanwhile, had rowed his boat directly for the small island in the middle of the lake. Rosalind made no objection. In fact, he had noted that her eyes sparkled and her lips smiled today. Her manner was almost flirtatious.

"You look very fetching in that particular shade of orange," he said. "Quite southern. I must take you to Italy for our wedding trip, Rosalind. Do you have relatives there?"

"Yes, several," she replied, smiling. "I have corresponded with them since my parents died there."

By unspoken consent they did not converse again until the boat had been secured to a tree branch that overhung the water at the island, and Sir Bernard had helped Rosalind onto dry land.

She looked down at her feet gingerly. "I do hope this is not just a stretch of swampy land," she said.

"Not at all," he replied. "George tells me there is even a pavilion hidden among these trees that was built for him and his brother when they were children."

He took her hand and led her among the trees. Almost immediately they could see the water at the other side of the island. But the pavilion was there, cleverly hidden among the trees. It was hexagonal, its roof supported by a wooden pillar at each corner. Wooden walls closed it in chest-high, but the upper half was open. There was a doorway but no door. They went inside, Sir Bernard stooping slightly so that his head would not graze the ceiling. Dried leaves crunched under their feet.

"No one has been here for a long time," Rosalind said. "Look, almost all the paint has peeled off the walls."

"What a shame!" he sighed. "I was hoping for a nice cozy structure in which to seduce you."

"Then I am very glad that it is as it is," she said severely, with a twinkle in her eye. "That was not at all a proper plan, sir."

He ducked back through the doorway. "I never said it was," he said. "I am finding Standen's house confoundedly crowded, are you not, Rosalind? I am a frustrated lover."

"I and my honor are eternally grateful for the crowd," Rosalind assured him.

"Well, for the moment at least you are my prisoner," he said with a grin, and circled her waist with his arm.

Rosalind laughed and punched him lightly on both shoulders with her fists. The next moment she was being very thoroughly kissed and clasped against the full length of him. She felt the kiss change tone after the first teasing moments. His mouth became urgent, his breathing faster. His hands roamed her back, molding her to him, and finally pressed down on her hips. Rosalind deliberately allowed the experience. She did not flinch even when his mouth trailed a hot path to her throat and his hands came up to cup her breasts through the thin muslin of her dress. But it was a clinical experience. She could not force herself to feel part of the embrace.

"A frustrated lover indeed," he said ruefully, and nibbled at her earlobe. "I cannot do any of the things I wish to do, love, in this standing position. And there is no grass on which we may lie down. Was ever such a pair of star-crossed lovers?"

"We almost rival Romeo and Juliet," she replied, pushing herself away from him in some relief. "And there are going to be several suspicious people on the bank opposite if we do not reappear soon."

"Ah, the voice of reality and common sense," he mocked as he took her arm and led her carefully back down to the boat.

The picnic proceeded with a great deal of gaiety when all members of the party had returned to the starting point. Sylvia's unusual quietness and Rosalind's forced high spirits did not attract any particular notice.

Sir Bernard Crawleigh, it seemed, was far from satisfied with the events of the afternoon. When the whole party arrived at the house, Rosalind would have ascended the staircase with the rest of the ladies to rest and freshen up for dinner. Her leg was feeling uncomfortably sore after the rather long walk. But her betrothed caught her by the hand and pulled her unnoticed to a reception salon opening off the main hall. He led her inside and closed the door quietly behind him. He drew her to him and kissed her.

"I begin to think it was a mistake to accept the invitation to come here," he said, holding her head against his shoulder. "I find being this close to you more disquieting than seeing you only formally in London."

"Well, in a few more days we will be back there, Bernard," she said, raising her head and lightly kissing his chin.

"Love, let me come to you tonight," he said, clasping her to him again urgently. "I shall make sure that I am not seen, and I can promise you a night of great pleasure."

Rosalind bit her lip painfully. "We are not married yet," she said.

"But we will be soon," he argued. "What difference can a couple of months make, love?"

"Bernard . . ." she began.

"Hush," he said, stopping her lips with his again. "Don't say no. I know it is only that maidenly modesty of yours that makes you hesitate. You want me, I know it. I shall come tonight and we will make love in peace and comfort."

"Over my dead body," a quiet but cold voice said.

Rosalind jumped away from her companion as if she had been scalded. Where was he? Sir Bernard Crawleigh cursed under his breath and stood with fists clenched at his sides, staring at the high back of a chair above which the top of a blond head was just visible.

"What in thunder are you doing here, Raymore?" he said tightly.

"I am here by invitation," the earl answered, rising to his feet and turning to face the couple who stood just inside the door. "I was shown in here to await Standen's return home. It seems the butler did not quite know what to do with me when I arrived two days earlier than expected."

"You might have made your presence known a great deal sooner," Sir Bernard said testily.

Raymore's face hardened. "It seems to me it was a good thing I did not decide to interrupt a lovers' tryst sooner than I did," he said coldly. "Miss Dacey is my ward, Crawleigh. I am responsible for her conduct until she marries. I find your behavior quite reprehensible. Were you not betrothed to her and within a few months of your marriage, I should feel obliged to call you out for the words you just spoke."

"I think it is well that you remember that Rosalind will soon by my wife," Sir Bernard said, obviously making an effort to hold on to his temper. "And remember, too, Raymore, that she is not a girl from the schoolroom. She is old enough to decide for herself the degree of intimacy she will allow between herself and her future husband."

"Please!" Rosalind interrupted. "Let us end this argument. Bernard, I gave you my answer. And, Edward, I would thank you to at least try not to treat me like a child. I resent your constant interference in my affairs. Soon I shall owe complete loyalty to Bernard."

Raymore's eyes flashed and he turned his attention completely to his ward. Rosalind steeled herself for the type of blazing row that always seemed to erupt when he and she were together. Fortunately, perhaps, for both of them, the door of the salon opened at that moment and Lord Standen walked briskly into the room.

"Raymore," he said, "I cannot think what my servants are about keeping you here like an unbidden visitor instead of showing you to a room and seeing to your needs."

Rosalind, glancing at her guardian, was amazed to see that in the few seconds since she had last looked at him, his manner had been completely transformed. He was bowing and smiling amiably.

"Think no more of it," he said, all affability. "I insisted on staying here when I realized that I was not expected today. And your butler brought me refreshment."

"I see that Miss Dacey and Crawleigh have found you and have been entertaining you," Standen commented.

"Yes, indeed," Raymore agreed, smiling genially at the couple.

"I shall excuse myself," Rosalind said, dropping a slight curtsy. "I feel rather tired after the picnic and need to freshen up before dinner."

All three men bowed. Lord Standen held the door open for her as she left the room with lowered eyes. Raymore noticed that her limp was more pronounced than usual.

The Earl of Raymore had come to Broome Hall determined to have a peaceful holiday. Both his wards were safely betrothed to eligible men. His responsibility was almost at an end. He was determined to keep his distance from Rosalind whenever possible. He wanted to observe her with Crawleigh to satisfy himself that both wished the alliance. But he knew that he could never be close to her without quarreling with her in most undignified fashion.

Now, as he soaked in a bathtub of hot soapy water in the room that had been prepared for him, his valet assembling the clothes he would wear to dinner, he was feeling irritated. He had been in the house less than an hour before he had been arguing with her yet again. Why could she not be more like Sylvia? The latter had apparently gone straight to her room on returning from the afternoon's outing, just as she should. And he could not in his wildest imaginings picture Standen making to her the sort of proposition that Crawleigh had been making to Rosalind.

He did not know quite what to make of that episode or whom to blame. He had been almost blind with anger at the time. That Crawleigh could quite coolly suggest that he spend the night in her bed suggested a want of proper restraint in him. But what did it suggest about her? Surely no man would dream of proposing such a thing to a girl who had not given him much encouragement. And the thought of Rosalind flirting with Crawleigh and inviting his intimacies renewed the earl's anger to such an extent that he scrubbed his arms quite mercilessly and soon had scattered soapsuds in a wide circle around the bathtub. His fury was not in any way mollified by the sudden memory of himself making similar advances to Annette when he was betrothed to her. She had been no innocent, either.

Rosalind had been looking tired. He had noticed the fact even before she had said so herself. Did that mean that her nights were already occupied with Crawleigh? He ground his teeth at the thought. But, no, he did not think so. The man's words to her in the salon had suggested that he still had not conquered her reserve. Or her artfulness!

Raymore, pouring a jugful of clear water over his head to take the suds out of his hair, tried to consider the situation rationally. She *was* a grown woman, as both she and her fiancé had pointed out to him. She was betrothed. She was no blood relation of his. Perhaps he should allow her to make her own decisions about her behavior.

But he could not! He got abruptly to his feet, reaching for the towel that his valet rushed over to hand him. Word was bound to get out if Crawleigh began spending nights with her. Tidbits of gossip like that were harder to keep secret than the man seemed to think. And even if she were a loose woman, Raymore decided, he was damned before he was going to have the fact bandied about among the whole *ton*. And what if for some reason the marriage never took place? She would be ruined. She might even bear an illegitimate child. She would certainly be a permanent millstone around his neck then. He determined to keep a very close eye on the girl in the coming days. Thank goodness at least that his other ward always behaved with propriety and blessed predictability.

Raymore dressed with care in formal evening dress: pale-blue silk knee breeches, silver waistcoat, and dark-blue velvet coat with white linen. He allowed his valet to arrange his neckcloth into complicated folds and insert a diamond pin into it. In his present mood he realized that he would probably ruin several carefully starched neckcloths before he would arrange one to his own satisfaction. Finally he descended to the drawing room, squaring his shoulders and setting his jaw. It seemed as if these few days in the country would not be such peaceful ones after all.

Rosalind had also dressed with care, choosing a gown of kingfisher-blue satin overlaid with sea-green lace, a color combination that looked startlingly attractive with her pale skin and dark hair. She was not sure why she had chosen to wear it tonight. She had been saving it for a special occasion and consequently had not worn it at all, though it had been delivered a month before. Perhaps she wanted to appear attractive to Bernard, whose proposition she had been forced to refuse quite publicly. Or perhaps she needed extra confidence to face the Earl of Raymore. She had been badly shaken to find him at Broome Hall two days before he was expected and under such very embarrassing circumstances. She preferred not to think about the meeting. She would have been glad of almost any other form of interruption. She had been shocked at Bernard's suggestion and did not know how she was to answer it. But Raymore of all people! She was glad that the two men had argued long enough for her to regain her poise. She had had the absurd urge when she first heard his voice to rush across the room to him to justify herself, to explain that *she* had not said or done anything improper. What a stroke of good fortune it was that she had not so humiliated herself.

Rosalind waited until the dresser had added the final touches to an elaborately piled hairdo, then made her way downstairs. She was deliberately almost late. She did not wish to have to make polite conversation in the drawing room with either Raymore or Bernard. She found that she had to cling more tightly than usual to the banister of the stairs. Her leg throbbed so badly that her whole body felt like a mighty heartbeat. She set a smile in place on her lips before entering the drawing room and accepting a glass of ratafia from a footman.

Rosalind's attention during dinner was taken by Sylvia. She was deliberately trying to ignore the presence of both Sir Bernard seated three places from her, and of Raymore seated almost opposite. There was certainly something wrong with her cousin. She was conversing with both Lady Standen and Sir Rowland Axby, but she did not have her usual sparkle. Rosalind doubted that anyone else would notice, but she had grown up more as a sister to Sylvia than as a cousin. And she recognized instantly that the girl was unhappy. Was Standen still displeased with her for the way she had behaved the night before at the dinner table? It seemed possible. The man set great store by his own consequence. Or had Sylvia discovered that she was not in love with him after all? Rosalind had never known the girl to be in love for more than a few weeks at the longest. And the match with Standen did not seem right. This time, though, Sylvie was in much deeper than she had ever been before. A betrothal, especially such a public one to a leading figure of the *ton*, would not be easy to withdraw from. Rosalind made a mental note to have a talk with her cousin before they went to bed. She held up her hand to refuse the helping of strawberries and Devon cream that a footman was about to set at her place. The pain in her leg was like a gnawing toothache. She could not concentrate upon eating.

Raymore noticed nothing strange about Sylvia's behavior, perhaps because he was sitting at the same side of the table as she and could not see her without leaning forward and turning his head. However, he was pleased to note that she was seated beside Lady Standen and that the two ladies appeared to be conversing. She was a crusty old bird, he understood. Standen might not be so eager for the match if his mother disapproved of his chosen bride.

He did watch Rosalind, though, without appearing to do so. He conversed politely with both Lady Theresa Parsons on his left and Letitia Morrison on his right. He felt an amused contempt for Lady Theresa, who was sending out very obvious lures in his direction. Women were all the same. Set a man with a title and wealth within their reach and they would use all the wiles at their disposal to trap him into matrimony. Rosalind was very subdued, he noted, probably feeling cramped by his presence. He drank from his wineglass and glanced across at her as she refused dessert. She would feel a great deal more cramped in the next few days if he had anything to say in the matter. She would find it far more difficult to meet her lover tête-à-tête.

In the drawing room afterward Rosalind played the pianoforte while Lady Theresa and Letitia took turns singing. Sir Bernard joined them briefly, but he did not have the chance for personal conversation, as Letitia was seated on the stool beside Rosalind sorting through a pile of music. Within a few minutes he was called away to make up a table of cards with Lady Standen, Susan Heron, and Thomas Morrison. Rosalind limped to a sofa and sank down thankfully onto it, trying to find a comfortable position for her aching leg. The Earl of Raymore seated himself beside her almost immediately and handed her a cup of tea.

Rosalind looked up in surprise and not a little alarm. "I trust you had a pleasant journey, my lord," she said with chilling formality.

He inclined his head but did not reply. "You have a headache?" he asked abruptly.

"Why, no," she replied. "What gave you that idea?" She had been quite deliberately smiling brightly all evening.

"You are in pain," he stated. "Do you think I do not know you well enough to notice the strain on your face?"

Rosalind was completely amazed. No one had ever known that she suffered occasionally from the old injury to her leg. Not even Sylvia or her aunt and uncle had ever guessed. She had always considered it a matter of pride to hide the fact from them. "My leg aches a little," she admitted.

"I would guess more than a little," he replied, no trace of sympathy in his voice. "Does it often pain you?"

"No, not often, my lord," she said. "Sometimes in cold or wet weather, or when I have had too much exercise."

"How far did you walk this afternoon?" he asked.

"The lake is about a mile away," she said. "We all walked there and back."

"And did neither Standen nor Crawleigh realize that the distance was too far for you?" he asked. Rosalind was surprised to detect a note of anger in his voice.

"I am not an invalid, my lord," she replied rather stiffly.

"Would you like me to help you to your room," he asked, "and have some laudanum sent to you?"

Rosalind had been wishing for just such an escape since she had come downstairs to dinner. Perhaps it was fortunate for her that Raymore asked rather than ordered.

"Would it be very ill-mannered to retire so early?" she asked, looking full into his face for the first time.

"Not at all," he replied, rising to his feet and extending a hand to her. "I shall make your excuses when I return."

Rosalind placed her half-empty cup of tea on the table beside her and put her hand in his. She found it surprisingly strong and supportive. She was able to rise to her feet without putting weight on the aching foot. He offered his arm and she leaned on it heavily as they left the room.

Sir Bernard Crawleigh, his attention distracted from the card game, watched them go, a frown creasing his brow.

Rosalind felt a powerful urge to rest her head against the broad and inviting shoulder that was so close to the side of her head. She supposed that the unusualness of having the pain recognized by another person was making her a little self-pitying.

Raymore paused when they came to the foot of the broad marble staircase that led to the upper apartments, and looked down into the drawn face of his companion. He said nothing, but quietly disengaged his arm from hers and stooped to lift her up into his arms. Rosalind said nothing, either. One of her arms, in a reflex action, went around his neck. She did not even feel surprise or outrage. Time and reason were suspended as he carried her up the stairs and along the upper corridor to her room. He set her gently down outside the door and they suddenly found themselves staring uncomfortably into each other's eyes.

"Thank you, my lord," she said.

"I shall have some laudanum sent up to you," he said at the same moment.

There was another awkward silence.

"Good night, Edward," she said, smiling slightly.

"Good night, Rosalind," he replied. "Go inside now and lie down. If the leg pains you in the morning, I shall have Standen send for a physician."

"These bouts do not last," she assured him. "I am sure I shall be better in the morning."

She smiled briefly again and went into the room. Self-pitying indeed, she told herself in mockery as tears that she could not control coursed their way down her cheeks.

11

As Rosalind rose early the following morning, she remembered that she had not had the talk with Sylvia that she had promised herself. She had intended to wait up until her cousin came to bed, but her leg had been aching quite severely and the temptation of the laudanum had proved irresistible. Rosalind had never taken any sedation in a similar situation before. She had been fast asleep long before anyone else went to bed.

Perhaps there was another reason why she had taken the draft. She had wanted to drug her mind. She was so used to hating the Earl of Raymore and believing that he did not possess one redeeming feature. It seemed out of character for him to be the first person in her life to know when she was hiding pain. How was she to reconcile that sensitivity with the cold, unfeeling man she had always known him to be? She did not want to like him in any way. If she did, the attraction she felt toward him would be dangerous. As it was, she had wanted to lay her head down on his shoulder as he carried her upstairs and breathe in the very masculine scent of him.

She had sobbed and sobbed after coming inside her room, but could not adequately explain to herself why she did so. Was it the pain? But she was accustomed to coping with that, although it did not happen very frequently. She had just felt hopelessly depressed. Consequently, when a maid had brought her medicine a mere ten minutes after Raymore had left her, she had taken it and lapsed into blessed unconsciousness soon after.

Now she felt considerably better. Her leg had stopped aching and she was cheered by the sight of a clear blue sky and sunshine when she drew back the curtains at her window. Her head was feeling a trifle heavy from the drug-induced sleep, but fresh air would soon dispense with that problem. She decided that she would take a brisk ride before breakfast. She doubted that anyone else was up yet.

Less than half an hour later, having washed, dressed, and combed her hair into a loose knot beneath her feathered riding hat, Rosalind was walking across to the stables, the loose gravel of the driveway crunching beneath her boots. The Earl of Raymore, seated alone in the breakfast room with yesterday's paper spread before him, saw her go. He frowned. She was up very early and seemed to be in a great hurry. Was she keeping a tryst? It was hardly likely this early in the morning, but he would not exclude any possibilities as far as Rosalind Dacey was concerned. She must be made to realize that she could not come and go with total freedom even if she was now in the country. Once she was married, it would be up to her husband to set the limits. In the meanwhile, she would have to accept the restrictions he chose to impose upon her. He folded the newspaper, threw his napkin onto the table, and rose to follow her.

Rosalind was impatiently tapping her riding crop against her boot waiting for a groom to finish saddling the stallion that she usually rode when Raymore entered the stable yard. The crop became still when she saw him.

"Good morning, my lord," she said warily. Why did he always have to look so disturbingly handsome? This morning he was wearing a close-fitting dark-blue coat with buff riding breeches and shiny black boots. A black top hat sat at a slightly rakish angle on his blond hair.

"Is it wise to ride when you are in pain?" he asked.

She was relieved to hear his voice. It had its old irritable tone. She could safely dislike him again.

"I am quite recovered this morning," she said. "A ride is just what I need."

"Not on that animal," he said decisively. "He is much too large and skittish for you. Saddle a quiet mare for Miss Dacey," he ordered. turning to the groom.

"I shall ride Prince, as I intended," Rosalind replied coolly. "He needs the exercise as much as I."

"Are you doing this to provoke me or to impress me?" he asked coldly. "You are not strong on common sense, ma'am, but surely even you must realize the folly of risking a fall when you already suffer the consequences of one."

She did not deign to reply, but seeing that Prince was ready, she crossed to his side and indicated to the groom that she wished to mount. Soon she was guiding the horse out of the stable yard. She did not even glance in the direction of her guardian.

"Hot headed fool," he muttered under his breath as he strode to the stall that housed his own horse and began swiftly to saddle it. A few minutes later he was urging his mount in the direction of a field, where Rosalind was holding her horse to a trot. He quickly caught up to her.

"At least, if you must be foolhardy. I shall accompany you and pick up the pieces," he called testily across to her.

She smiled frostily back. "I plan to give this horse a good workout once he has warmed up," she said. "Do you think you can keep up with us, my lord?"

"You do not have to show off for me, Rosalind," he growled. "Your present pace is quite fast enough."

She laughed and increased her horse's speed slightly.

He should have told her to go ahead, that it mattered not to him if she broke her neck, Raymore realized. She was so headstrong that she would do anything just to defy him. Why, in heaven's name, had he been blessed with her? It was bad enough to be

landed with two female wards under any circumstances,
but when one of them was Rosalind Dacey, the situation became a nightmare. His peace of mind was completely shattered. He had lain awake half the night
before puzzling over his feelings for her. She was everything that should repel him. He had never admired
dark-haired women and her hair was almost black. He
liked sweet, fragile faces that promised submissiveness.
She had strong features, flashing dark eyes, and a stubborn chin. He had always disliked tall women. She
reached to his shoulders and was far from fragile. He
had seen her and touched her often enough to know
that a voluptuous figure lay beneath the loose, flowing
clothes that she favored. He hated women who talked a
lot. She was not a prattler, but when she did speak, it
was with the assertiveness of a man. And then there
was that limp.

Why, then, did he feel this impossible attraction to
the girl? It was years since he had been tempted by a
lady of quality. His tastes had drawn him to women of
the theater, with whom he could very quickly satisfy his
appetites. There was no way he could rid himself of the
desire he felt for his ward. In fact, he felt quite humiliated even to admit to himself that he did want her. He
must concentrate on his dislike of her, he reminded
himself as he kept urging his horse to a slightly faster
speed to keep pace with hers. His rose!

Suddenly he found himself left behind as Rosalind
spurred her mount into a gallop. She did it partly to
show him that she cared nothing for his admonitions.
Yet she had intended when she left the house to blow
away the cobwebs of her mind. She bent low over the
horse's neck and urged him on ever faster and faster.
When she saw a hedge approaching, she made no
attempt to avoid it but soared over with a feeling of
great exhilaration. She felt again the thrill of speed and
uninhibited motion. On horseback she could forget her
disability; she was the equal of anyone. She was aware
of Raymore half a length behind her. The need to stay

ahead of him added to her excitement. With Flossie she could have done so with ease.

There was another hedge at the far side of the field through which they now raced. There was also a five-barred gate, higher than the level of the hedge. Rosalind turned her horse's head so that she galloped directly toward it.

Raymore saw her intention at a glance. He gritted his teeth and knew a moment of blank terror. She would kill herself. Even if the horse did not catch a leg on the top bar and plunge them both to the ground, she would never be able to keep her seat over such a height, mounted as she was on a sidesaddle. He considered trying to head her off, but that would mean risking collision and almost as much danger.

He took the hedge at the same time as she soared over the gate with inches to spare. Rosalind immediately pulled back on the reins and eased the horse to a walk. She had turned its head so that it could keep to the cooler shade beside the hedge. She leaned forward and patted its neck.

The next moment a very firm gloved hand grasped the reins and her horse was pulled to an abrupt halt. The Earl of Raymore was off his own mount almost as quickly. He reached up, caught Rosalind by the waist, and almost dragged her to the ground. The horses wandered off, side by side, in search of some longer grass on which to graze.

Before Rosalind could make any sort of protest, she was being shaken by hands that held her shoulders in a bruising grip. Her head flopped back and forth like a rag doll. Her riding hat fell to the ground and her hair cascaded down over her shoulders and face.

"Damn you to hell!" Raymore was shouting. "You could have killed yourself, do you realize that? You hotheaded, stubborn fool!"

When he finally stopped shaking her, Rosalind had a hard time catching her breath and her sense of balance. She clung to his arms in self-defense. "Stop treating me like a child," she cried, her voice shaking. "I am mortally sick of your constant spying and scolding. Leave me alone!" She struggled to free herself from his grip but only found herself hauled firmly against his chest, her hands imprisoned between them.

"By God, Rosalind," he said between his teeth, "I shall teach you that you cannot bait me and get away with it."

His mouth was savage on hers, as it had been the last time, she remembered. But that last time he had not tumbled her immediately to the ground, his weight pinning her to the grass and depriving her momentarily of breath. He had not then proceeded to dispense with her upper garments so that almost before she understood his intentions his hands were on her naked breasts, his mouth and tongue plundering her own before trailing a hot path down her throat and to her breasts. But then that other time her hands had not unbuttoned his coat and roamed over the thin silk of his shirt to feel the firm muscles of his chest, the rippling muscles of his arms.

"Rosalind," he was murmuring over and over again. "My rose! My red rose!" His hands twined in her thick dark hair until his fingers rested against her scalp. He turned her head up to him again and traced her parted lips with his tongue before covering them with his own and exploring the warm excitement of her mouth.

"Edward," she moaned when he lifted his head again, "oh, please. Please!"

He had to have her. He would go mad with longing if he had to wait just one moment longer. He had to be one with her, had to be inside her. He eased his weight half off her and reached down to pull up the skirt of her heavy riding habit. His hand caressed her slim legs as his mouth sought out the pulse at the base of her throat. She twisted her hands in his hair and gasped out his name.

His hand stroked and caressed its way up one leg to the knee, along her warm inner thigh, over the tight muscles of her stomach to the fastenings of her under-garments at her waist.

She wanted him so desperately. He was moving so slowly, pulling loose now the ribbons that kept him away from her. Finally his warm and gentle hand was against the bare flesh of her stomach, moving to one side to trace her hip before continuing its descent. Rosalind was raw sensation. She would explode if he did not release this tension soon. She arched her hips against his hand, parting her legs, willing him lower.

He raised his head and she gazed into his passion-heavy blue eyes. Beautiful eyes that she could drown in. "My rose!" he murmured. The eyes and voice heavy with feeling, the hand worshiping her body. So different from usual. From usual! Rosalind was suddenly jerked back to reality. She was lying under a hedge in an open field in broad daylight, almost naked to the waist, her skirt bunched up around her hips, within a few moments of being bedded by the Earl of Raymore. And inviting and responding to his advances every step of the way. With a cry of panic, she pushed at his chest and rolled to one side, pulling her skirt down with shaking hands as she did so.

"Rosalind!" he protested in bewilderment.

"Go away! Leave me alone!" she cried, leaping to her feet and, her back to him, pulling her blouse around her and buttoning it up. "Do you think I am a servant or a milkmaid to be rolled on the ground like this? I am the niece of the former Earl of Raymore and your ward. I am betrothed and soon to be wed. Do you hate me so much that you must ruin me and spoil my one chance of a respectable future?"

She babbled on, not knowing half of what she said. Finally her jacket had been buttoned up again and her hat and riding crop gathered from the ground. In her frenzy she had tried to find enough hairpins in the grass to pin up her hair again, but it was a hopeless task. She limped across to where Prince was grazing and mounted unassisted into the sidesaddle. Without a backward glance at her companion, who had not uttered a word since her outburst, she spurred the horse into a gallop across the field.

Raymore, who had been sitting with his head resting on his updrawn knees, looked up as she moved away. What a fool he was! She was easily the most accomplished horsewoman he had ever seen, as he would have realized earlier had he not been blinded by irrational fears for her safety. She was true grace and beauty as she disappeared from sight, dark hair streaming out behind her.

And, God, more than a fool. A prize idiot! He loved her. He loved Rosalind Dacey, the woman to whom of all others he felt most antagonistic. Of course! He must have felt it from the start, and some inner instinct of self-preservation had reacted with such terror that he had convinced himself that the opposite was true, that he hated her. God help him, he had lost, cruelly lost, every woman to whom he had entrusted his love and now it was happening again. But this time he had lost her before ever having her. He had done everything in his power to make her hate him, and hate him she did. He had used every effort to find her a husband, to be rid of her before he was forced to recognize his love of her. And she was now betrothed to a man with whom she seemed quite contented and who obviously desired her. And he had just insulted her beyond endurance. The terrifying experience of expecting her each moment to break her neck had snapped his control. If she had not broken away when she had, he would be lying with her now, his seed inside her, contemplating the worst dilemma of his life. He would have been forced to marry a woman who hated him, keeping her away forever from the man with whom she could be happy.

He had lost again, and through his own stupidity this time. Raymore looked up at the blue sky and laughed harshly. But the smile on his face faded quickly and he rested his forehead on his knees again. He could not get that song out of his head. Words that had eluded him for days were suddenly there with cruel clarity:

> And I will luve thee still, my dear,
> While the sands o' life shall run.

Rosalind!

Sylvia had passed a restless night. She felt extremely foolish having discovered that yet again she had only imagined herself in love. But this time it was impossible to get out of the entanglement that she found herself in. Lord Standen was a man of principle and impeccable reputation. Their betrothal had been publicly celebrated in London at his sister's ball and was being celebrated this week. She had been accepted by his mother. Plans for a wedding in the autumn were already being made. She could not possibly tell him now that she did not wish to be his wife.

Perhaps the situation would still be tolerable if it were not for her terrible discovery of the day before. She could do worse than make this marriage. Lord Standen would be a good husband, she believed, even if rather strict. She would have a good home, all the luxuries she could want for the rest of her life. She would occupy an enviable position in society. The fact that she did not love him need not doom her to misery.

But the fact that she loved his brother surely would. She was not really surprised that she had not realized the truth until the day before. Nigel Broome was so different from any of the young men with whom she had fancied herself in love during the past few years. They had all been handsome, charming, fashionable. Nigel was so ordinary: only passably good-looking, only of medium height, and earnest rather than charming in manner. She had liked him from the first, had developed a close and warm friendship with him. Only the afternoon before, when they were together in the boat, had she known that he was far more than a friend to her. He was the man with whom she wished to spend her life. She did not care that with him she would not live in mansions or have several carriages or dressing rooms full of gowns. It would be enough just to be with him, to share his dreams, to look after his comforts.

But there was little use in dreaming. Even if she could summon the courage or audacity to break off her engagement to Lord Standen, she could not then marry his brother. Such behavior was unthinkable. And even if she had not accepted Standen's proposal in the first place, she doubted very much if Cousin Edward would have countenanced her marriage to Nigel Broome. His birth, of course, was as good as Lord Standen's, and he had an income of his own, she knew, though he was not a wealthy man. But the fact was that he was a younger son with no particular prospects, and she was sure that her guardian would consider him unworthy of the daughter of an earl.

There was nothing for it, it seemed, but to accept her fate. But Sylvia felt desperately lonely. At one time during the night she had considered going into the next room and waking Rosalind. But she remembered Cousin Edward telling Lady Standen in the drawing room that her cousin had retired to bed with a headache.

When she awoke the next morning, Sylvia felt an immediate sinking of the heart as memory flooded back. She dreaded telling anyone of her problems, but the need to confide in someone was overwhelming. She dressed in haste, without summoning help, and brushed impatiently at her blond curls. She would go talk to Rosalind before going down to breakfast. Rosalind always seemed to know what to do, although Sylvia did not think that anyone could offer her any real help. Rosalind's room, alas, was empty. She must be up and riding early as she often used to do at home.

She went downstairs, but shook her head at the footman who would have opened the doors of the breakfast room for her. She could hear voices inside and did not think she could cope with the need to be sociable just yet. She wandered through the front door, which stood open to the morning sunshine, and started to cross the main driveway to the formal gardens that were laid out south of the house. She stopped when she saw Raymore striding toward her from the direction of the stables. He was staring at the ground, looking pensive. He did not look his usual arrogant self at all, in fact. On impulse, Sylvia stopped and waited until he was close enough to notice her.

"Good morning. Edward," she said brightly when he looked up. "Have you been riding so early?"

"Yes," he said, "it is a beautiful morning."

"May I speak to you for a few moments?" she asked hesitantly. "Or are you very anxious to go in to breakfast?"

"I am not hungry at all," he said abruptly and, offering her his arm, led her into one of the grass walks of the garden.

"Cousin Edward," Sylvia said with a deep breath, "I am very unhappy."

Unhappy, he thought, turning to glance down at the pretty girl on his arm. What did she know of unhappiness? She had doubtless been pampered and petted all her life and had no conception of what pain and misery were. "Oh?" he prompted chillingly.

"I fear I have made a dreadful mistake," she said, staring at the ground ahead of her.

"A mistake?"

"I do not wish to marry Lord Standen," she said.

Raymore stopped walking and turned to look down at her incredulously. "Is this some kind of joke?" he asked. "Why, pray, do you not wish to marry?"

Sylvia's syes were filled with tears. "Don't be angry with me," she pleaded. "I cannot love him, Edward. I thought I did, truly, but it is not so. Oh, what am I to do?"

"What are you to do?" he thundered. "Why, you are to marry the man, of course. Love! What does that have to say to the matter? Do you believe you would be one whit the happier with a man whom you loved? You would only be inviting misery and betrayal. I want to hear no more of this nonsense. Do you understand?"

"Edward," she began, a tear spilling out of each eye.

"The connection is eminently suitable," he went on. "You are doubtless the envy of every unmarried girl in London. You will live in the style to which you are accustomed, and even more elaborately. I will not tolerate any withdrawal from this betrothal, Sylvia. Such a move would publicly embarrass Standen and sully your own reputation. What other man would be willing to look at you for the remainder of the Season?"

"I am sorry," she said. "I did not mean to anger you. Please forgive me. I shall try to feel as I ought."

Raymore relaxed slightly. He had certainly not expected trouble from this girl. But at least she was more biddable than her cousin. She just needed firm handling. She would have it from him until she was safely married, and he believed beyond a doubt that Standen would put up with no nonsense once the ceremony was over.

"Come," he said, his tone somewhat softened, "let me escort you to the house. Have you had breakfast yet? I imagine that you are suffering from prenuptial nerves. Believe me, you will live to thank me for promoting this match."

"Yes, Edward," she said, taking his arm and allowing herself to be led back to the house.

Susan Heron and Letitia Morrison, in the breakfast room, were planning yet another morning visit to the village. Sylvia declined to join them, saying that she would wait for Lady Theresa to get up and Rosalind to return from her ride. They would find something to do together.

But Sylvia did not wait for either her friend or her cousin. As soon as she was alone, she left the house again and wandered in the direction of the trees, where she could think without interruption. It was hopeless, of course. She could see that she was doomed to marry Lord Standen. And there was no possible way she could ever marry Nigel. But there was no harm in dreaming, was there? If only there were some way of making everyone see with great clarity that she and Lord Standen were not suited. If only everyone could agree that she must break her engagement to him. And if only miracles would happen and everyone would urge her to marry Nigel.

Sylvia stopped and stood with her arms stretched around the trunk of a tree. She laid a cheek against the bark. It was impossible, of course. Unless . . . An arrested look came over her face. She stood thus for several minutes, hugging the tree. Anyone who had observed her both enter the woods and leave them a half-hour later would have noticed that there was more spring in her step as she strode back to the house, more color to her cheeks and sparkle to her eyes.

"I was beginning to think that you were never going to rise, sleepyhead," she called gaily to Lady Theresa, who was standing in the doorway, blinking in the bright sunlight.

12

Lady Standen had planned a grand dinner and ball for the following evening. She wished to introduce her future daughter-in-law to the foremost families of the neighborhood and to make a formal announcement of the betrothal. The whole house was in an uproar of excitement at the elaborate preparations that were being made. The chef was preparing all the food himself, the gardener was cutting flowers enough to decorate the dining room and the ballroom, and all the servants were engaged in cleaning and helping.

The guests were glad of the distraction. The weather was cold and blustery, the pleasures of the countryside beginning to pall on those who were eager to participate in the last whirl of activities that the Season had to offer in London. Sylvia and her two friends fluttered gaily about the house, helping with floral arrangements and exchanging details of the gowns they were to wear that night. The men played billiards and wisely stayed out of the way of the main activities. Lady Standen and Letitia Morrison spent most of the day in the morning room, sewing and chatting cosily. Only a few went about their lone pursuits.

Nigel spent the day visiting his brother's tenants and paying a lengthy call at the school, where he helped out an overworked teacher by listening to some of the youngest children read. He deliberately occupied himself away from the house. He could not resist his beloved's plea to stay, yet he could not be near her. It was a personal torture to see and hear her, and to know that soon she would be his brother's wife and beyond his reach forever. And it went against his sense of honor to be in her presence while harboring forbidden feelings for her. He would have to attend the ball tonight. It would be most unmannerly of him to stay away. But tomorrow he must go, a day before the rest of the party broke up. He must find an opportunity to tell her so tonight.

The Earl of Raymore played billiards for part of the day, but soon after luncheon he secluded himself in Standen's library, where he drew down volume after volume, trying to interest himself in a pastime that was usually among his favorites. Nothing would do. Each book found its way back onto the shelf when less than a page had been read. He should leave. It was torture to be in the same house as her. In London, he could at least leave the house and spend a whole day away. Here that was impossible. Luncheon and dinner yesterday had been an acute embarrassment. He had stolen a glance at her only a few times, and though she had not been looking at him on any of those occasions, he knew that she too felt desperately uncomfortable. He did not even have the consolation any longer of believing that he disliked and hated her. And he could no longer persuade himself that she was ugly. Her startling southern beauty made everyone else at the table look insipid, even Sylvia. He knew what that dark hair looked like falling in heavy locks around her face and over her shoulders, making her skin appear like alabaster. He knew how her eyes and lips looked when they were dreamy with passion. And he knew how very womanly her body was beneath the flowing gown.

He needed a few days to accustom himself to the knowledge that he loved her but could never have her. For a while she had responded to his lovemaking, but she had made it very clear before leaving him that she hated and despised him. And she had conversed almost exclusively with Crawleigh during dinner. Afterward, in the drawing room, she had sung for a while, but not for the entertainment of the room at large. Her songs had been quietly directed at her fiancé, who leaned against the pianoforte the whole while gazing into her face. Raymore had been tense, though he appeared to be relaxed as he made up a table for piquet. He was terrified that she would sing the song about the rose. He would not be able to stand that. He was greatly relieved when she moved away from the instrument and joined Crawleigh on a love seat a little removed from any other members of the company.

Despite his need to distance himself from Rosalind, Raymore knew that he must stay. He had joined the party only two days before. It would be entirely rude to leave before the end, especially on the day of the ball. He must be present as the guardian of the girl whose betrothal was to be celebrated. And his talk with Sylvia the morning before had bothered him. He had thought her to be a thoroughly predictable young lady. He had expected her to be mindlessly satisfied with any marriage, provided the man were eligible, wealthy, and tolerably good-looking. He was not seriously alarmed, as he believed the words she had spoken to him had been prompted by prenuptial nerves. He could think of no rational explanation of why she would suddenly wish to withdraw from her engagement. However, he felt that his presence was necessary. He must certainly watch to see that she did not do anything foolish before she had time to recover from her strange mood.

Rosalind was not alone on the day of the ball. She was out riding with Sir Bernard Crawleigh, and she was in a deliberately gay mood. She had just agreed, in fact, that their wedding should take place during early August in Shropshire, where his parents lived. They did not enjoy city life and would be far happier to organize the wedding among their friends, he explained. Rosalind had her own reasons for agreeing. She did not want a big society wedding. The thought of limping down a long church aisle watched by all the prominent members of the *ton* horrified her. And she wanted to move permanently away from the Earl of Raymore's home as soon as she possibly could. She did not wish to have to move back there after the summer while her wedding was organized. She did not wish to have him give her away. It would be quite intolerable to have to walk down the aisle on his arm. She hoped that he would not come to Shropshire.

They spent the whole morning riding, going even as far as the hills that rose to the north of the estate. Sir Bernard told her about all the places to which he planned to take her during their wedding trip to Europe.

"I must take you to Austria," he said. "You will love Vienna. And in Italy, of course, Venice is the city of romance. You shall ride in a gondola, Rosalind."

"And Rome?" she asked eagerly. "Will we go there too, Bernard?"

"How could we miss it?" he replied.

By the time they arrived back at Broome Hall Rosalind was feeling quite cheerful. She had certainly made the right decision. In four or five weeks' time she would be married and traveling as she had always dreamed of doing. She would be with Bernard, who was always cheerful and attractive and who understood her. Once she was married, she would be able to forget about the Earl of Raymore. She would be safe from him.

Rosalind was very grateful to Bernard for urging her to agree to bring forward their wedding. He had suggested it the evening before at the end of a nightmare day. She had been desperately in need of some distraction. She had spent most of the day alone. After leaving Raymore, she had ridden, not even aware of the direction she took or the landmarks she passed. She had tried to outride her thoughts, but the visions crowded in: Raymore dragging her from her horse, his hands iron hard on her arms, his face furiously angry; shaking her until she thought she would lose consciousness; kissing her and caressing her on the ground; calling her by name, calling her his rose. Her face grew hot as visions of her own response came unbidden to mind. As soon as she had felt his mouth on hers, she had been lost, given up entirely to mere physical responses. His weight on her when he took her to the ground had been such an erotic experience. She had wanted him with a raw passion.

She might have stopped him from unbuttoning her jacket and her blouse, but she had eagerly cooperated. She had had to feel his hands on her bare flesh, on her breasts. She had not even been ashamed of their fullness as she had been ever since she had realized years ago that she was developing far more than any other girl she knew. She had wanted him to see her, to touch her. And she burned with shame now at the memory of the way she had allowed him to raise her skirts. She had even lifted her hips so that he could pull away the fabric. She had wanted him so desperately, had chafed at the tantalizing slowness with which his hand had moved up her thighs. And she had been close, so close, to losing herself completely. Some instinctive part of her womanhood told her that they had been within moments of the ultimate touch, the one to which every- thing else had been building.

And she had desired it, desperately wanted it, with Raymore! The thought was terrifying, nauseating. Was she so depraved, so out of control of her own reactions, that she could have allowed him of all people to make love to her? She could not even have accused him of ravishment if the act had been carried to completion; she had been an eager partner.

She found it very difficult to understand her own behavior. She knew that she was physically attracted to her guardian. He was Alistair in appearance, after all. But surely mere attraction should die when one found the person cold and unlikable. And what of him? He disliked her just as much as she did him. Why, then, had he made such violent love to her on two separate occasions? Did he experience a similar sort of uncon- trollable passion? It was hard to believe because she knew that he was a man of impeccable taste in beautiful things, and she was far from lovely. Was he merely trying to punish and humiliate her? She would have believed so, but his behavior had not seemed cold and calculating. He had spoken to her, almost as if he did not know that he did so, calling her his rose. What had he meant by that? Was it a reference to her name?

Rosalind could not find any interpretation of Raymore's behavior that satisfied her. But she did know that their relationship was dangerous. They could not be in each other's presence without quarreling, and when they quarreled, this disturbing passion flared. She had to get away from him, and stay away.

She had contrived to spend the afternoon alone as well, keeping to her room. complaining of a recurrence of her headache. At dinner she had been relieved to find herself seated next to Sir Bernard. Only by talking and joking with him could she cope with the terrible ordeal of having to share a table with the Earl of Raymore. And after dinner, in the drawing room, her fiancé had taken her apart and asked her if she could be ready for a wedding the following month when they visited his parents. He had made a joke of the proposal. Since he could not get her to bed this side of the wedding, he said, he would have to move the wedding ahead in order to save his sanity.

"Of course," he had added with a grin, "the offer that you so heartlessly rejected yesterday still holds for to-night. Will you, Rosalind?"

She had slapped him playfully on the hand. "Patience, sir," she had said. "All good things come to those who wait, you know."

"I shall hold you to those words," he had replied.

While Rosalind had crossed to the tea table in order to pour tea for them both, Sir Bernard had watched Raymore with narrowed eyes as the latter contemplated the cards in his hand, apparently engrossed in his game. From his bedroom window he had seen the earl ride after Rosalind that morning. It had been a full hour before he returned, alone. He had not stayed with her. But still, an hour!

There were more than thirty people invited to the grand dinner before the ball. All the leading gentry of the countryside had been invited. Sylvia was dressed to perfection. She wore white satin covered with delicate Brussels lace threaded with silver. The gown, with its high waist, low neckline, and short puffed sleeves, emphasized her delicate beauty. Rosalind was pleased to notice that her cousin was looking happier than she had looked for days. In fact, she positively glowed. She must, then, have convinced herself that her betrothal was right, that she really did love Lord Standen.

Rosalind herself wore a gown of bright turquoise. She had had it made hurriedly for this very occasion, after she had accepted Bernard's offer. And for the first time she had allowed Madame de Valéry to shape the gown to her figure. She did not have to hide herself any longer. Nobody could dispute the fact that Sir Bernard Crawleigh was a fashionable member of society. He had chosen her to be his bride. It did not matter that she limped, that she was unfashionably dark, that she did not have the sylphlike figure of the ideal debutante. He had chosen her. She had therefore decided to be ashamed of her appearance no longer.

She was rewarded by a look of frank admiration from her betrothed as she entered an already crowded drawing room. "I say," he said, "you will make me the envy of every man present tonight." He raised her hand to his lips.

Rosalind smiled determinedly into his eyes. A sixth sense told her that Raymore was also in the room already, but she could not risk looking around and meeting his eyes.

Lord Standen was circulating in the room, Sylvia on his arm, introducing his bride-to-be to his neighbors. They made an extremely handsome couple, Rosalind thought. His ice-blue coat, white satin knee breeches, and silver waistcoat complemented Sylvia's outfit to perfection. They looked like a bridal pair.

Sylvia was seated at dinner at the right hand of Lord Standen, instead of at the foot of the table next to his mother as she had been all week. She made a great effort to talk to him during the meal and flushed becomingly when he rose at the end to introduce her formally as his betrothed to the company. She looked at Nigel for the first time at that point. He was smiling at her, but she knew him well enough to detect that the smile was strained. She smiled warmly back at him. All will be well, she wanted to tell him, if only my plan works. It must work, she thought as she turned to answer a comment made by the guest sitting to her right.

Rosalind had the great misfortune to be seated next to the Earl of Raymore. She was most dismayed and vastly annoyed with herself for not having taken an active interest in the preparations earlier in the day as the other ladies had done. Perhaps she could have discovered the seating plan and had it changed while it was still possible to do so. Raymore too seemed taken aback to find himself seated next to her. For the whole of the first course they studiously devoted their attention to their other neighbors. Rosalind listened to a monologue on the corn crop delivered by a Mr. Phelps, who was openly delighted to discover such a receptive audience. Raymore submitted himself to an exhaustive interrogation on the latest hairstyles and fashions in gowns and bonnets by an eager little matron whose husband would apparently never agree to take her to town. Both held themselves turned stiffly away from the other. Each felt an electric awareness of the other.

Raymore was finally forced to turn to his ward when the little matron leaned across him to ask Rosalind to pass the salt.

"You are looking extremely handsome tonight," he said stiffly after the salt had been passed.

Rosalind darted him a startled look. "Why, thank

you, my lord," she said. It was the first time she had looked directly at him since he had held her in his arms. He looked breathtakingly handsome himself, she thought, looking away in confusion as her quick glance took in the black coat, which molded his shoulders as if he had been poured into it; the elaborate, diamond-studded folds of his white neckcloth. His hair looked gleamingly blond in contrast to his coat.

"I trust your foot has not been paining you lately?" he asked.

"No, thank you," she replied. "I am quite well now." She had a sudden, alarming urge to giggle. What a ridiculous conversation to be holding on such a festive occasion. "Did you make final arrangements for your concert while still in London?" she asked.

His face relaxed almost into a smile. "Yes," he replied. "I believe it will be a great success. Dr. Hans Dehnert has agreed to perform."

Rosalind turned to gaze at him, wide-eyed. "Hans Dehnert?" she repeated. "You mean the Austrian pianist? He has agreed to play for you?"

He smiled openly. "Are you surprised?" he asked. "I can be very persuasive, you see, when a matter is important to me."

"I have dreamed and dreamed of being able to hear him play Mozart," she said, cheeks flushed with excitement. "He will play Mozart, will he not?"

"Exclusively," he assured her. "It was the one condition he made, and I would have requested it, anyway. I, too, shall be hearing him for the first time, though he will come to the house for a few days before the concert to acquaint himself with my pianoforte and the room in which he will play."

"And may one listen to him?" she asked eagerly.

"He has specified not," he replied. He grinned suddenly. "But there is an anteroom, you know, from which one can hear sounds made in the music room as well as if one were right there."

Her eyes sparkled into his. "Dare we?" she asked, and they grinned at each other like a pair of conspirators.

A footman stretched out an arm between them in order to refill Rosalind's glass with wine. His presence broke the spell with great thoroughness. Raymore's face sobered as he continued to gaze into his ward's eyes. She stiffened, blushed, lowered her eyes, and turned jerkily away. Mr. Phelps was waiting to recapture her attention with news of enclosures that he had been making on the eastern portion of his land.

Lady Standen stood with her son and Sylvia in the receiving line when the other guests arrived later for the ball. Sir Bernard Crawleigh led Rosalind to a sofa and seated himself beside her. She felt self-conscious again. These people were strangers and had not seen her before. She had intercepted several curious glances. However, she raised her chin and refused to be daunted. Let them stare. Lady Theresa, she noticed, was smiling dazzlingly and chatting with the Earl of Raymore. He was looking bored, as he usually did in such situations.

It was much later in the evening when Sylvia, dancing with Lord Standen for the second time, complained of the heat. "I feel I shall surely faint if I do not have some air," she told him.

"I ordered the doors to be left closed, my dear, because the evening is quite raw and I would not wish any of the ladies to take cold," he replied.

"But I must go outside," she said. "Please take me into the garden for a while. Your guests will not miss you." She held her breath. Would he reply as he had the many times she had rehearsed this scene with herself?

"I could not desert my guests in the middle of a ball," he told her kindly. "Perhaps if you were to sit down and I were to bring you a glass of lemonade, you would feel better my dear?"

"Perhaps," she answered faintly.

He led her solicitously to a chair close to the windows and seated her before moving away to the refreshment room. Sylvia smiled at Nigel, who was standing a short distance away, not dancing. He came across to her uncertainly and bowed.

"Are you not feeling quite the thing?" he asked.

"Just a trifle faint," she assured him. "Standen has gone to fetch me some lemonade."

When it arrived, she sipped on it awhile while both men watched her. She looked up at Lord Standen with pleading eyes. "If you cannot take me outside, may Nigel accompany me?" she asked. "Just for a brief walk?"

"I was about to suggest the very same thing," he said. "Nigel, do you mind?"

Nigel hesitated. He looked quite taken aback. "It would be my pleasure," he said, bowing in Sylvia's direction. "You will need a shawl, Sylvia, or even a cloak."

"I shall have one brought from your room," Lord Standen agreed.

Having given his orders to a footman to have a maid fetch a cloak from Lady Marsh's room, Lord Standen also ordered that one set of French doors be thrown back for the comfort of his guests. The crowded ballroom. laden with flowers, had become unpleasantly stuffy.

Five minutes later, Nigel led his charge, well-protected from the chilly evening air in a pink cloak, out onto the terrace. Rosalind noticed Sylvia leave and felt a twinge of uneasiness. It had seemed for a few days as if her cousin was happy with her betrothal, but Rosalind had never been quite certain of the role played by Nigel Broome in the relationship. The Earl of Raymore also saw his ward leave but was not alarmed. The girl had appeared happy tonight with Standen, and, as he thought, the man was taking pains to look after his own. Raymore had noticed how he had delegated to his brother the task of escorting Sylvia out of doors.

It was only much later that anyone still present indoors realized that neither Nigel nor Sylvia had returned to the ballroom.

Nigel's arm was tense beneath Sylvia's hand. He walked her in silence along the terrace and turned to walk back again.

"Let us not go in yet," she pleaded with him. "Let us go down onto the lawn, Nigel."

"It is cold," he said. "You will catch a chill."

"No, I will not," she said. "Please, Nigel."

They descended the stone steps to the grass below and she turned and strolled—aimlessly, it seemed—in the direction of the trees to the east of the house. It was a dark night, but occasionally moonlight flooded down on them as broken clouds scudded across the sky. They said nothing but an awareness grew as they moved farther and farther away from the light and music of the ballroom. Again Nigel moved to turn back when they reached the line of trees.

"Take me to the lake," she said. "I want to see it in the moonlight."

"No," he said, strain in his voice. "It would not be wise to go farther. This is not easy for me, Sylvia."

"Nor for me," she said, turning to him and clasping her hands. "Nigel, please. This may be our only remaining chance to be together—for just a short while."

He gazed at her out of tortured eyes. Then he caught her to him, holding her head against his chest, resting his cheek on her curls. "My love," he said shakily, "I cannot bear this."

He allowed her to take his arm again and they walked through the trees until they came to the edge of the lake. It took a little more persuasion to convince Nigel to take out one of the boats, but eventually they were out on the lake. Sylvia gazed happily at the moonlit water, rough and choppy in the wind. She ran her hand experimentally through the water. It felt disconcertingly cold. Her heart started to thump uncomfortably loud as she silently measured the distance to the island. Soon now!

"Nigel," she said, looking up to find his eyes fixed on her in an agony of longing, "do you truly love me?"

"Don't ask me to say it," he said. "Please, Sylvia, I am trying not to think of it."

"I need to know," she pleaded.

"Yes, I love you," he said.

"And you would wish to marry me if I were free?"

"It is the dearest dream of my life," he said.

"Nigel," she cried, "hold me, hold me just once."

She leapt to her feet and almost launched herself at his chest. He had time only for a startled exclamation and a "Look out!" and they were both in the water, sputtering and coughing as their heads came above the surface. Nigel tried to grab for the overturned boat, but Sylvia clutched at his coat and he was forced to abandon the boat in order to save her from panic. The island was close by. Nigel swam for it, dragging Sylvia along with him. They lay on the bank for a few moments, coughing and gasping.

"Are you all right, love?" he asked finally, pulling her sodden form close to him and pushing the soaked strands of hair away from her face.

"Y-yes," she stammered, becoming more and more miserably aware of the icy coldness of the gown and cloak that clung to her and of the cold wet velvet of Nigel's coat, against which her cheek was pressed. "Are you?" She had thought of the wetness and cold, had tried to think of some way of landing them on the island in dry clothes, but there had seemed to be no other way.

"It has not floated too far away," he was saying. "I can swim to it, love, and bring it back here. I shall have you back at the house in a half-hour."

"No!" she shrieked, clutching at his sodden sleeve. "Don't leave me, Nigel. You will be drowned for sure and I should have to watch you. Please, please stay with me."

"It might be morning before they find us," he said.

"You will have pneumonia by then, love. There is no other way."

"No," she said. "Stay here. We will keep each other warm as best we can."

If Sylvia had ever imagined that the situation would be romantic, she was to be rudely disillusioned. They moved to the pavilion, where at least they would be shielded from the worst force of the wind. Nigel wrung out as much water as he could from Sylvia's cloak and his own coat, and Sylvia squeezed the folds of her dress. They lay on the hard floor for the rest of the night, covered with dried leaves and the decidedly damp cloak, huddled together, but too miserable with cold to feel any spark of desire.

Sylvia had not planned to confess quite so soon, but she found that, loving Nigel as she did, she could not deceive him any longer. She told him that she had carefully plotted all the happenings of the last hour.

"Even the tipping of the boat?" he asked incredulously.

"Yes," she admitted, "even that. I could not think of any other way to get us stranded here, you see, Nigel."

"But why?" he asked. "Do you not realize that you will be hopelessly compromised, love?"

"Yes," she said against the curve of his neck.

"George will never marry you now," he said seriously. "I shall be forced to."

"Yes," she said.

There was a short silence.

"Sylvia," he said, "I shall be forced to marry you. I shall be forced to marry you! You little schemer!"

"I did ask you if you truly wished to before I tipped the boat," she said anxiously. "You do, Nigel, don't you?"

"Little schemer!" was all he would say in reply. "I can well see who will rule our household if I do not put my foot down very firmly right at the start."

"No, really, Nigel," she said, moving her cheek away from the thread of warmth she had found against his neck. "I shall be very good and very obedient. I was desperate on this occasion, you see."

He kissed her on the lips for the first time. Unfortunately, it was not the most auspicious occasion for a first kiss. They were soon desperately trying again to find some measure of warmth against each other and beneath the damp cover. Sylvia fell into a light doze just before dawn. Nigel, whose arm soon became badly cramped beneath her neck and whose velvet coat brought more discomfort than warmth, did not sleep at all.

13

―――――――――― ‥●‥ ――――――――――

During supper Lord Standen had tried to find his brother and his fiancée, without alerting anyone to the fact that they were missing. He circulated among the tables, smiling graciously at all his guests, took a turn in the garden, walking completely around the house in the process, circulated among his guests again, and then searched all the rooms in the house except the bedrooms and the servants' quarters. There was no sign of them anywhere.

Finally, as the dancing began again, he thought it wise to consult Raymore. Perhaps two heads would be better than one. He strolled across the ballroom, nodding at acquaintances as he went, and joined Raymore, who was standing talking to the parson and his wife. Standen too talked with them for a few minutes until he had the opportunity to draw Raymore aside. The two men went to the library.

"Your ward has been missing for almost two hours," Standen said, coming straight to the point. "She left the ballroom to walk in the garden with my brother for a few minutes. Neither has returned."

"Yes, I saw them leave," Raymore replied, "and have been uneasy myself at their continued absence from the company. I assumed, since you did not seem concerned, that there was some simple explanation."

A few minutes later both men were outside, searching in different directions, rather more thoroughly than

Standen had looked before. But there was no sign of the truants.

Back in the library they felt growing concern. Raymore was too worried to be angry, but he had a growing suspicion that Sylvia's disappearance had something to do with her talk with him the day before. Had she run away? But how would she have persuaded young Broome to go with her? He was a dull, sensible young man who would hardly allow himself to become a willing accomplice of a silly young girl. There was one person who was likely to know the truth. Lord Standen sent a footman to request Rosalind's presence in the library.

Rosalind did not immediately see Lord Standen as she entered the library. She was aware only of her guardian standing across from her, looking handsome and grim, his hands clasped behind his back. What now? she thought as she felt her heart begin to beat uncomfortably.

"What is it, my lord?" she asked coldly, and caught sight of Lord Standen at the same moment. She looked inquiringly at him.

"Rosalind," Raymore said sternly, "your cousin disappeared more than two hours ago. She is with Nigel Broome, we believe. Do you know anything of her whereabouts?"

Her eyes widened. "I noticed she had not returned," she said. "I have been worrying."

"But that does not answer the question," Raymore said. "If you know where she is, you must tell us."

"I do not know." she protested. "How should I?"

He strode across the room until he stood before her. He took her chin in his hand and raised it until she could not escape staring directly into his eyes. His touch was not gentle. "I know you resent my authority," he said. She noticed that his eyes were like blue ice chips. "But you must understand that Sylvia's reputation and perhaps her safety are very much at stake. You must tell me what you know. Now!"

"I am not a foolish girl, my lord," she blazed, grasp-

ing the wrist of the hand that held her chin. "Of course
I do not know where Sylvia is. Do you imagine that I
have helped her plan some escapade, perhaps even an
elopement? You cannot know me very well."

His grip tightened. His lips became a thin line.

Lord Standen broke the tension. "Miss Dacey," he
said, "I must believe you. I have the highest regard for
your good sense. But please think. Perhaps you know
something without realizing it. Does your cousin have a
favorite place where she might have gone?"

Rosalind thought. "No, I know of none," she said.
"Are you sure that she has not run away, perhaps
returned to London or even Raymore Manor? She is a
rather impulsive girl and can change her affections quite
rapidly."

Standen flushed. "You mean she may be running
from me?" he asked stiffly. "I think it hardly likely,
ma'am. I can offer her all the worldly goods she can
want and she has been well-received here by my mother.
I can only believe that some accident has befallen them."

"Have you checked the stables, Standen, to see if any
horses or carriages have been taken?" Raymore asked.
"I cannot imagine how I did not think of doing so
myself."

"Has anyone been down to the lake?" Rosalind asked.
"Would they have gone there?"

It was agreed that Standen would go to the stables
and Raymore to the lake. Rosalind begged to go with
him, but he very firmly refused. She was forced to
return to the ballroom, smiling sociably as she returned
to the sofa that she had occupied for most of the evening.
She was confiding to Sir Bernard what had happened
when Standen joined them, smiling easily.

"There is no horse or carriage missing," he said. "I
am afraid that I shall have to remain here, as the ball
will be ending within the hour. I do not wish anyone
else to know what has happened. I informed Mrs. Ev-
anston a moment ago that Lady Marsh has been forced
to retire with a headache." He smiled and moved away

to solicit the hand of a neighbor's wife for the set that
was forming.

"That is a cool customer," Sir Bernard murmured to
Rosalind. "I would wager that it will not go well for the
little Sylvia when she is finally found. Propriety comes
before all else in Standen's book."

"Yes," Rosalind agreed, "but I cannot help agreeing
that a scandal should be averted if at all possible."

"Have they eloped, do you think?" Sir Bernard asked.

"You mean hired a carriage somewhere else?" she
asked. "I fear it. From the start she has been more
attached to Nigel than to his lordship, I believe, though
I did not suspect love."

She was feeling almost frantic by the time the Earl of
Raymore reappeared in the ballroom when some of the
guests were already taking their leave. He did not cross
the room to her, but she did contrive to catch his eye.
He shook his head imperceptibly.

Almost another hour had passed before a search party
could be organized. By that time all the outside guests
had left. Lord Standen had decided that he must enlist
the help of all the men of the house party, and some of
the servants. Inevitably, the whole household knew the
story before much time had elapsed. The ladies gathered in the drawing room and ordered tea. The men
began to search, on foot and on horseback. Even Rosalind rode out with Sir Bernard after Raymore had left
and could not object. One servant was dispatched to
the village to inquire discreetly whether any vehicle or
horse had been hired during the night.

When dawn was already lightening the eastern sky,
several members of the search party had gathered
despondently in the main hallway. There did not seem to
be anywhere else to search.

"Come, Axby," Mr. Morrison said wearily, "let us go
down to the lake. It should be easier now to see any sign
with daylight coming."

"I searched there earlier," Raymore said. "I walked
the bank in both directions as far as I could go. But go

again. Perhaps I missed something. The boat was still safely tied up by the bank."

"Boat?" Rosalind queried. "You mean boats, my lord. There are two."

He blanched as he looked into her frantic eyes. "There was one at the bank," he said.

All who were gathered in the hallway made immediately for the doorway. Rosalind, feeling sick with apprehension, also rushed forward. Raymore stopped her.

"No," he said firmly. "You must stay here."

"I must go," she cried. "Oh, do not be cruel. I cannot wait here. Please! I must come."

He caught her by the arms and looked earnestly into her face. "You must stay here," he said. "If you walk all that way, you will hurt yourself and be an invalid. Then you will be of no use to anyone. You may be needed. As soon as we find out something, I shall send someone running back to inform you. Now, promise me you will stay."

"Yes," she whispered, mesmerized by his eyes. "Bring her back safe, Edward."

He squeezed her arms and after a moment's hesitation kissed her softly on the forehead. Then he was gone.

The growing daylight helped the search party find the missing boat within the next hour. They found it overturned, knocking against the bank one mile away from the place where the other was moored.

"They might have swum to shore too," Mr. Morrison said hopefully. "Can Lady March swim, Raymore?"

"I have no idea," the earl replied. He was feeling physically sick. She was dead! They would find her body some time during the day, perhaps by dragging the bottom of the lake.

"But Nigel can," Lord Standen was saying, "and has swum in this lake many times. As children we got more than one strapping from our father by challenging each other and swimming to the island."

"Could they be on the island, Standen?" Sir Bernard Crawleigh asked, shading his eyes and peering across the water.

"It seems a sensible place to start," Mr. Morrison replied. "Let us look there first, George, and then organize a thorough search of the banks."

The Earl of Raymore and Lord Standen jumped into the dry boat and the latter rowed them across the water toward the small cluster of trees that made up the island.

"There is a small pavilion in the center that we used as children," Lord Standen said. "If they are indeed here, they would probably go there for some warmth and shelter from the wind."

Raymore said nothing but strained his eyes to see into the trees.

Nigel heard their voices and the splash of the oars as they approached. He shook Sylvia and leapt to his feet. By the time the boat had reached the shore and before either man could climb out onto land, they were greeted by the sight of a sadly bedraggled pair coming through the trees toward them. Sylvia's hair was matted against her head, a few dried curls fanning out wildly in the breeze. Her face was pale and mud-streaked, her gown a sad ruin of limp, damp lace and silk. Nigel looked no better. His silk knee breeches were wrinkled; his velvet coat was shapeless and dark with wetness. He held Sylvia's cloak in the hand that was not around her waist.

"Thank heaven you have found us," she said weakly.

Raymore was on the bank in one leap. "Thank God you are alive," he exclaimed. He whipped off the heavy black cloak that he wore, enveloped her in its folds, and held her shivering form against him. "Thank God," he said again, hugging her closer. "Rosalind will be so relieved."

Lord Standen was still sitting in the boat. "What is the meaning of this, Nigel?" he asked stiffly.

"The boat overturned in the rough water," Nigel said, looking the picture of misery as he watched another man tend his darling. "Fortunately, we were close to the island and I managed to swim here with Sylvia."

"But what, in God's name, were you doing on the lake in the middle of a ball?"

Raymore interrupted what looked like becoming a lengthy interrogation and suggested that they take the two victims back to the house with all speed, where they might change into dry clothes and tell their story in greater comfort. "Will this boat carry four?" he asked Standen.

"Yes," his lordship replied. "provided everyone sits still." He looked significantly at his brother.

True to his word. Raymore dispatched Sir Bernard Crawleigh back to the house at a run to reassure the ladies that all was well. Several of them were on the doorstep waiting when the search party finally emerged from the trees, Nigel walking disconsolately beside his brother, Sylvia being carried the last part of the way by Raymore.

It was decided that Nigel and Sylvia retire to their rooms immediately for a hot bath, a change into dry clothes, and a hot drink. Standen suggested that everyone else do likewise, since all had had a sleepless night.

"This afternoon we can find out exactly what happened," he said. "For now it is enough to know that both are safe."

Rosalind went into Sylvia's room a little later to see how she did. Her cousin was sitting up in bed drinking a cup of steaming milk while a maid emptied a bathtub that stood before a roaring fire.

"How are you, Sylvia?" Rosalind asked.

"It is so lovely to be warm," Sylvia replied. "I do believe I might escape without catching a chill, Ros."

"Was it deliberate?" Rosalind continued. "I mean, did you intend to get marooned?"

Her cousin hesitated. "I would have told you," she said, "but I did not want to put you in the position of having either to betray me or to protect me by lying. Cousin Edward did question you, did he not?"

"But why, Sylvie?" Rosalind persisted. "If you had changed your mind, why did you just not have the courage to tell Lord Standen so? Why involve poor Nigel?"

"Because if I had just broken the engagement, Nigel would have felt honor-bound to stay away from me," Sylvia said earnestly. "Please understand, Ros. We love each other."

"Are you quite sure, Rosalind asked. "What will you do this time when you fall out of love?"

"Oh, I shall not," her cousin assured her. "This is different, Ros. I had no idea of loving Nigel when I first met him. The feeling grew on me, you see. I know I cannot expect you to believe me, but time will tell. I shall love Nigel for ever and ever, I swear."

Rosalind squeezed her hand and took the empty cup from her. "Whatever the explanation," she said, "you have had a terrible ordeal. Go to sleep now."

The ordeal was not over for Sylvia. When she was summoned to the library in the late afternoon, she found that she had to face three grim-faced men. Raymore and Lord Standen stood facing the door, their backs to the fireplace. Nigel stood looking out of a window.

The Earl of Raymore spoke first. "Nigel has told us, Sylvia, that he suggested that boat ride so that you could have the best of the cool air and that the boat tipped in the choppy water."

"That is not so," she said, agitated, looking swiftly at Nigel's back. "It was I who suggested the boat ride, and I tipped the boat when I moved suddenly. I am truly sorry, Edward, that I caused such anxiety, but Nigel was entirely the gentleman. He was not in any way to blame."

"However it was," Raymore continued gravely, "the fact remains that you were alone for several hours with a man who is not your husband or your betrothed."

"Oh, but nothing happened," she assured them with wide, innocent eyes. "We merely tried to keep each other warm. We were so wet and cold, you see."

"Lady Marsh," Lord Standen said. His expression when she turned to him was wooden. "I deeply regret the fact that this happened when there are so many guests here as witnesses. Nigel has offered to do the honorable thing and marry you. I am forced to agree. I much regret having to do so, and I am sure that it will be painful to you to end our betrothal thus. However, I can assure you that my brother has a steady character and a competent income. He will be able to support you and will make you a good husband."

Sylvia hung her head.

"Well, what do you have to say?" Raymore asked a trifle impatiently.

She looked up at Standen. "I am sorry," she said. "This will cause you great embarrassment, my lord, and you have always been kind to me. I shall do what you consider right."

The tears in her eyes looked genuine enough, Raymore thought. Little minx!

"I should like to make my offer in private, please," Nigel said, his back still to the room.

"Of course," said Lord Standen. "Raymore?"

When the two men had left the room, Nigel turned to face her at last. His face was white and drawn; the tears in her eyes had begun to spill over onto her cheeks. They stood and looked at each other for a few moments, then rushed into each other's arms.

"I did a terrible thing, did I not?" she said a while later. "Is he hurt, do you think, Nigel?"

"Yes, at the moment," he said gently. "But remem-

ber, Sylvia, that he does not know that we love each
other and really wish to marry. He could still have
insisted on marrying you himself without causing any
very great scandal. I have the deepest respect for my
brother and believe him capable of love. But this time
I do not believe his heart has been deeply touched. Honor
and reputation mean more to him on this occasion."

"And do you truly wish to marry me?" she asked
anxiously.

He looked down at her with a fond smile. "I am
supposed to do the asking, remember?" he said.

"Oh," said Sylvia.

"Will you do me the great honor of marrying me, my
love?" he asked, putting his forehead against hers.

She fingered the buttons on his jacket. "I shall always
love you," she said quietly, "and I shall spend my life
making it up to you for not really giving you a choice."

"Does that mean yes?"

"Yes."

He tilted his head and brought his lips down to cover
hers. Soon she was being clasped very tightly in his
arms. Her own arms were wrapped around his neck.

"It will have to be soon," he said breathlessly much
later, "the wedding, I mean. George mentioned tomorrow."

"Tomorrow!"

"Is it too soon?" he asked anxiously. "Perhaps you
want more time to consider?"

"No, Nigel," she said. "I wish it might be today."

He kissed her again.

The wedding took place the following morning in the
village church. Only the house guests were present.
Both Nigel and Sylvia made an effort not to appear too
radiant. For the sake of Lord Standen's pride, they had
decided the day before, they must make it seem as if
the marriage had been forced upon them to a certain
extent.

The Earl of Raymore gave his ward away. He watched

her closely during the ceremony. She was conducting herself very well, he thought. He had been very much afraid that she would be bubbling with excitement and reveal the truth to all the world. But she was putting on a very good act. She seemed almost subdued, and Broome looked about as solemn as the earl had ever seen him.

Raymore had not credited this particular ward with so much intelligence or courage. It must have been her plan. Broome would never have dreamed up an idea that was in many ways quite shady and dishonorable. Little minx! The earl found himself feeling unexpectedly amused. He should be furiously angry, but he had to admit it was a pleasant surprise to find that Sylvia was not just a milk-and-water miss. He wished them happiness.

When he sat down, his own part in the ceremony complete, Raymore was very aware of Rosalind beside him. Crawleigh was at her other side. He found himself dreaming of saying the words of the ceremony with her. It would be good to be standing there with her, to lead her outside afterward and drive away with her. She would be his. He would take her away, far away from any people they both knew, and show her all the beauties of Europe. She would appreciate all the art treasures that he had gazed at in wonder on his own grand tour as a younger man. It would be such a pleasure to show them to her, to see that look of animation and true delight that he had seen so rarely. It would be good to share jokes with her, like the one they had briefly enjoyed at the dinner table when he had hinted that they might listen unseen to Hans Dehnert practicing for his concert. It would be good to have the right to touch her and love her whenever he wished.

Raymore half-turned to her as the vicar pronounced Nigel and Sylvia man and wife. He could not believe that she did not feel the same vibrations that he felt. Crawleigh was just reaching over to clasp and squeeze her hand. They looked into each other's eyes and smiled.

Fool, Raymore thought. What a fool he was! There must be some strange flaw in his character that he always became attached to women whose attentions were directed elsewhere. And Rosalind most of all. She had never even pretended to like, or even respect, him. And it seemed that she loved the man whom she was to marry in a short while. He would not be able to attend that wedding. He could not give her away to another man when he wanted her so much for himself. He would have to think of some excuse when the time came.

Rosalind was also relieved to see Sylvia behave in a proper manner. It would have been very bad *ton* for her to show the excitement and happiness that she was evidently feeling. Rosalind was very familiar with that tense look about her cousin and the heightened color of her cheeks. It always meant that the girl was bursting with exuberance. But it really would not do for Lord Standen to suspect the truth. It would be even worse if any of the guests did so.

Rosalind felt relatively happy for her cousin. She should be uneasy. Sylvia had fallen in and out of love so many times in the last few years that it should be highly likely that she would regret her marriage within a few months. And Nigel did not have a great deal to recommend him to a romantic young girl. He was not unusually good-looking or elegant or fashionable. He possessed no great charm, no great wealth, no outstanding prospects. He was not at all, in fact, like any of the men with whom Sylvia had fancied herself in love. Perhaps it was this fact that reassured Rosalind. Sylvia had certainly not fallen just for an attractive exterior this time. She really did seem to love the man himself.

The Earl of Raymore sat down beside her, and Rosalind forgot her cousin. She was suddenly uncomfortably conscious of his closeness. How annoying! Why did she not have the same awareness of Bernard, who had sat beside her since they entered the church? She still heard the words of the service, but she heard them with Raymore in mind. What would it be like to be standing there with him? She pictured them, her hand in his, his eyes looking into hers, speaking his vows. It would be suffocating. Rosalind's heart was thumping uncomfortably against her ribs. She had to concentrate to control her breathing. What would it be like afterward to know that she belonged to him, that she forever owed him loyalty and obedience? It was a terrifying thought. But she could not shake from her mind that strange, tender moment when Sylvia was lost and Raymore had gripped her arms reassuringly and kissed her on the forehead.

Rosalind felt a dreadful urge to turn her head and look up at the man who sat so still beside her. There seemed to be such an overpowering magnetism pulling between them. Bernard's hand suddenly covered hers and squeezed it. She looked up into his face with a guilty start and smiled warmly.

After she looked away again, back to Sylvia and Nigel, Crawleigh looked over her head at Raymore, who was also watching the newly married pair. Bernard frowned slightly and returned his attention to the service.

14

It felt strange to be back in London without Sylvia. Cousin Hetty was delighted to see Rosalind, and the poodles yapped around her ankles in noisy welcome when she stepped into the hallway of the house on Grosvenor Square. She found herself borne off to the drawing room and plied with tea and all the latest *on-dits* in equally large quantities. Then it was her turn. Cousin Hetty wished to know every detail of Sylvia's strange courtship and wedding.

"I am so chagrined that it all happened when I was not there," she said, tickling the stomach of a small dog that lay in ecstasy on her lap. "Of course, if I had been there, dear, it would not have happened at all. I always had an eye for those two and would certainly have made sure that they were not allowed to leave a ball-room together. That Lord Standen! The man must be blind as a bat. I cannot say I am sorry, though. He and dear Sylvia did not suit at all. He needs someone to tease away his stuffiness. Your little cousin is too timid. Though, bless her soul, she was not too timid to go after the man she really wanted, was she, dear? I do believe Mr. Broome will be just right for her, do you know? He is quiet and serious enough to make her believe that she has all her own way, but I believe he is a man to rule his own home. She will be happy, won't she, Pootsie?" Cousin Hetty smiled sagely down at the little dog.

Rosalind did not have to contend with the presence

of the Earl of Raymore on that first day back. He hac
returned to London the day before, on the afternoon o
the wedding. Rosalind had traveled with Susan Heroi
and her ladies' maid, Sir Bernard Crawleigh ridin;
beside the carriage for most of the way. When sh
entered the house, only Cousin Hetty was there t
greet her. There was no sign of Raymore, either then o
for the rest of the day. Rosalind was immeasurabl
relieved. There would be increased embarrassment t
be in his company with Sylvia no longer there, to knov
that she alone was now his ward, though there was n
relationship whatever between them. She dreaded fac
ing him.

For his part, Raymore was keeping a careful distanc
from his own home. Although there had been no mate
rial change since his journey into the country, he some
how felt now that it was almost improper to share :
house with Rosalind. Knowing that he loved her, ad
mitting to himself that he wanted her, he could no
share a roof with her in comfort. He must stay away a
much as possible. Then, too, he did not relish th
thought of being in her company when all they ever di
was quarrel. He would not now be able to enjoy match
ing wits and tempers with her, knowing that she hate
and despised him. He would want to catch her in hi
arms and turn her anger to passion. His rose!

He spent the morning of her return at the House c
Lords. He did not attend very frequently, finding th
long and ponderous debates somewhat tedious. H
went to the racetrack in the afternoon and watched som
races without any great interest. He made no bets. Si
Henry Martel was there and persuaded his friend t
return with him to dinner.

"Elise will be delighted," Sir Henry assured his friend
"I took her to the opera last evening and I have drivei
with her in the park two or three afternoons, but she i
unable to enter into too many activities. She will no
hear of hiring a wet-nurse, you see, and consequentl
can leave the baby only for a few hours at a time."

"I admire her dedication," Raymore, said, maneuvering his curricle around a phaeton whose wheel had become hopelessly sunk in a muddy rut. "Many women would be all too ready to give up the care of their child to a mere servant."

Sir Henry Martel shot his friend an amused glance. "What, Edward?" he said. "Do you actually have something favorable to say about a female?"

Raymore looked mystified. "I have always respected your wife, Henry," he said.

The evening was a pleasant one. Raymore found himself almost envious of the quiet domesticity of his friends. They were not ostentatious in their love of each other, but there was an obvious affection between them and, more important, they shared a friendship. It was strange, he thought, that he had never noticed these things. Although he had always treated Lady Martel with courtesy, he had constantly pitied his friend for being leg-shackled. He had never been able to see that there could be any real happiness in marriage. Of course, it was different for him. He could never hope for such contentment. For some reason, he could not inspire any woman with deep and lasting love and loyalty. It was probably just as well that way. He was not at all sure that he could risk entrusting all his happiness to one woman.

He left before he felt he could have outstayed his welcome. He could not go home. She would surely be there by now and he would be obliged to go to the drawing room to greet her and converse for a while. It was impossible. He did not feel like going to one of his clubs. Neither cards nor drink appealed to him tonight. He finally went to the theater, although he knew he would have missed at least the first two acts. Elise had told him that there was an impressive new actress playing Ophelia. Raymore was impressed, too. He wandered backstage at the end of the performance and easily attracted her attention away from other would-be admirers congregated in the green room. As he left her bed and her room in the early hours of the morning, he reflected that such a relationship was far superior to the one he had been thinking of for the last few days. This way he could walk away perfectly satisfied without putting any part of his real self at risk.

The following day Raymore had to be at home during the afternoon to greet Dr. Hans Dehnert, who wished to try out the earl's musical instruments. It was important to him, he said, to use the actual pianoforte he was to play and in the actual room in which he was to perform. Only four days remained until the concert.

Raymore came face to face with the ladies as he entered the house and they were leaving the dining room after luncheon. He removed his hat and bowed to them, keeping his eyes on Hetty. "Hans Dehnert will be here this afternoon," he told her. "You need not concern yourselves, though. I shall have him shown directly to the music room. I believe he will want use of the room for the next three afternoons."

"Oh, how I look forward to hearing him," Rosalind said warmly. "Maybe it is a good thing that Bernard is coming this afternoon to take me to Kew Gardens. Otherwise I might be tempted to seek out that anteroom you told me of, my lord."

He shot her a brief glance. She caught a flash of amusement in it, but he did not hold the look. He seemed strangely uneasy, she thought. He was soon striding to the staircase and mounting the stairs two at a time.

The afternoon at Kew was not a success, though Rosalind was hard put to it afterward to explain to herself exactly what was wrong. She had been delighted at the prospect of escaping from the house and the constant threat of coming face to face with her guardian. She had dressed very carefully, choosing a new dress of bronze muslin and matching parasol, and a chip-straw bonnet whose ribbons of orange and yellow complemented the outfit. Sir Bernard looked at her with frank admiration as she descended the staircase to join him in the hallway. He growled playfully into her ear before lifting her into the seat of his high-perch phaeton. The afternoon was perfect, a slight breeze and a scattering of fluffy clouds relieving the heat of July. The gardens were breathtakingly beautiful.

Sir Bernard teased her about the concert that she would be forced to attend. "Now I know why your cousin married in such haste," he said, grinning broadly at her. "She saw it as the only escape from an evening of boredom. You should have lured me to that island, my love. We might be safely in Shropshire, too."

She smiled back at him. "Ah, but you see," she said, "I would not miss the evening for worlds, so you have been made to wait, sir."

"Even when the entertainment has been arranged by your tyrant of a guardian?" he goaded.

Her smile faded. "But I cannot dispute that his taste in the arts is impeccable," she said earnestly. "I must feel privileged to be associated with him in that way."

They drove in silence for a while until Sir Bernard turned to her again with determined cheerfulness and began to talk on one of his favorite topics: the places he planned to take Rosalind on their wedding trip.

"Oh, shall we be able to see the art treasures at Versailles and the Louvre?" she asked with enthusiasm when he mentioned Paris.

He smiled indulgently. "If you wish, my love," he agreed. "I was planning to take you to all the leading modistes and milliners so that you might turn every head with envy when we return to London."

"So that everyone might notice me limp along?" she asked with a smile.

He frowned. She asked if they might go to Florence when they reached Italy. There were so many art treasures there that she had dreamed all her life of seeing for herself.

Sir Bernard chuckled. "Am I to have a bluestocking for a wife?" he asked. "I had thought to head for Venice, where we might ride in a gondola and I might fill your head with romance."

"That would be lovely," she agreed. "And St. Mark's is in Venice. Will we see it, Bernard?"

He sighed with mock exasperation. "Do you know, Rosalind," he said, "I believe I should deputize Raymore to take you on this wedding trip in my place. You and he would lap up all the dry dust of Europe and believe that you had shared a feast. But you may see any place you wish by day, my love, provided that your nights belong to me." He leaned toward her with a wicked leer on his face and tried to kiss her.

Rosalind slapped his wrist with her closed parasol and laughed. "Sometimes I think you are no gentleman, sir," she said with mock severity. But his words had given her a sickening jolt. The very idea of being on a wedding trip with Raymore! The thought made the bottom want to a fall out of her stomach.

Sir Bernard would not come into the house on Grosvenor Square with her, claiming that he had some business to attend to before dinner. Rosalind was not sorry. She was feeling unaccountably depressed. She wanted to be alone. She was craving, in fact, a session alone in the music room. Although she had played the pianoforte at Broome Hall, she had done so only in the presence of other people. There had been no chance to play for herself. Now she needed the mental discipline of playing something that offered challenge, the emotional release of playing something full of feeling. Surely Dr. Dehnert must have left already.

She talked briefly with Cousin Hetty in the drawing room, then excused herself by saying that she needed to rest before dinner. It was not a total lie, she told herself. What better way to rest than to devote an hour to music? She made her way to the music room, listening carefully as she neared the door to make sure that it was not still occupied. She opened the door cautiously, then stepped inside and closed it behind her. Soon she was bringing Bach to life on the harpsichord.

By the time she moved on to the pianoforte to tackle the Moonlight Sonata, which she had not played for more than a week, Raymore was listening. He had not left the house after the arrival of the Austrian pianist, although he had left the musician alone in the music room. And he had stayed at home afterward, having decided that he would leave only in time to keep a dinner engagement. He had seen Rosalind return to the house while he was standing at the window of his own apartments. Instinct told him that she would soon seek out the music room. She was playing the harpsichord when he stopped outside the door. He let himself quietly into the anteroom.

Her playing was not good at first. The days without practice had affected her precision. Worse, she appeared to be in a mood of some agitation. She stumbled over phrases that should have given no problem; her timing was inconsistent. As the minutes passed, though, she became more absorbed in the exercise. She played the piece through without error. But more than that, she had put the whole of herself into the interpretation of the music.

Rosalind sat slumped over the painoforte, rubbing her eyes wearily, and finally looked up. The Earl of Raymore was standing in the doorway, his hand still on the doorknob. She jumped to her feet, pushing back the stool with such haste that it tipped over and fell to the floor with a clatter.

"Oh!" she said, bending down to lift the stool to an upright position. "My lord! I, um, er . . ." She broke off in confusion and stared at him, waiting for the explosion.

"That is the best I have heard you play," he said.

She tensed. He must be more than usually angry to speak so quietly. "In the drawing room I play popular music only," she said. "I hardly consider it music at all."

"I meant here," he said. "This is the best I have heard you play here."

Rosalind paled. "You knew I have used this room before?" she asked.

He inclined his head and walked a little way into the room, leaving the door open behind him. "I want you to play that sonata on Friday night," he said.

"On Friday night?" she repeated uncomprehendingly. "Friday is the night of your concert, my lord."

"Precisely," he agreed. "I wish you to play at my concert. Rosalind. I usually have more than one artist. You will play at the end of the first half, before refreshments are served."

Rosalind bit her lip and moved around the pianoforte until it was between her and her guardian. "You mock me," she said.

He looked annoyed. "Nonsense," he said. "I am serious. Why should I come in here merely to tease you?"

"Then you wish to humiliate me, my lord," she said, anger flaring in her face. "You would have me walk—limp—to this instrument in full sight of all your highborn friends just so that I might make a perfect cake of myself. You are an evil man, sir."

"What a very foolish woman you are, Rosalind," he said, moving forward so that only the pianoforte stood between them. "Common sense should tell you that that is the most ridiculous accusation you have ever leveled against me. Even if I did wish to humiliate you—which, by the way, is a thoroughly silly idea—would I choose to do so at my own concert? I am sure you are aware that I have spent years building up its reputation as one of the Season's most brilliant cultural events. I choose you because you are good, because I wish to share your talent with my friends."

She glared at him. "I do not trust you for a moment, my lord. My music is very private to me. It is not for sale, not for public consumption. How dare you come here to spy on me. That anteroom, of course. Oh, how dare you!"

"Rosalind," he said, a stubborn set to his jaw, "may I remind you that this *is* my house."

"Yes," she cried passionately, "and *this* is your music room, and *this* is your pianoforte, and *I* am your property. Am I to be allowed no privacy? Must you claim even my soul?"

She limped clumsily around the end of the pianoforte and made for the door. Raymore moved too and caught her by the arm. Rosalind was sobbing as she turned and struck at him with her fists. "I hate you!" she cried. "You would reduce me to nothing. I have no identity when I am with you. You would overpower me completely if you could. Oh, I shall send to Bernard and beg him to take me away from here even if we must run to Gretna Green. Let me go. Let me go!"

Raymore let her fury run its course. He let her pummel his chest and rave at him, but he kept hold of her arms. Finally, her sobs prevented her altogether from speaking, and he pulled her against him and held her head against his shoulder. He rocked her comfortingly until the sobs had subsided.

"I had not meant to order you to play," he said gently against her hair. "It was a request. You are an artist, Rosalind, a very talented performer, while I am a mere patron. I ask you very humbly to honor me by playing for my guests on Friday. I will not force you or badger you. It will be your own decision. But please remember that, although no performer myself, my taste is well-respected. If I say you are good, you may feel confident that you are good."

He grasped her arms and put her a little away from him. He looked down into her tear-stained face with great gentleness. "I am sorry that you hate me," he said. "I would not wish it. But please do not rush into a runaway marriage, especially to Gretna, when no one is opposing your wedding in the first place. You may think now that you do not care what society says, but in time you would be embarrassed to find that those who marry over the anvil are not readily accepted socially. And there is no need, Rosalind. If my presence is so intolerable to you, I shall stay away. You need not see me more than in passing between now and Friday, nor afterward, until you leave for the country with Crawleigh. Will that please you?"

Rosalind looked into his eyes but could not answer. The lump in her throat was choking her. With one hand he gently put back a strand of hair that had fallen across her face.

"Go now," he said, "and think over your decision, if there is anything to think about. Will you send word to me tomorrow? But whatever you decide, you may use this room whenever it is not in use. I give you my word of honor that I shall not come near. I will intrude no further into your soul."

She was still looking into his eyes, her own large with unshed tears. He bent slowly and covered her mouth with his in a gentle and unhurried kiss.

"Go now," he whispered, releasing her mouth, and he turned away so that she would not be made self-conscious when she limped the distance between the pianoforte and the open door of the music room.

Rosalind lay facedown on the bed sobbing her heart out and not knowing quite why she did so. Perhaps it was the feeling she had had during the afternoon that all was not as it should be with Bernard. It was hard for her to pinpoint exactly what was missing. There was a feeling that perhaps their friendship was all of the surface. She knew that he did not share her love of music and art; she did not share his interest in high fashion and hunting. Once the first romance of their marriage lost its novelty, would they have enough in common on which to build a deep and lasting relationship? Such thoughts were absurd, of course. How many girls of her class had the opportunity or time to find a man to whom they were totally suited? It was silly to aim for the ideal. Her own marriage would certainly be no worse than the majority she saw around her. In fact, it was likely to be better than most. Sir Bernard Crawleigh was a good-natured, intelligent man who would always treat her with consideration for her feelings, she believed. It was pointless now to start feeling uneasy about her forthcoming marriage.

Anyway, she really had no choice. If she broke off her engagement, she would be in the charge of the Earl of Raymore for the rest of her life. The prospect of spending two more weeks in his home was intolerable. She could not possibly contemplate a lifetime of such torture. Perhaps that was the problem, was it? She was totally lacking in freedom. All her life she had been ruled by men, as in fact all women must be, but never had she felt the restraints more than now.

It was the Earl of Raymore, of course, who had provoked her tears. She really did hate him. He had insinuated himself into every part of her life in the short time she had known him. She had thought that at least her music was hers. Music had always been very private to her, a channel for the outpouring of her spirit. She was badly shaken by the knowledge that he had listened to her in the past weeks and that he had passed judgment on her skills. Would she be free of him even when she married? She almost doubted it. He was constantly in her thoughts to plague her. She was constantly remembering their arguments, thinking of other things she might have said on various occasions. She was constantly comparing him to the dead Alistair of her dreams and to Bernard. If she ever again felt dissatisfied with the placid nature of her relationship with her betrothed, she must murmur a prayer of thanks that there was none of the turbulence that marked her encounters with Raymore. If ever she felt that there was some emotion missing in her embraces with Bernard, she must be thankful that there was not the passion that turned her into mindless fire with her guardian.

That was what she resented most about him. If he had always been the cold, arrogant, demanding man that was his normal self, she could at least respect him for a certain integrity. Her emotions would not be placed in turmoil. But there had been too many inter-ludes of passion, when they had both behaved as if they could not possibly live one moment longer without each other. She still flushed hotly with embarrassment when she thought of that morning at Broome Hall when she had almost given herself to him completely. She could not forgive him for using her so. And then, most con-fusing of all, were those rare occasions when he was gentle, almost tender. She had tried to forget the night of Sylvia's disappearance when he had kissed her brow, apparently in a gesture of comfort. But what about his behavior of this afternoon? All her defenses had come crumbling down with his gentleness, with the humility he had shown when talking about her talent. His kiss had almost destroyed her completely. She had wanted to cling to the lapels of his coat and pour out her heart to him just as if he were a normal man who would understand and sympathize. For a moment she had felt as if she had glimpsed a different man, a warm and compassionate human being.

It was clearer to her now, of course, why he had behaved so. He was a man who must have his way. For some reason that eluded her, he had decided that she must play at his concert, but she had almost thwarted him. He must have learned already that neither cold-ness nor anger would move her, and had consequently turned to other tactics. He was trying gentleness, hu-mility, concern. Despicable man! She thumped the bed with her fists. How could he so coldly use the physical appeal that he must know he exerted over her?

She was almost resolved to refuse to play for him on Friday night. She could not give him the satisfaction of feeling that his blandishments had succeeded. Anyway, she could not possibly perform before a large and criti-cal audience that would include the great Hans Dehnert. Even so, a little niggling thought at the back of her mind kept reminding her of one thing that he had said. His concert was very dear to him. He would not have asked her to perform if he did not truly believe that she was worthy. Whatever his personal feelings for her, he must consider her talented. And she could trust his judgment; he was one of the most respected patrons of the arts in England, she had learned since moving to London. She had a chance to play in the same concert as Hans Dehnert! The thought was overwhelming. Although she still believed that she would say no the next day, or, better still, give him no answer at all, part of her was glad that she did not have to make a final decision until the following day.

Rosalind got up from the bed and rang for a maid to bring her some fresh water. She had only a little while in which to repair the damage her tears had done to her face before going down to dine with Cousin Hetty and preparing to attend the opera with Sir Bernard and a party he had invited.

15

The Earl of Raymore was true to this word. Rosalind saw nothing of him between the time of their meeting in the music room and the concert on Friday evening. The day following her encounter with him she was still as undecided as she was the day before about what her reply would be. She wandered into the music room in the morning and played some music that she found undemanding. She sang a little. But she could not bring herself to even try the Beethoven. She wandered out again little more than a half-hour after she had begun.

In the afternoon she decided to pay a call on Lady Elise Martel. She had not seen her since before going into the country. They spent a pleasant half-hour exchanging news and cooing over the baby, whom Lady Elise had brought down from the nursery for her guest's inspection.

"I have a terrible problem," Rosalind said finally, "that I am hoping you can help me solve."

"Yes," Lady Elise said, "I have noticed that you are preoccupied. Trouble with Sir Bernard, my dear?"

Rosalind hesitated. "No," she said, "it does not concern him. It is that my guardian has asked me to play at his concert on Friday evening."

Lady Elise gasped. "You mean on the pianoforte?" she asked.

"Yes."

"He has heard you play?" Lady Elise continued. "You are that good?"

"I have never thought of myself as a very good player," Rosalind said. "I have always played to please myself, you see. I have always found that playing both relieves my emotions and helps me build self-discipline. It is challenging to play a difficult piece perfectly."

"But you must be good if Edward says you are," her friend assured her. "What is the problem, Rosalind?"

Rosalind pondered. "It is as if he intruded into the most private part of my life," she said. "He has been listening to me all these weeks, you see, without my knowing it. I am honored to know I could play on the same program as Hans Dehnert, but . . . Oh, Elise, I cannot allow him to just take over my life. I have to keep part of me for myself. I am not explaining myself very well, am I?"

Lady Elise absently stroked the curled hand of the child who slept on the sofa beside her. Her eyes were wide and fixed on Rosalind. "Oh, you explain yourself very well," she said. "Tell me, my dear, do you feel the same about Sir Bernard?"

"About Bernard?" Rosalind repeated, frowning slightly. "No, of course not. He has never tried to bore into my very soul."

Her friend nodded several times but said nothing.

"Elise?" Rosalind queried.

"Have you realized that you love Edward?" Lady Elise asked quietly.

Rosalind could feel the blood draining from her head. "Love Edward?" she said, appalled. "Of course I do not love him, Elise. I hate him with a passion."

Lady Elise did not comment. She leaned back on the sofa and regarded her friend with gentle amusement. "And it just might be that your feelings are returned," she said. "Henry told me that Edward has been behaving strangely in the last few days. He dined here two nights ago, you know, and seemed quite happy to be here, though he was the only guest. He appeared almost reluctant to leave, in fact. Well, how famous!"

Rosalind leapt to her feet. "Please do not say such

things," she said. "Oh, do not make sport of me. I detest the earl. Nothing will make me happier than to leave his house in two weeks' time knowing that I never have to return again."

"Please sit down," her friend said. "I am sorry, Rosalind. I did not mean to distress you. Come, I shall ring for tea. But before we drop the subject entirely, please do consider accepting Edward's invitation. It would be a shame to have the talent you must possess and not share it at least once with a discerning audience."

It was a piece of advice that Sir Bernard Crawleigh echoed a couple of hours later when he took Rosalind driving in the park. She did not mention to him any of the emotional overtones of her interview with Raymore the afternoon before, but merely told him that she had been asked to play and had to give her answer that day.

"I say," Sir Bernard said, "much as I dislike the man, Rosalind, I must respect his judgment on music. You must be good."

She shrugged. "He seems to think so."

"You must accept, you know," he said. "I must confess that I have been looking forward to the evening as a crashing bore, but knowing you are to play, I shall definitely be interested."

"What if I make a mess of it?" she asked doubtfully.

"I told you," he answered with a grin, "I respect Raymore's judgment. How does he know you are good, by the way?"

"He has been listening to me," she said, a thread of anger in her voice. "Without my knowledge, of course."

He grinned again. "I'll wager you were furious when you found out," he said. "I wish I might have seen that interview. Did you strike him, Rosalind?"

"Yes, I did," she replied, her face hardening.

He laughed outright. "Famous!" he said. "He did not hit you back, though, did he? I should have to call the fellow out if he did, you know, and I am not altogether sure I would like that. He is a better shot than I."

Rosalind said nothing.

He looked at her more closely. "Did he hit you, Rosalind?" he asked.

"No," she said, looking down at her hands. "No, he did not strike me."

He continued to look at her for a while before turning his attention back to the horses. Several minutes passed before they again engaged in light chatter.

When she returned to the house, Rosalind went to the drawing room and seated herself at the escritoire there. She wrote a short note to the Earl of Raymore, telling him that she would be honored to play at his concert on Friday evening. She gave the letter to the butler, with instructions that it should be handed to the earl as soon as he returned to the house. She then went to the music room, where she began to practice the Moonlight Sonata with a furious kind of dedication. Only the gathering gloom later warned her that it was time to go down to dinner.

Raymore had passed a wretched day. He had spent more than an hour at Jackson's boxing saloon working off some of his physical and emotional energy, but apart from that he had avoided company. He had ridden early in the park, dined at home, alone, in the library, and sat in the same room all afternoon while Hans Dehnert practiced upstairs. He left the room and the house only when he heard Rosalind come in after her drive with Crawleigh.

He had certainly made a mess of things the day before. He wanted Rosalind to play in his concert on Friday evening because she had a great deal of talent. She had more than technical excellence; she had the rare gift of being able to put the whole of herself into the interpretation of what she played. Yet it seemed very doubtful that she would play.

For several years past Raymore had developed skill at persuading the most temperamental artists to play at his musical evenings. Hans Dehnert had been one of his most difficult conquests. Yet with Rosalind he had botched things so badly that he felt like a schoolboy again. He had walked in on her at a moment when she was obviously caught up in a very private experience. He had revealed to her that he had been spying on her for weeks. And then he had somehow given the impression that he was ordering rather than asking her to play for his guests. He could not have miscalculated more badly. He could fully understand her anger. He would be bitterly disappointed if she refused his request. And, in fact, it looked as if she was going to do worse than refuse. It seemed that she was going to ignore him altogether.

But that was not the worst of the matter for Raymore. He had wanted the day before to begin to make amends for the high-handed way he had treated her in the past. He knew that he had no chance of winning her love, but he had hoped to show her that at least he esteemed her and saw her now as a worthy and talented person. He had hoped that she might come to like him so that they could part on friendly terms. He had not wanted to lose her altogether. He had hoped that perhaps, as friends, they might meet in the future.

But he had succeeded only in hurting her deeply, in making it seem as if he wanted to destroy her sense of self. She had seen his actions as an unforgivable example of tyranny, spying on her in her most private moments. She hated him now worse than ever, and he could hardly blame her. He was consumed by an agony of remorse. He had had no right to listen to her all those times, uninvited.

Holding her in his arms the day before had been a terrible agony, because he knew as he did so that it would be the last time he would ever touch her. He had known that as soon as she recovered from her fit of sobbing he would tell her that he would stay away from her, never force his presence on her again. And even then he had not been able to resist one final act of self-indulgence. He had kissed her.

And fare-thee-well, my only Luve,
And fare-thee-well, a while!

The words of that song would haunt him forever, he felt. The next line would never apply to him, though: "And I will come again, my Luve." He would never be able to come to her again now. Once she was gone, he would probably never see her again, except for a chance glimpse at some *ton* event when she was in town, perhaps. And she might as well be gone already. He had pledged not to see her while she remained in his house, except on Friday evening, if she still planned to attend his concert.

Raymore thought about Sir Bernard Crawleigh. He hated to think of Rosalind belonging to him. The man was pleasant enough, he supposed, and he would certainly never ill-treat her. But there was no depth to the man's character. He still kept a mistress at an establishment that he owned. Raymore had checked quite carefully into the matter within the last week. And Crawleigh had made a lengthy call there since his return to London. The fact did not call for any great alarm. Crawleigh might be a perfectly decent husband despite the existence of a mistress. He would merely be doing what a large number of other husbands did. But it was not good enough for Rosalind, Raymore decided. She was very special: intelligent, talented, very cultured. She needed a man who could match her passion for the beauties of life. And Crawleigh was definitely not that man.

Had she chosen him freely? Had he himself pushed her into the betrothal by making such an infernal to-do over the episode in Letty's summerhouse? Had his treatment of her in general forced her to consider marriage to Crawleigh a welcome escape from his guardianship? Or did she love the man? It was impossible to know the answer.

But Raymore made a decision. Before he left the house, he wrote a letter, which he left with the housekeeper to deliver to Rosalind the following morning. He would have liked to speak with her himself, but he could not for two reasons. He had promised that she would not have to see him before Friday night. Also, he knew from experience that any meeting between the two of them was bound to flare into an angry quarrel. He did not wish to quarrel with her ever again. He wanted to love her.

Both letters were received the following morning. Rosalind was sitting at the breakfast table alone when she broke the seal of hers. She could not understand why her guardian would be writing to her unless it was in reply to her own note. Perhaps he had changed his mind and did not wish her, after all, to play at his concert. She read:

My dear Rosalind,
In reflecting on our conversation of yesterday afternoon, it has occurred to me that you might have engaged yourself to marry Sir Bernard Crawleigh only as a means of escaping my control over your affairs. I would not wish to drive you into an unwelcome marriage.

If your heart is engaged, I sincerely wish you joy of your union. But if not, I urge you to put an end to the betrothal. I shall send you home to Raymore Manor next week and allow you to live there for the rest of your life as if it belonged to you. I shall release to you control of your fortune and engage never to enter the property without an express invitation from you. You can be free, Rosalind. All this I am willing to put in legal form if you so choose.

Believe me when I say that I wish only what is best for you, and that I remain now and always,
Your servant,
Edward Marsh, Earl of Raymore.

Damn him, she thought, crumpling the paper and holding it tightly in her hand. He was determined, it seemed, to keep her mind and her life in turmoil. She had disliked him from the start. but at least then he could always be relied upon to behave consistently. She had labeled him as a cold man, totally devoid of all the finer feelings in life. It would have been more comfortable for her peace of mind if he had not recently begun behaving as if he had a heart. Even two days ago it had been hard to continue hating him, but at least then she could convince herself that his gentleness had an ulterior motive. But what could be his motive this time? He must already have had her letter telling him that she would play at his concert. She could not explain his letter in any other way than by seeing it as a sincere attempt to give her some freedom of choice about her future. Oh, damn him!

And what about the choice he had given her? Why did everyone seem intent upon putting doubts in her mind just at a time when she was feeling less than certain about her own feelings? She wanted to marry Bernard, of course she did. He was handsome, kindly, good-humored. He was the only man who had ever shown a real interest in her, if one discounted Sir Rowland Axby and the strange advances of her guardian. She could be happy with him. Only a few months before, she had resigned herself to a life of spinsterhood, believing that no man could tolerate her disability and her dark, unfashionable looks.

But first Lady Elise and now Raymore were attempting to make her take a closer look at her feelings. She did not wish to do so. She was terrified of doing so, in fact. She wanted to be safe. Lady Elise had even made the quite absurd suggestion that she loved the Earl of Raymore. And she had always considered her new friend to be a woman of good judgment. She was not going to stop to think about him. She was already too disturbed by the uncharacteristic nature of his behavior in the past two days. She would not think anymore.

Rosalind spread the letter on the table before her and folded it carefully into its original creases. She would not think about him or about her betrothal until Saturday. She had only two days to prepare herself for the concert. It was imperative that she be calm so that all her concentration could be given to her music. She rose from the table, her breakfast untouched, and went to the morning room to write a letter to Sir Bernard, canceling a dinner engagement with him that evening and explaining that she needed to be alone until Friday evening to prepare her mind as well as to practice her music. Then she went to the music room to make the best use of her time until the Austrian arrived.

For his part, Raymore was handed Rosalind's note when he returned very early to his own house. He had spent the night playing cards, or most of the night, anyway. Late in the evening he had kept an appointment to escort the new actress from *Hamlet* to dinner and then to her home. He completely mystified and enraged her when, after a half-hearted conversation of ten minutes' duration, he picked up his cloak and took his leave of her without having so much as touched her Her anger was somewhat mollified when she saw the number of bank notes he had deposited on the table where his hat had been, but she still made straight for a mirror after he had left and gazed at her own image, wondering what defect had turned away such a desirable protector.

He was done with such unsatisfactory liaisons, Raymore decided during the course of the night. Occupying a woman's body could bring him no further delight unless the woman herself was the object of his love. When Rosalind was gone, he would make an honest effort to find himself another woman whom he could love. He doubted that it was possible, but he would take the risk. He had been absent from life too long.

Rosalind's note delighted him. She had given him a last chance to show her that he esteemed her for herself. He must be very careful of the way he introduced her and of what he said to her afterward, if he had a chance to speak to her at all. Most of all, he wanted her to see that his assessment of her talent was correct. If she received the acclaim that he expected, she would have restored to her the confidence that her lameness and the loss of her parents had deprived her of at a very early age.

Tired as he was, Raymore took the stairs to his room two at a time and rang for a hot bath.

The next two days were intense ones for Rosalind, who practiced morning and night and shut herself into her room during the afternoons. Nothing was to be allowed to disturb her concentration. At first she found that her playing was full of mistakes and that the music itself was lifeless. She had to make a determined effort to control her nervousness. There was really no need to be afraid. The people who were coming on Friday night were coming, not in the hope that she would fumble, nor in order to criticize. They were coming to be entertained. And she was not even the star attraction. She was capable of performing well. *He* had said so and she must trust his judgment. Strangely, Rosalind found in the end that the best calming influence on her was to see his face before her, the rather austere aquiline features, the intense blue eyes, the blond hair. It was a face that could be trusted, as far as her music went, anyway. She played for him. She would play for him on Friday.

Finally even the Earl of Raymore faded into the background of her consciousness and the music lived for itself. It seemed no longer as if she played the music but as if the music released her into life and freedom.

Cousin Hetty, fretting over the fact that her charge had neither received company nor ventured out of doors for three whole days, decided on the Friday morning that she must take a firm hand. When Rosalind could not be persuaded to recognize her need of any new purchases for the evening, she herself had to make up a list of imaginary items that she needed. She could not possibly shop alone, she assured her charge. That would be most dreary. And positively none of her acquaintances rose before noon. Would Rosalind please spare an hour of her time?

Rosalind went with great reluctance. When they returned to Grosvenor Square at noon, it was to find that they had visitors awaiting them in the drawing room. Sylvia and Nigel had returned to London a day earlier than planned when Nigel's sister, Letty, had written to tell them that Rosalind was to play at Raymore's concert. They had traveled all night, having received the news only the day before.

"But we could not miss it, Ros," Sylvia said, throwing her arms around her cousin. "It is perfectly splendid news. I said to Nigel when I heard, 'How I wish I could be there,' and he said, 'Pack a bag; we are going.' And here we are."

Rosalind looked from one to the other of the newly married pair. They both positively glowed, despite the lines of tiredness that smudged the eyes of both. If they had made a mistake, they certainly had not discovered it yet. And somehow Rosalind did not believe that they had made a mistake.

"I always knew you were out of the ordinary, Ros," her cousin continued. "I never persevered with my own playing because I felt so inferior to you. But even so, this is a signal honor for you. Nigel says that Edward's opinion on music and art is very highly respected."

"My love," Nigel said now, "you are so tired that you must be sleeping on your feet. And if my guess is correct, Rosalind has her mind on other matters today than prattling with us. Let us go and get some sleep before this evening."

"As you wish, Nigel," his bride agreed, smiling radiantly at him. She placed her hand in his.

"Are you not staying here?" Cousin Hetty asked.

"No, ma'am," Nigel replied. "We stay at my brother's home for a few days before moving back to the country. When summer is over, we will find a house of our own. And I plan to make a start with a boys' school for the poor."

"Sylvie," Rosalind said, hugging her cousin, "I am so glad you returned today. I shall feel far less lonely and overawed tonight knowing that you are there."

"Nigel said you would feel that way," Sylvia agreed, and allowed herself to be led away by her husband.

"That little puss has got what she wants, at any rate," Cousin Hetty remarked as she and Rosalind made their way to the dining room for luncheon. "She has no business looking so happy. But then, I always did have a soft spot for young love. One sees it so rarely nowadays."

The Earl of Raymore did not dine at home. He had decided to keep his promise to Rosalind to the letter. He had not set eyes on her since that afternoon in the music room. He stood at the entrance to the music room now, greeting his guests as they arrived. The room was lit brilliantly by chandeliers that held hundreds of candles. Gilt chairs to accommodate the guests were set out around the room. He was nervous. Never had he succeeded in presenting someone of quite the caliber of Hans Dehnert at one of his concerts. He hoped that the setting would be to the man's liking. But it was Rosalind who caused his feeling of trepidation. He did not doubt her skill, but he knew her to have a somewhat volatile temper. How would she stand up to the strain of such an occasion? Had he pushed her too far?

He longed to see her again. Yet he dreaded it, too. It would be the last time, except possibly for the farewell he would take of her next week or the week after. He doubted that she would want him to attend her wedding, and indeed he did not wish it himself.

She finally appeared on the arm of Crawleigh. He recalled then that her fiancé had been engaged to dine at the house. She was looking pale, but there was a determined set to her jaw. She wore the same rose-pink gown that she had worn to her come-out ball. Her dark hair was piled in intricate swirls around her head, a few tendrils carefully curling over her temples and along her neck. She looked the picture of beauty to the man on whom her eyes were riveted.

Rosalind hardly knew how she had reached the music room. She knew that she was leaning rather heavily on Bernard's arm and that she was limping more than usual. She was in the grip of a blind terror. She could not go through with it, she thought. She would be sick. Every moment she thought she would have to tell Bernard to turn back. Then she caught sight of the Earl of Raymore standing inside the doorway of the music room looking reassuringly cool and confident. He had told her she could do it. And he did not appear worried now that he had made an error. She fixed her eyes on him and felt some of the warmth returning to her body.

He looked back at her, smiled, and bowed. "Rosalind," he said, taking her hand in a steady, warm one, "how are you feeling? Crawleigh?"

She made a grimace that passed for a smile. "Terrified," she admitted.

He placed her hand on his arm and led her to an empty chair in the front row. Sir Bernard followed them. "I should be worried if you were not," Raymore said softly. "You will play magnificently, I promise you."

"Will I?" she asked, looking up at his reassuring smile.

Hans Dehnert arrived soon afterward. There was a stir among the assembled guests as he crossed the room and seated himself at the pianoforte. Rosalind stared in surprise. She had expected someone seven feet tall. Could this slim little man with the receding hairline and nervous hands be the great pianist about whom she had heard so much?

After Raymore had introduced him and he began to play, Rosalind could understand his fame. He brought Mozart alive with his playing. One almost immediately forgot the player and saw, heard, and felt only the music. For a half-hour she sat enthralled as he played first

the pianoforte and then the harpsichord. But the cold-
ness began to creep back. Soon it would be her turn.
How would she be able to get up and cross the expanse
of floor to the instrument? How would she be able to
play? How could she follow such a performance as this?
She could not. She must somehow signal to Raymore
her change of heart. Without knowing it, she began to
clench and twist her hands in her lap.

Sir Bernard covered them with one of his. "Steady,
love," he murmured. "You will be good."

His reassurance did not help much. By the time she
joined in the applause for Hans Dehnert, she hardly
knew what she was doing. When Raymore got to his
feet, she stared at him as at a lifeline. He looked back.

"We shall hear more from Dr. Dehnert later, after
refreshments," he told his guests. "I am sure you feel
the same delight as I do that there is more to come. In
the meanwhile, I wish to introduce to you a new talent
that I discovered under my own roof. Miss Rosalind
Dacey is a true musician, in the sense that she plays for
the music alone, not for an audience. However, she has
consented to play for us this evening. In a few moments
you will all share with me the honor of hearing her
perform. Rosalind?"

He was standing before her, his hand outstretched.
Rosalind placed her own in it and rose to her feet. She
had not taken her eyes from his. Raymore resisted the
temptation to draw her arm through his and pull her
close to his side so that her limp would be somewhat
disguised. Rosalind Dacey did not need to disguise one
defect when there was so much beauty in her. He led
her to the pianoforte and seated her.

She could not begin. Her fingers would depress the
wrong keys. She would not be able to move her fingers;
they were cold and stiff. She could not remember the
music. She stared at the keyboard for a moment in
blind panic. Where was he? Where had he gone?

She looked up and locked eyes with the Earl of
Raymore. He was not smiling. He was sitting very still.

But there was a look in his eyes that she had not seen there before. It warmed her and calmed her completely. He believed in her. She would play for him. She would show him that he had not made a mistake.

She lowered her fingers to the keys. For the first few bars she played correctly but somewhat tensely. She was playing to the Earl of Raymore. But soon her eyes closed and she forgot everything except the music that was creating itself beneath her hands. She was surprised at the end of it when the sound of applause interrupted her thoughts, prolonged applause that was more than merely polite.

Raymore was not applauding. My God, he thought. she has improved almost beyond recognition in four days. He rose to his feet only when he saw her slightly bewildered face. He crossed the room and bent over her. "You were magnificent," he said. "These people will want an encore, Rosalind."

"An encore?" she echoed. "Oh, no, please. I have not practiced anything else."

"Will you sing?" he asked, still bent over her, speaking for her ears only.

"Sing?"

"Will you sing the song about the rose?" he asked. "For me, Rosalind?"

She looked up at him, startled. "You mean the one by Mr. Burns?" she asked.

"Is that who wrote it?" he said. "That Scottish fellow, Robert Burns? Will you, Rosalind?"

She had no time to think. The audience had quietened down. "If you wish," she said.

"Miss Dacey has agreed to sing an encore," Raymore told his guests. "It is a song by Robert Burns that I have grown to love."

Rosalind followed him with her eyes until he sat down. The song about the rose. He had called her his rose on that morning at Broome Hall. She had thought it a shortened form of her name. Had he been referring to this song? Had he listened to her sing it and did he think of her as Mr. Burns had thought of his Jean, or whoever the girl was who had inspired the poem?

She sang the song, her contralto voice soft and rich in the hushed room. But she was aware only of the man who sat looking at her, his face expressionless, his eyes full of that new look that she now wondered more about. And before she had finished singing, she knew the truth. She did love him. He had become as essential to her being as the air she breathed or the music she played. She watched her hands during most of the song. When she did raise her head, it was at him that she looked, growing wonder in her eyes.

It is unlikely that many of the invited guest noticed. They were enjoying the novelty of hearing a simple love song after the intense music that they had been hearing for more than an hour. But Lady Elise Martel noticed and exchanged a triumphant smile with her husband. And Sylvia Broome noticed and darted a look of wonder at Nigel. He appeared engrossed in the song. And Sir Bernard Crawleigh noticed.

During the first half of the time set aside for refreshments Rosalind's attention was taken by a large crowd of people wishing to congratulate her on her performance. Finally, though, Sir Bernard was able to steer her back into the music room and to a couple of chairs on the side of the room farthest from the refreshments.

"I must speak to you in private," he said. "This may not be quite the time. I should be allowing you to bask in people's praise. You deserve it all, you know, Rosalind."

"What do you wish to say, Bernard?" she asked.

"I see I must get to the point," he said. "I wish you to break our engagement, my dear."

"Bernard?" she asked, her eyes wide.

He smiled rather crookedly. "I am sure you must have suspected that I had no intention of getting married this early in life," he said. "That does not mean that I do not desire you as a bride. And I would have made the best of it. In my way, I love you, Rosalind.

But the marriage would not be good for you, my dear. Your heart is engaged elsewhere. I am not even sure that you realize it. But you would in time, and I should hate it to happen after you had married me."

Rosalind was staring at him, her face pale. "With whom am I in love?" she asked, her voice sounding distant to her own ears.

"With Raymore, of course." he said, "damn his eyes."

Rosalind stared dumbly back at him.

"I cannot break the engagement," he continued. "It would be very bad *ton*. You must do it, dear. But do not feel guilty. I regret never having possessed you, Rosalind, but in a few days' time I shall no doubt feel relieved at my own renewed freedom." He attempted a grin, which appeared rather lopsided.

Rosalind was searching for an answer, but it was too late. The guests were reassembling and Hans Dehnert was taking his place at the pianoforte again. She sat next to Bernard for the full hour of the second half of the recital without hearing one note of the music. She sat in an agony of guilt and confusion. Could it be true? How could she love a man she detested, a man she had felt suffocated by for as long as she had known him? How could she have failed to recognize the truth a long time ago? And what of Bernard? Was he hurt? He pretended not to be, but she suspected that it had not been easy for him to release her from their betrothal.

She stole several surreptitious glances at Raymore, who sat with his eyes directed at the floor. It was hard to tell from his expression whether he was engrossed in the music or a million miles away in thought. She remembered Lady Elise telling her a few days before that it was possible that he loved her. Could it be true? The idea seemed too fantastic. They had disliked and despised each other so strongly at the start. And how could a man who was himself so physically perfect and who cultivated beauty around him love her? It could not be.

It was at that moment that their eyes met across the music room. Each looked away hastily. Rosalind felt as if a shock had passed through her. What was she to do now? She would have to end her betrothal to Bernard. Then, what? Should she accept Raymore's offer to send her back to the country? It was what she had longed for from the start. But she would never see him again. Could she bear the thought of that? There was just no alternative. She would soon be free, but free only to leave forever the man she loved.

Rosalind heard loud applause all around her and realized, with a start of guilt, that the recital was over. She had missed the chance of a lifetime! She applauded with everyone else and stood talking with friends reluctant to leave long after Raymore had escorted the Austrian pianist outside to his waiting carriage.

Bernard succeeded in having a private word with her before he left. "I shall expect to hear from you tomorrow," he said. "Please think carefully, Rosalind. I should be delighted to be held to our engagement, but I think, my dear, when you have had time to consider, you will find that I am right."

She put her hand in his. "Yes," she said, "I shall write to you tomorrow. Good night, Bernard."

He bent and kissed her hand.

"Well, I ben't altogether sorry ter see the back of Lunnun," Ben was saying. "What say you, lad?"

"The streets be too hot 'n dusty fer me," the footman agreed. "Reckon young Jenny'll like the country, then?"

"She'll like it iffen you be there," Ben replied, leering sidelong at his companion on the box of Raymore's traveling carriage. "Yer'd better set yer poppers back, lad, iffen yer wants a last glimpse o' Lunnun. We lose 'er over yonder rise."

The footman obediently cast his eyes back on the London skyline that had set his jaw hanging with wonder only a few short months back.

"Someun be in a big hurry," he commented, jerking

his thumb at a distant horseman who was galloping hard up the hill a mile or so behind them. "He ben't a highwayman, eh, Ben?"

"Nay," said the other. "Road's too open 'ere fer gen'lemen o' the road."

Inside the carriage Rosalind sat gazing sightlessly out the window. A smart little maid sat in the opposite corner, watching eagerly the passing scenery. She had never been out of the city before.

She had finally got her wish, Rosalind was thinking. She was on her way home. She was free. Within a few days she would have picked up her life where she had left it before coming to London. She could ride Flossie, paint, revel in her music, read to her heart's content. And although Raymore Manor would never legally be hers, she was assured sole possession of it for her lifetime.

She had had a short and uncomfortable interview with Raymore two days before, the day after the concert, at her own request. She had told him that she had ended her betrothal and that she wished to return to the country. He had made no comment, put up no argument, merely agreed to make all the arrangements for her journey. And he had promised to send his man of business into the country the following week to give her a signed copy of his agreement to allow her undisputed possession of Raymore Manor during her lifetime. This man would also go over with her the details of her fortune, so that she might decide for herself how she wished to manage it. It had been a purely businesslike meeting. The concert and the tense bond that she had felt with him on that evening might never have been.

The two days before her departure had been busy ones. In addition to helping the maid, Jenny, who was to accompany her on her journey, to pack her trunks, she had to write to Sir Bernard Crawleigh and pay calls on Lady Elise and Sylvia and Nigel. There had not been a great deal of time for reflection, but there had been enough time for some very disturbing thoughts. The great irony of her life, she discovered, was that

when she had finally gained the freedom she had longed
for for more than a year, since the death of her uncle,
she no longer wanted it. She wanted only Edward!
Somehow the thought of riding without him to scold
her, playing the pianoforte without him to praise her,
living without him to constantly stimulate her emotions, seemed very dull. He had become the focus of
her life, but she had fought so hard against losing the
privacy that had surrounded her all her life that she had
not recognized the fact that she loved him. Edward
Marsh: strong-willed, well-educated, cultured, so very
attractive. She could never be happy with a lesser man.

But then, she thought with a sigh, still staring out the
window, there would never be any other man. She was
going home to the life of a hermit, the life she had
chosen for herself. Back to her dreams of Alistair, except
that now he had changed name and had acquired a far
more forceful character than Alistair had ever had. She
would remember him as he had been a couple of hours
ago as he said good-bye to her. He had said very little.
His face was serious and controlled, but not cold as it
had been when she first knew him. He had shaken her
hand, wished her a safe journey, and finally, as an
afterthought, had bent and kissed her on the cheek.

The carriage bounced on its springs as the coachman
drew it to a sudden halt. As the horses slowed down,
both Rosalind and Jenny became aware of the louder
sound of galloping hooves.

"Oh, lawks, madam," Jenny yelped, "highwaymen!"

"Nonsense," Rosalind replied, "this is daytime on an
open and well-traveled highway."

She did start forward in alarm, though, when the
sound of hoofbeats suddenly stopped and the carriage
door was flung back.

"Don't have hysterics, my girl," the Earl of Raymore
said to Jenny, "it is just me. Out you come and up on
the box with Ben and Harry."

Having lifted the girl out, Raymore vaulted into the

carriage and shut the door behind him. Rosalind sat on the edge of her seat, saucer-eyed, staring at him.

"It's no good," he said, obviously greatly agitated. "I cannot let you go."

She sat back in her seat and turned her head to look out the window. "I see," she said stiffly. "Has Sir Rowland made a more tempting offer, or do you have someone else picked out for me?"

"The latter," he said.

Her head jerked back in his direction. "No," she said, "I am not for sale. You promised, my lord."

"I am the one offering," he blurted. "I love you, Rosalind. I don't think I can live without you."

"You cannot love me," she denied. "I am ugly and I limp."

His jaw clenched. "I will not have you describe yourself that way," he said. "You are your own worst enemy, Rosalind. You are beautiful, quite exceptionally lovely, 'like a red, red rose.' He must have known you, Robert Burns. And do you still limp? I confess I have not noticed lately."

"No," she said, her face pale, "it is not true. You know it is not true, Edward. People would laugh at you."

His jaw was still clenched. "You know," he said, "when I realized finally that I loved you, I thought I would never wish to quarrel with you again. Right now I am holding onto my temper with all my willpower. Why do you do this to me?"

"I belong at Raymore Manor," she said stubbornly, "where no one can see me and where I can do the things I love doing."

"Come back to London with me," he said, "and I shall see to it that you spend the rest of your life doing what you like doing. But not in loneliness, Rosalind. You have too much to share: your musical talent with the world, your passion with me."

She darted him a startled look.

"You have proved your worth, love," he said. "You

are well-admired in London. I want to marry you in St. George's, and I want you to walk the whole length of the aisle toward me, with your chin up and your eyes on me. Will you?"

"Oh, Edward," she said, laughing but with tears springing to her eyes, "what an absurd picture you paint."

"Will you?"

"Are you sure you really wish to, Edward?" she asked wistfully. "It is not just that you have fallen in love with my music?"

He smiled. "It is not my pianoforte, much as I value it, that I long to take to bed or to Florence and Milan and Rome with me. I believe you will make a much warmer and more passionate companion, Rosalind. You have become part of my life, love, whether you wish it or not. You are like the other half of my soul. I cannot face living without you."

"I do love you so," she said almost in a whisper.

They sat and stared at each other from opposite corners of the carriage for long moments.

"Come here," he said finally, and when she came, he pulled her down roughly across his lap and met her open mouth with his in a kiss that immediately had passion flaring between them.

Ben had to expend some energy steadying the horses when the carriage suddenly lurched. He addressed the head of the horse most distant from him. "If I ever understands the quality," he said, "I'll know I've up an' died an' gone to 'eaven. 'Is lordship just took 'is leave of 'er two hours past."

Jenny sighed. "Lawks, it's so romantic," she said.

The Earl of Raymore leaned his head out of the carriage window at that moment. "Is the girl comfortable up there, Ben?" he called. "Will you tie my horse behind and return to Grosvenor Square?"

Ben and the footman exchanged knowing glances and Jenny peeped shyly up into the latter's face.

"Now," said Raymore, shutting the window and settling Rosalind more comfortably on his lap, "what was I saying?"

"I don't believe you were saying anything, my lord," she replied, twining her arms around his neck.

"Really?" he said, his eyebrows arching above very blue eyes. "What was I doing, then?"

"This, Edward," she said, threading her fingers through his thick blond hair and feathering a kiss across his lips.

"Ah, yes," he said, "I remember." His fingers began to remove one by one the pins that held her hair on top of her head. "I have noticed that you have not answered my question. I am determined that you shall marry me, Rosalind. As your guardian, I strongly disapprove of your present behavior with a man who is not even your betrothed. If you do not say yes immediately, I shall have to use coercion, you know." He brushed his lips tantalizingly across hers. "Well, what do you say?"

She looked down at him, her heart shining from her eyes. "You had better try coercion, my lord," she said, shaking her hair loose as he removed the last hairpin.

About the Author

Raised and educated in Wales, Mary Balogh now lives in Kipling, Saskatchewan, Canada, with her husband, Robert, and her children, Jacqueline, Christopher, and Sian. She is a high school English teacher.

SIGNET Regency Romances You'll Enjoy

Other Regency Romances You'll Enjoy